The Second Meeting

In the middle of the nomad camp Marisola's former opponent sat in a hide-upholstered chair on a carpet rolled out in the shade of an awning.

She stopped and afforded him a polite nod.

He stared at her but did not respond.

"So, besides being cowards, the Ulaan have no manners, either." She swung around and sat on the carpet beside his chair. "I suppose you must be the barbarians we thought you were."

Kitten scanned the nomad's mind. *This one is quite Sensitive, and he is thinking furiously. Something is going on but he doesn't know what, and that makes him cautious.*

"It is good to be cautious in an unfamiliar situation. Many a hotheaded young leader has failed to learn that. Some day you will be a fine War Leader for your people."

His back straightened. "I am Husam al Din, the Sword of the Faith, and I am already the War Leader of my people."

"I am Marisola da Falken, Sword Hand to the Cloud Cat of the Leute. I had assumed you were the War Leader. Perhaps some day you will become a good one."

He broke his pose and looked down at her. "You are determined to test my patience. Is this a demonstration of the feeble diplomacy you village folk depend on?"

"Perhaps it is a courting ritual. You'll just have to find out."

"Let's not rush into things. I have not decided if you are worthy of my attention."

"And I have pretty much decided that you are too rude to be worth mine. Perhaps we should stick to diplomacy for the moment. It has a better chance of success."

This is not diplomacy as I have ever seen it practised. Nor courting, come to think of it.

Cloud Cat

Gordon A. Long

Airborn Press
Delta, 2018

Cloud Cat

Gordon A. Long

Published by
Airborn Press
4958 10A Ave, Delta, B. C.
V4M 1X8
Canada

ISBN 978-1-988898-11-7

Printed by Amazon Direct Publishing

Cover Design by Gordon A. Long

This is a work of fiction. All the characters and events portrayed in this book are fictional (except for the cat), and any resemblance to real people or incidents is purely coincidental.

...except for the cat.

Contents

Prologue

Forty years have passed since Eirlin the Healer helped the Sword who calls herself Kitten save the throne from destruction. Now Fang, Eirlin's Scalpel, has gained maturity. The tensions between the Inderjornese and Maridan nobles have retreated from open conflict to their usual squabbling.

So Kitten finds herself needed less and less. She spends much of her time hanging over the fireplace in the Great Hall at Falkengard while Ecmund and Perica raise their family. But while she awaits the next time her services will be required, she has found a useful way to spend her days...training a new Hand for the war that is sure to come.

1. War

The war arrived suddenly at Falkengard Castle.

Kitten was with Marisola in the practice room, involved in a complex series of moves: getting up a good sweat, their minds sliding toward the true blending of Sword and Hand. *Well, Hand-in-training, who is training up very...*

...what was that? Kitten's attention was tugged away by a familiar feeling. Her jolt of terror froze the girl in mid-lunge.

DANGERDANGERDANGER!

Marisola reached for her robe, but the Sword's urgency blasted her out the door dressed as she was.

Close the gate! Horsemen coming fast!

As Marisola's feet hit the cobblestones of the bailey, she was voicing Kitten's warning.

"Close the gate! Attack! Horsemen coming. Close the gate!"

Even as the girl crashed her powerful shoulder against the massive door, Kitten knew it was too late. There were only two soldiers on duty, and the gate swung far too slowly. The horsemen were closing in, now. Roughly dressed men on shaggy little ponies, but riding fast for all that. The soldiers needed time.

There was only one solution.

Outside!

Marisola slipped around the swinging gate and sprinted forward to meet the first attacker. If he was surprised to be challenged by a scantily clad woman, he had no chance to show it.

Duck right!

The teeth of the squealing horse missed Marisola by a hand's breadth, and her sudden shift sent the rider's sword whistling through empty air.

He will raise his left foot.

As the horseman slid down on the safe side of his horse he pulled his near leg up, and Marisola spun and sliced. Kitten jumped to her task.

The pony screamed again and shied away from the bright sword that scored its ribs, severing the girth. The rider, his saddle slipping one way and his mount the other, fell heavily.

His sword has a flaw. Break it. Put your knee right...there. Good. Now toss the pieces at him and motion him to go. He is a young hothead, thinking to achieve fame through being the first at the kill. He will live to learn wisdom.

"Glad you're so thoughtful of him. I'm the one in trouble."

The horsemen had stopped their attack to watch this little scene, and the timbers thumped home to secure the bolt-studded gate. The castle was safe.

And Kitten and Marisola were outside the door, alone with fifty nasty horsemen who whooped and hollered and milled in a rough half-circle around them.

"Which one?"

Him.

"You really know how to pick them, Sweetheart."

She strode towards the heavy-shouldered barbarian, the only one who sat his horse stock-still. He wore a short-sleeved fish-scale hauberk and a conical helmet with plated earflaps. A banner of black horsehair streamed from the top. More important, his right hand held a short, curved sword that looked very useful.

No bows.

Marisola spared a glance at the other attackers, who had not yet nocked their arrows. She made a commanding gesture at the helmets peeking over the battlements, and the castle bowmen relaxed their taut strings. Then she faced her enemy.

He grinned, tossed his reins down and leapt from his horse.

Do the glissade. I want to read him.

As the big man's weapon reached out, Marisola caught it tip to tip and ran the Sword the full length of his, keeping firm contact all the way. Just before the hilts clashed she circled under and withdrew, pushing in the opposite direction. It was a disconcerting move that often left an inexperienced opponent open to a quick thrust. Kitten did not expect it to work in this case, but it gave her the time she needed to read the man's aura.

Now Marisola stood back, her grin matching the puzzled frown that began to form on the dark, handsome face.

They have a legend. I will sing.

"I will dance, then. It should be entertaining." She glided forward, the grit cool and firm under her bare feet. She rapped a sharp double beat against his blade, and Kitten started her song.

At first their opponent did not register the sound, intent as he was on the opening passes of the duel. Marisola tried a quick cut-thrust-cut pattern that he parried easily, but every time their weapons met the Kitten boosted her hum until his own blade was ringing in sympathetic vibration.

Now it was beginning to bother him. Kitten could see the sweat stand out on his forehead and feel the uncertainty in his moves. *Press harder.* The ringing soared upward into an unearthly shriek, swooping and circling with the movement of her blade.

The barbarian champion shook his head, took two quick paces back. Marisola held in garde, ready for his next move.

Kitten kept the sound building and building, layer upon layer of agony. Their opponent began to lose interest in them, his eyes darting left and right. The other horsemen

3

shifted in the saddle, their mounts circling against tight reins.

Marisola regarded the man in front of her as the shriek started to hurt her own ears. He shook his head again, then flipped his sword up, catching the blade below the hilt, his arms wide in a gesture of hopeless submission.

The sound slowly faded.

He has more value to us alive. Let him go.

"You don't want him? I certainly don't want him. Let's get rid of him." She tossed her head, her chin pointing towards his horse, fidgeting nearby. With a thankful nod, almost a bow, the barbarian sheathed his sword, swung into the saddle and shouted a single word to his men.

The whole pack turned as one and galloped away as if all the devils in the world were after them.

The Sword's song ebbed slowly, fading to a moan as the dust settled, finally leaving Marisola in silence, alone with a slashed barbarian saddle in the empty court before the castle walls. She stood there, allowing the faint breeze to cool the sweat from her body, Kitten purring in her hand.

"That went rather well."

Your performance was appropriate to your training.

"What did my training have to do with it?"

I didn't spend eighteen years filling your head with romantic nonsense only for my own entertainment.

"You didn't? I sometimes wondered. I thought maybe you were bored and using me to keep your ideals alive."

War always comes, Dear One. Your people have been at peace for too long. I had to be sure you were ready.

"You knew war was coming."

What is there to know? War always comes.

"That's a very pessimistic way of looking at things."

Realistic, my dear. The world is like that.

"No it isn't. Grandfather told me…"

I know what Ecmund told you. That I am young and impressionable, and you must be careful what you say around me in case I turn into a bloodthirsty, soul-stealing minion of evil. My Hand always did have an exaggerated sense of his importance in the overall scheme of things.

"You can't talk about my grandfather like that!"

Why not? If I may quote your great-uncle Tyrbrand, I am an 'exceptionally rude and talkative young sword, with a lot of learning to do.' I have tried to foster that impression. It gives me latitude.

"I can just hear him saying that. Don't you love the way he speaks?"

I don't recall being quite so impressed at the time.

The gate behind them creaked open and Marisola turned at the sound of running footsteps.

"Careful, Chavito. It would be a poor end to the story if you impaled yourself on your sister's Sword after it was all over."

Xavier brushed Kitten aside and seized his sister, held her close. "I thought they had you. What happened? Whatever made you come out here?"

She shrugged. "A calculation. It was us out here or them in there. I guess you saw the rest."

"Yes. Curse this inventory Father wants. I was in the far storeroom when the alarm went up. I got to the battlements just as you signalled the bowmen to stand down. Why did you do that?"

"Because if everyone started shooting, I would be very dead, very quick, with nothing I could do about it. Kitten and I had it figured out already."

"What did you have figured out?"

"That we could handle it. Once the gate closed and they stopped charging, it wasn't war any more. It was a challenge, and someone would have to answer it."

"How did you know they believed that? I've never seen them before."

"I hadn't either, but Kitten says they all act the same. She told me about that sort, and how they work."

"You mean you believe all those tales she used to tell you? I thought you grew out of that."

"Aren't you glad I didn't?"

"Can't say I'm arguing now. Did they include that wailing sound?"

"I've never heard that one before."

I took it from his memories.

"She took it from an old legend she found in his mind. I guess there was once another magic Sword." Then Marisola frowned. "...Kitten?"

Yes, Dear One?

"Did he shout, 'Witchcraft' to his men?"

He did.

"In his own language. Why could I understand him?"

Because his language is very close to Leute, which I understand very well.

"Oh."

"All right, all right. Let's get you inside. We can't have the hero of the battle standing around in her underwear."

She regarded her practice smock and knee breeches, then slapped his arm with the back of her hand, perhaps harder than she needed to. "This isn't underwear!"

He winced. "Any more sweating and it won't make much difference."

She looked down at her chest. "You always say that if my breasts were as thick as my arms they'd attract some attention."

"You have definitely been hanging around the soldiers too much. I'm going to ask Father to pack you up and send you off to Great-Aunt Eirlin the Capital."

"Fine idea." She sheathed the Sword. "Soon as the war's over."

"What war?"

"The one that just started."

"Oh. That war." He put his arm around her shoulders and, with one last grimace at the surrounding forest, pulled her back towards the gate. Kitten hummed quietly in her scabbard.

2. Prepare for Battle

The first person to meet them inside the gate was Lord Ecmund. He eyed Marisola quizzically. "And what are you doing wandering about in your nightwear?"

"I am sooo sorry, Grandfather. I slept late. Almost missed the battle."

"Hmph. Well, give me my Sword and go and change your clothes before the soldiers start getting ideas. We've had enough of our family marrying out of the Blood lately."

"Speak for yourself."

"Exactly. Someone has to make up for my disgrace in marrying into the Maridon nobility. Might as well be you."

He reached out, and she passed Kitten to him. As their hands touched on the pommel, the Sword allowed the rush of his pride to wash over the girl. She glanced up at her grandfather, seeing the faint twist of his lips. With a quick kiss to his cheek, she was away.

She fought well.

"I should hope so. You and Jesco have done a fine job of training her."

It is also in the Blood.

"I'd like to take some credit."

She will be the fighter you never were.

"And never wanted to be, remember?"

So now you have your wish.

He stopped walking. "What do you mean by that?"

You're supposed to be the intelligent one. You tell me.

He grinned and resumed his way up the stairs into the castle. "I never did cure you of that lip."

Swords don't have lips.

8

"How can you give out so much of something you don't have? Now, back to the topic. Did you mean what I thought you meant?"

Yes. The time has come. War is here, and there is need for a Hand to wield the Sword.

"Marisola? But she's so young, so…"

She is at the prime of her life. She will become wiser and stronger, but she will never be so fast, never so unafraid. Now is her moment, Ecmund. There is no time for discussion. Do you know who those riders were?

"Some scruffy band of nomads, wandered down off the plains."

How I wish that were true. That was a scouting party of Ulaan.

"Ulaan? Surely not."

The trappings are unmistakable. You know what a scouting party of fifty Ulaan means.

"A larger party close behind."

Thousands upon thousands. Enough to sweep Inderjorne beneath the feet of their ponies and roll her up in their dust as they have done with countless peoples before.

"What can we do?"

Run to the mountains and hide with the Leute, who are able to deal with invaders. Lock yourselves up in the peaks and hope they keep moving. Then come down and bury the dead and try to start your civilization again from the bottom. If you don't get wiped out by the scavengers who follow.

"And if they don't keep moving?"

Surrender your women to their beds and your necks to their swords. Which order doesn't matter.

"We are talking about Inderjorne, here, not some valley of farmers. We have our mercenary guards. The king can raise levies from every noble. The people can field thousands as well: better organized, better armed."

Nonetheless. A Hero and a Sword will be needed. Even then, we may not be able to turn the tide away.

The old lord sighed. "Well, Kitten, I suppose this day had to come. Is there some kind of ceremony?"

Not really. The old Hand falls in battle, the new Hand picks up the Sword and fights on.

"Falls in battle?"

Figure of speech. I can't see you riding into battle, somehow. A waste of good brainpower.

"Thank you for that."

My pleasure.

"So. Where to start?"

Very soon you will send for Marisola. You will give her the Sword, and the two of you have time to shed one tear, or whatever you need for your soft human hearts. Then we will call a meeting and send messengers to the Capital and to the lords who hold the northern border. As quickly as possible. The Ulaan Horde moves fast, and minutes count.

"Then why are we wasting this time, chatting?"

You needed a moment to collect your thoughts. You have had your moment. Get moving.

"Yes, O mighty commander. I hear and obey."

You're beginning to get the picture.

3. Handover

Lord Ecmund sat in his plain chair beside Lady Perica's ceremonial one, his Sword lying across his knees. Marisola stood in front of him in the echoing, empty Great Hall of Falkengard. They regarded each other.

"Well, Grandfather? What do we do?"

"No idea. I bought her from a merchant. He belted her scabbard around my waist, and away I went. Kitten, is there a ceremony?"

Usually there is no necessity.

"What do you mean?"

A living Hand does not often give up his Sword.

"Oh."

Ecmund smiled. "We have a living Hand this time, and he has not wielded the Sword for many a year."

You never did wield me. Not in a real battle.

"Only the once, and only one blow. Not much of a Hand."

You always did what was right.

"I remember the lesson. 'A strong hand in war, a strong voice in council,' or something like that."

You have been a strong voice in council for forty years. You don't need me for that.

"So there we have it, Marisola. You have already taken over the duties of the Hand, as I have long ago relinquished them. Now you have fought together and won. The Joining has happened."

"Has it?"

I suppose it has.

"Don't worry, my dear. I won't miss her or want to interfere. I have my place in Inderjorne, and it doesn't involve the use of any sword, let alone a magic one. Today you have proved your worth." He stood and held out the Weapon. "So give your grandfather a hug, belt on your Sword, and the two of you go out where you are needed."

She leaned forward and gave him a brief, firm hug. Then she stood straight and adjusted the belt around her waist.

Kitten molded herself to the familiar contours. *It feels different, doesn't it?*

"Yes. It feels right."

That's because it is. You and I will be a perfect Joining. We will win honour and glory, and perhaps an even more distinguished Name.

Marisola broke the tone of the occasion by slapping Kitten's hilt and winking at her grandfather. "Isn't the one you have good enough?"

I am very happy with it, thank you. But one should never rest on one's laurels.

"A fine attitude."

So let us go out and win this war in some glorious and heroic fashion.

The old man raised his hands in benediction. "Hopefully one that doesn't get too many of us killed."

I wouldn't dream of it.

4. Persuasion

"Marisola!"

The Hand paused at the end of her lunge: her wrist solid, her Sword point motionless. "Yes, Mother?"

"What are you doing?"

Marisola glided back into the garde position, then lowered her weapon. "I'm paring potatoes for dinner, Mother. Can't you tell?"

Caterina Skonric Delfontes strode across the practice floor as if she had every intention of becoming their next opponent, despite the fact that she was dressed in a well-bred lady's travelling garb. "You will not talk to me in that flippant way, young lady."

Well, she hasn't changed any. Kitten pictured a large yawn and stretch, complete with arched back and extended claws.

The girl's shoulders relaxed, and a grin twitched her lip. "Mother, it is quite some time since you gave up trying to make me a young lady and I've been talking to you like this most of my life. Why don't we drop the pretense and just get along with each other?"

The older woman's stride faltered, and she frowned. "That's an uncommonly mature response, my dear. Perhaps there's hope for you yet."

Marisola shrugged. "That approach won't work either, but at least it's civilized. How are you, Mother? It's good to see you. Was there any trouble on the road from Koningsholm? We thought two days for the post rider with the message, and then four days for someone to come back. You rode late and early to make it in three." She sheathed her Sword and took her mother's arm, leading her over to the table where the towels hung.

"We did. I have not lost my muscle tone, but it was a tiring ride."

Marisola dried herself thoroughly, then slipped on a short, embroidered jacket. Settling the Kitten comfortably at her hip, she regarded her mother. "All right. Now that you and Father are here, I assume there will be a meeting?"

"Yes. Xavier said he would bring us up to date on this problem."

"Good old Chavito. Always has everything orderly. The sooner we get started the better. Let's go."

Her mother did not follow. "Why are you wearing that weapon?"

Marisola strode back to Caterina and stood, one hand on Kitten's hilt, facing the older woman squarely. "There you go again, Mother, asking questions you already know the answer to. We don't have time for this. Come." She turned abruptly and paused, ready to start towards the door.

After an instant's hesitation Caterina stepped up beside her. "Why is there such a rush?"

"Because we are at war, Mother. We have been for five days, and nobody has done anything about it. That is the great disadvantage peaceful people have when faced with an aggressor. The enemy has prepared himself for war, physically and emotionally. The victims take too long rousing themselves to an equal state, giving the attacker crucial time to achieve ground that is harder to retake at a later date."

Her mother said nothing for several paces. Finally she glanced at her daughter. "I can't argue with that. How do you know such things?"

"I have heard Uncle Tyrbrand tell that lesson twice recently within your hearing, so you needn't be surprised. But that's not it." She glanced over at the stern face beside her.

Yes, this is the time to tell her.

14

"I have had the best military training in the kingdom, given by an expert, starting when I was four years old. I know a huge amount about tactics and fighting, from single combat to realm-wide warfare. I can plan battles on foot, on horseback and with fully armed knights. If there is something I don't know, I have an extensive information source literally at my fingertips. Most important, I know how difficult it is for leaders to stir peaceful folk to a battle pitch. And you are one of the leaders who will be tasked with that responsibility, so there are things you need to be aware of as soon as possible."

Caterina frowned. "The king was quite urgent about me getting out here quickly..." She stopped dead in the middle of the hallway. "But that does not explain why my daughter is acting like she is some kind of general. There are plenty of tasks to be done, young lady, and striding around brandishing a sword like a minstrel in a comedy will not be useful!"

Kitten sent a quick upper-lip curl to her Hand. *She really is hard to persuade, isn't she?*

We expected a change? I've been living with this all my life. I don't think I'm about to make any progress.

Then it's up to me.

You!

Oh, yes. I have a distinct advantage over you. Plus the element of surprise.

You do?

Find us a place to sit. It's time your mother and I had a chat.

"Marisola...? Well? Are you going to stand there staring into space?"

The daughter glanced around. "I have a little experience prepared for you, Mother. We need a quiet spot. The bench in this alcove will do. Come. Sit."

It was not a request, and Lady Caterina obeyed, eyeing her daughter with interest.

"Don't speak. Just put your hand on Kitten's hilt."

"Kitten...?"

"That's right. My Sword."

"But that's your grandfather's..."

"Mine, now. It's her nickname, really. She has several more glorious ones, but Kitten is the one the family uses."

"Just what is going...what? What is happening?"

Good evening, Lady Skonric. I'm sorry I have never contacted you before, but I do try to limit the number of people I speak to, and the occasion never arose. I suppose I should say Lady Delfontes, but it's a hard habit to break.

"Habit? What are you...? Who are you...? You're the Sword, aren't you? Don't worry, I know all about you. Why are you speaking to me now, after all these years?"

As Marisola says, we don't have time for the niceties. You need to be brought up to date on many things quickly, and your reluctance to cooperate is getting in the way of our efforts to plan the defence of the kingdom. No, don't respond. I have a tale you need to hear. It won't do Marisola any harm to know this either.

Lady Caterina, I have a long and close relationship with the Skonric family. Lord Theobald Skonric was my first Hand. I was created for him.

"Theobald? He was Lady Caterina Skonric's husband, a century and more ago."

The only distinguishing point in his life, I'm afraid. His career was cut short through no fault of his own. However, his marriage to the original Lady Caterina laid the pattern of my life for the next few decades.

"You knew my ancestor, Lady Caterina?"

I did. I was there when she and Theobald met, and I was there for several other firsts that we need not discuss in the presence of the innocent mind of my Hand.

After Theobald was killed in battle defending Inderjorne from invaders, there was a regrettable period when I was unable to do anything to help the realm. Then, and some might say it was through luck, I was reunited with Lady Caterina and her son, Johannes. We had a long and useful relationship, but Lord Johannes was a very different type of person from his father, and we were not the ideal Joining. It was Lady Caterina who helped me stabilize the border with Marida and enforce the peace for many years.

But that was years ago, and since then I have had many adventures and many Hands, some good, some bad, many indifferent.

"Including my father-in-law. Is Lord Ecmund one of the good ones?" The woman glanced at her daughter.

He and Perica did a wonderful job of teaching me the ways of humans. Lady Eirlin the Healer and Lord Magician Tyrbrand as well. But as a Hand Ecmund was rather remiss. Do you know he never once fought a proper fight with me? He has been my Hand for forty-two years, and our only accomplishment at arms was to break an enemy's sword. Come to think of it, that was a great training for me as well.

But now we are in a different kind of battle. Ecmund's diplomatic skills will be useless against the Ulaan. A different sort of Hand is needed. The availability of a potential Hand with the blood of the Skonrics running in her veins is such a happy coincidence as to defy logic. It almost makes me wonder if it is pure chance that everything has come together at this point at this time.

Lady Caterina gave an unladylike snort. "If you considered being attacked by an overwhelming foreign foe at a moment in our history when the kingdom is completely divided into warring camps, you wouldn't consider this so lucky."

And thus my task is complete.

"What...?" The woman stared at her daughter. "What does she mean?"

Marisola rose from the bench. "You are now ready to take your place in this battle. Thank you, Kitten."

The woman stared at her daughter. "What was that about her task?"

"Kitten told you. She wanted you to be ready to take charge in this battle."

"I don't need an uppity Sword to prepare me to do my duty!" Caterina rose and started down the hallway.

You don't like to think you were manipulated.

"That's right." She strode out faster, towing her daughter along. "And don't you forget it."

5. Council of War

"But Kitten, can't you give us any more information than this?

Kitten regarded the stubborn minds that faced her. Lady Perica, the head of the family. Lord Ecmund, her husband. Jesco Halfhand, the old swordsman. *At least the warrior agrees with me.*

Marisola, we do not need more information! Kitten blasted out the idea with such power that even Lord Jandro, the least Sensitive of the group, started. He sent a guilty glance at Lady Caterina, his wife, and sat straighter.

These are the Ulaan. When they send out advance parties of fifty horsemen, they are on the move, and only the combined forces of the whole realm have a chance against them! Tell everyone!

Marisola surged to her feet, but Ecmund raised a calming hand. "Sit, my dear. Now is not the time for the Hand and the Sword."

"Yes it..."

"No. When your time comes, I will tell you." He turned to the rest of the group. "Caterina, now the main task is for a younger generation, for you and Jandro and even your children, but you have less experience with Kitten than any of us. Please believe me, I have never seen her so worried. Ask Jesco if you don't believe me."

Why would she listen to Jesco? She stays out of his way.

Precisely, my dear Cat. Ecmund sent her a private grin. *Watch.*

The lady turned her attention to the old swordsman, who was toying with the hilt of his plain steel sword with his right hand as if wishing he had enough fingers remaining there to fight as he once had.

"Well, Uncle Jesco?"

He rasped out his bark of a laugh. "Why would you listen to me? You've scarcely given me the time of day in twenty years."

The woman's face paled, and her hands gripped the edge of the table. "Because you are a renowned swordsman, and the time for minor differences is past. My delicate sensibilities must take second place to the needs of the kingdom."

"Don't like what you might see in my mind?"

"Do we have to do this right now?"

He chuckled. "No, we don't. For what it's worth, I don't blame you. Sometimes I don't like being in here myself. So I'll answer the question you haven't asked yet. From what I can gather — and I have had considerable experience with this Cat — the Sword is absolutely certain in her analysis of the situation." He shot the lady a frown. "Kitten is tied by multiple threads to this realm and to this family. She could no more go against those bindings of loyalty and love than she could..." He tossed up his hands. "I can't think of anything more unlikely."

His eyes probed hers. "So if Kitten says there's an army of Ulaan coming, I, for one, am shaking in my boots. She's got a hundred years and more of military training, and whatever she tells us to do, that's what we'll do in the end or we'll suffer the consequences. Have I made it clear enough for you?"

Then he gave his twisted grin. "And lest you think she's using some kind of influence on me, you should know that she doesn't like being in my head, either. Probably that's to her credit."

Lady Caterina glanced around at the hopeful eyes regarding her. "Fine. You're not the sort of people to go running off in all directions over nothing. The response of the king and the lords in Koningshof is insufficient. What are we going to do?"

Marisola tossed up her hands. "What Kitten says. We need an army. A huge one."

"So she says. An army consisting of every knight, mercenary, archer and peasant foot soldier we can scrape together. We need them all here, and we need them quicker than it has ever been possible to organize an army before. How do you suggest we do that? It takes two days for the fastest messenger to reach the capital. If his Majesty still doesn't hear the urgency, then it's two more days wasted, and we have to go in person. That will take too much time."

Ecmund laid a finger on Kitten's hilt. "I hate to ask, but you solved this problem in an emergency before. Could you form a merge and speak as far as Koningshof...?"

Perica had stayed silent all this time. Now she shook her head. "I'm not sure, Ecmund. We had more power then. Kitten? Can you reach the capital with this group?"

Kitten regarded the minds around her. *There is no one here with Eirlin's power, but there are more of us, and we are all family. Your minds should be much easier to manage, and the urgency of our message will help. That is not the problem.*

Lady Perica frowned. "What is the problem?"

Ecmund, I have told all of you too many times. If she hasn't listened to me, maybe she'll listen to her husband.

The lord shrugged. "You know as well as I do, Perica. Kitten doesn't like using her power to merge a group together. Some time in the past she did it and it went wrong."

"But this is an emergency! The fate of the Kingdom of Inderjorne is at stake."

Kitten sighed. *That's what they always say. "Only this emergency. Just this once." However, I have to agree, since you use my own strongest argument. Inderjorne is at risk. I will do it.*

Perica gave her serene smile.

You always look like that when you get your way.

The smile did not fade. "How do we reach the king?"

Ecmund laid a hand on his wife's. "There is only one group in the kingdom that could hear us from this far away. The Magician and the Healer."

Right. And they are family, too. This will be easy.

Perica reached out a finger and tapped her hilt. "And the last time you did this you passed out for an hour. You be careful, Cat. We need you."

Thank you, my Lady. I appreciate your concern. Now, your daughter-in-law is looking confused, and your son is counting the arrows in his armoury instead of listening, so perhaps you would organize this little séance?

Perica straightened her back, and her eyes probed theirs. "Jandro, pay attention. The rest of you listen carefully. You are about to see family legend with your own eyes and feel it considerably deeper than that. Kitten has the ability to focus our minds into a group that is far more powerful than even our single minds added together. It is a dangerous and taxing exercise for her, and for some reason that we still don't know, she is reluctant to do it. However, this is an emergency, and she is willing.

"We are going to broadcast an emotion. That is all. At this distance and with this group, there will be no ability to speak."

"What emotion?"

"Urgency. With a certain amount of fear. We have to get through to them how important this is. We need help, and we need it now!"

Caterina sat straighter. "Fine. What do we do?"

"We listen to Kitten."

22

Thank you, Perica. You have prepared them as well as possible. Marisola, please draw me and lay me on the table. My scabbard dulls my powers somewhat. Thank you. Now, everyone reach out and touch me. Try to stay away from the sharp bits. While we are merged, you may not be aware of what is happening in this room.

Good. Now I will reach out to Tyrbrand. I want you to concentrate on him. Think of his face if that helps. Try very hard to concentrate on him and nothing else. This is the most difficult part for me. Human minds are always wandering. Jandro, I know you have spent little time with him, but concentrate on what you remember. That's it. Good.

Now I reach out, farther and farther...there! Did you catch that? We have his attention. Just hold on now. We have no idea what he might be doing.

Careful! Hold on. That other aura is Eirlin's. Now there are two of them, and I will try to concentrate on both. Start the feeling of urgency. Start it now.

Kitten could feel the questioning from the Magician and the Healer, but it was so faint she wondered if anything was getting through.

Try harder. Think of something that really worries you. Think of what would have happened if those Ulaan had come before Marisola could get out there. Think of...

BIG CAT! YIKEYIKE YIKE! PERICA-ECMUND-SWORDSMAN...YIKEYIKE YIKE! CATERINA? LADY CATERINA! YIKE YIKE SLURP YIKE!

The human minds could not hold on, and Kitten knew better than to try. Their concentration exploded in all directions, and the contact was broken.

Silence settled over the room while everyone focused on reality.

"What the hell was that?" Caterina was scrubbing her cheek with her hand. Then she rubbed her fingers together in surprise. "I feel like I've had my face licked!"

23

The others laughed. Perica laid a hand on her daughter-in-law's arm. "That's the element of the situation we forgot to consider. Fang."

"Eirlin's Scalpel?"

"Afraid so. It seems he is more powerful than we realized. What do you say, Kitten?"

Much though I'd love to give his yappy little muzzle a decent scratch, I think this will simplify things.

"How?" Caterina frowned. "He destroyed the small amount of contact we had achieved."

Perica grinned. "Did you feel how strong he was?"

"So, what do we do?"

"I suggest we wait. It will take them a while to get him calmed down, but once he gets over his excitement, he has reasonable control. It may feel like shouting across the Main Hall with a hunt forming up in the bailey, but I suspect we'll be able to talk."

I have to agree. If he doesn't calm down, I'll calm him. And speaking of that...Marisola?"

"Uh...what? Are you talking to me?" The girl's head came up, her eyes striving to focus.

You will have to excuse us for a moment, folks. There is another new mind who is finding this situation difficult.

Concerned glances followed the young Hand as she stumbled out the door into the hallway.

Easy, girl. Don't rush. We don't want to be too far away when Tyrbrand calls us. Also, we don't want to run face-first into a wall. How are you feeling?

"Terrible. All that was happening in my head. People were talking outside, and saying almost the same thing inside, but it was different somehow, so I couldn't understand anyone!"

Ah. I did not know. I have always used my Hand as part of the process, and I didn't realize that you would be unprepared.

24

"I'm sorry. It's just that…"

Do not blame yourself. Speaking with a large group of people is not normal for me, either, but I have had practice. Now that I know, I can use your power less. Having Fang in the group will make that easier. You will get better at it as you go along.

"I certainly hope so."

Of course you will. Just concentrate on my mind and ignore the rest. Feel free to speak aloud if that makes it easier. It is polite in any case, because the less sensitive members of the group do not receive your thoughts clearly. Are you ready to return to the fray?

The girl straightened her back, her grip firming on Kitten's hilt. "I'm ready."

Good, because I feel a small black nose nudging me. Hello, Fang. Are you calm, now?

The thought came faint but clear. *Ready, ready, Big Cat. The Smith and the Healer are here.*

Marisola strode into the workroom and laid the Sword on the table. As each member of the family joined her, the message cleared more.

Ah. That's better. Tyrbrand's creaky voice projected stronger than it sounded face to face. *"I suspect you have news of the invasion."*

Perica nodded to her husband.

Yes, Tyrbrand. Kitten has had experience with this people. She says that when they send out raiding parties that size, it means the whole army is coming. This was a deep foray by one of their battle leaders to size up the land and incidentally demonstrate his bravery and leadership for the fighting that will ensue.

So we have a major attack on the way. Your message said that. I informed his Majesty.

It is more than an attack, Magician. Kitten formed the image of a sweeping claw. *If their past is anything to go by, they have come to take over the realm.*

The king wonders if there is any chance of putting up a front and then paying them off.

The king fails to realize the danger. These people have no diplomacy. Strength of arms is all they know. We must meet force with force, blade with blade. And it will require all the power of all our realm. The time for petty rivalries is over.

I will inform his Majesty in the strongest possible terms, though I doubt that this will sway the radicals of either side. I sometimes think they'd see the realm fall into chaos rather than allow their rivals to rule it.

Please make him believe, my Lord Magician. Even with all our might, we may not be able to stop this army.

I will do my best. Ecmund, I assume you have sent scouts?

Marisola and I took care of that long before Caterina and Jandro got here. They have not reported in, yet. That very fact makes me nervous.

No news is rarely good news in a war. Eirlin and Fang would send their affection, but they are concentrating on the bond so that I may speak. Now that we can, please keep in touch.

The Magician's presence faded, to be replaced momentarily by a wash of slobbery affection and serene love. Then the link washed away in a blur of colour and sound.

As they took their hands off the Sword, everything returned to the cold reality of the stone-walled room. They looked at each other for a long, silent moment.

Ecmund finally shook his head. "I am not a man of war. I have nothing to suggest."

Jandro, too, was silent.

Kitten scanned the room, found a small flame and nurtured it.

Lady Catarina's head came up. "I am not a woman of war, either, but if I must become one to save Inderjorne, someone please tell me how."

Jesco leaned forward, all business. "Well spoken, my Lady. That is how Inderjorne always survives." He regarded the group. "Ecmund, start your mill cutting timbers. Big, heavy ones; it doesn't matter what kind of wood. Think of anything that can defend against huge numbers of horsemen with light weapons. Get the village bowmen together and turn your carpenter shop over to them. They will be crucial in any pitched battle. The nomads have little armour, and their horses have none."

He turned to Perica, Jandro and Xavier. "Start gathering supplies for a siege, preparing the castle. You know the drill."

Tell the farmers to harvest anything close to ripe. The enemy will eat or destroy whatever is growing. Might as well deny him the forage for his mounts.

Caterina frowned. "We have such little information. What has happened to our scouts? I thought you sent out your best woodsmen."

Marisola shrugged. "Leof and Maer are wonderful in the forest, but not as fast as they used to be. It depends on how close the enemies are. If they are still in the plains to the north, it will take our scouts longer to find them. The open country will slow our men down. They are woodsmen."

"But what about more reconnaissance?

Ready, Hand?

Marisola stood. "Uncle Jesco?"

He rose as well. "There doesn't seem to be much for us to do around here."

"No. Shall we take a small ride?"

27

"A little sweep out to the north for a couple of days."

"I think so."

"Just a moment, young lady!"

The girl faced her mother, one hand on Kitten's hilt.

"We are at war, as you have taken pains to inform me. You will not leave this manor without appropriate escort."

"What do you consider appropriate, Mother?"

"I have no idea. That is why you are taking Jesco, I presume. But I do have a suggestion. They should be the most Sensitive soldiers you can find."

A chuckle spread around the room. Jesco winked at his cousin. "Not bad, is she, Ecmund? And she hasn't even heard of 'I am the wind in the trees' yet."

A faint blush stained the lady's cheek. "Exactly. If it's what it sounds like, and Kitten can use the Sensibilities of everyone..."

"She can. Two bowmen, one axeman, one extra swordsman. I know who to take, all Sensitive to some degree."

That is enough. A full troop would slow us.

"Especially as we get farther north. The smaller manors would have trouble finding fast horses for a larger group to trade off."

Lady Caterina stood. "All right. You assign your men and do your talking over an early lunch. You have a long afternoon ahead of you."

There was no argument, although Kitten sent her Hand a wry claw-stretch. *Shaping up, isn't she?*

6. Danger To the North

An hour later their little expedition was mounting in the bailey of the old castle. Marisola paused to hug her mother and father, then started to turn away.

Jandro's arm did not release her. Instead he pulled her aside. "One more point, my dear."

"Yes, Father?"

"I don't know much about war and things like that. But this castle is already in condition – your brother and I tend to that every day – and by the time you return it will be as prepared for war as the best minds in the realm can make it." He took her by the shoulders. "Just you be sure you return to it." His usually pleasant face held stern lines.

"Yes, Father. This is only reconnaissance. We're not looking for trouble, and Kitten will see that nothing takes us unawares."

Do not worry, my Lord. She is far too important to waste so early in the campaign.

Jandro's eyes widened. "Your words don't fill me with confidence in the long run, but for the moment, that's what I wanted to hear. So, off you go. Your mother is very worried about you, but she must play the role of war leader, so she will not show it."

Marisola felt a lump in her throat. "But you can." She threw her arms around her father again, then leapt to Tariq's saddle. He snorted but stood firm; he was used to that sort of antic.

"Everybody ready?"

Jesco tipped a finger to the brim of his hat.

She nodded to Lord Ecmund and Lady Perica and spun her steed, heeling him to full speed out of the castle gate and down the road.

They ran at a gallop for the next six hours, slowing only when there were no manor houses where they could trade their mounts. Marisola's last horse was a hammer-headed roan with a bone-jarring trot and no match for her beautiful Tariq, but he showed no signs of tiring, slogging ahead with dogged determination.

She glanced over at Jesco. "This horse. He refused to run when I asked him to, but once he got going, he refuses to stop."

He laughed. "Like driving a pig down an irrigation ditch. The best method is to persuade him you want to go the opposite way."

"What's our plan, now?"

"We don't have one. We've made good time: about fifteen leagues. Lesser Walden is only a few hours ahead. We'll keep pushing, because as soon as we get within range of the enemy we have to leave the road, and that slows us down. Our only advantage is to stay in the woods. They are plains people. They will mainly stick to the roads and fields."

"Bad for the farmers, good for us."

Rider coming. Kitten broadcast the message, and the four troopers behind pulled up in unison with their leaders. *Solo. Tired horse.* She listened. *Inderjornese. He's only half awake, so I'm not getting any information.*

Jesco pointed right and left, and their party slipped in among the trees on either side of the road, the bowmen limbering their weapons.

The rider plodded around the corner ahead, then seeing the open straight stretch, pushed his mount to a faint trot.

It's Maer. As the scout approached, Kitten sent a pleasant feeling of greeting so when Jesco kneed his horse onto the road, the old hunter did not startle.

30

"Jesco. What brings you so far north?"

"You. What have you to report?"

Maer winced. "Not much, but we figured we'd better send what we have."

"You're right. They're getting twitchy back at the castle. What did you find?"

"The nomads are farther away than we thought. Still out on the open prairie, several hours' ride north of Waldheim Castle. We couldn't get close to them." Maer gulped. "Edouard got too close, and they caught him. He tried to get away, but those little ponies they ride are really fast. They ran him down and shot him out of the saddle. I saw it happen."

"He's dead, then?"

"Arrows in his back."

Better for him.

Jesco nodded. "Better dead than captured. What did you see from where you were?"

"They're all over, so it's hard to count. Hundreds of campfires spread for leagues over the prairie. Leof and Gunter are going to ride around them, staying far out. Then they'll report back."

"Fine. You keep going, but pick up the pace. Change horses at every manor. Stay in Woldbarg tonight, but I want you back at Falkengard by noon tomorrow."

Maer's eyes rolled up to the side as he calculated. "I can do that if I rest up tonight. Any message to pass back from you?"

"How far are we from Lesser Walden?"

"Two hours north."

"At the speed you were going."

"This horse is on his last legs."

"He's done his duty, that's for sure." Jesco slapped the scout on the shoulder. "Your news is good. If the enemy is farther away, we'll stay at Lesser Walden tonight and try to spot the other two scouts tomorrow as we continue to Waldheim Castle. Then we'll go in closer, get an idea what's happening."

"Don't go too close, Jesco. Especially not with Lady Marisola. It isn't safe!"

"Don't worry about us. We're not taking any risks we don't need to." Jesco grinned. "Now, your horse has had a rest, so you get yourself to Woldbarg for a well-deserved sleep, then hotfoot for home in the morning."

"Aye, Jesco. Glad to be headin' in that direction."

"See you there." He turned to Marisola. "Let's ride. We'll check out the defences at Lesser Walden tonight and make the Castle by noon tomorrow. Be interesting to see how Lord Waldheim is doing."

She gave him an upside-down grin. "Scared to death and not showing it, I'd guess."

As he should be.

They heeled up to a trot.

Kitten.

?

Can you do something about this horse?

I can hardly train him to a smoother gait. Would you settle for strengthening your legs and dulling the pain from other parts of your anatomy?

I could use that.

* * *

They stayed at Lesser Walden, a tiny, well-built fortress that backed against the mountains of the Leute, and spent the evening discussing the situation with the Lord Walde, a young man but capable, in Kitten's estimation.

At least he doesn't think he's a hero.

Marisola grinned. *Only room for one hero in this war, is there?*

Yes, and it better be us, or the whole realm is in trouble.

They woke in the morning stiff and aching, but forced themselves onto the road in good time.

On a fresh mount with an easier gait, Marisola's muscles soon stretched out and her spirits rose. They chatted in a more relaxed manner as they trotted along.

Waldheim Castle was another throwback to the age that had created Falkengard. A blocky, grim fortress of heavy stone, it sat on the crown of a hill overlooking a fertile valley. Farther to the north the valley opened wider and wider, and the hills faded down to disappear into the rolling prairie and the mists of distance.

Marisola looked up as they rode through the dark granite walls. "This castle was built to defend the valley. Turns out it was a good idea."

Jesco scanned the area. "Can't see a bunch of horsemen having much luck. Do the Ulaan know anything about siege engines?"

Not that I am aware of. It has been many years, though, and even the most primitive of barbarians modernize when it suits them.

Jesco clucked to his panting horse, and they clopped across the drawbridge. "Wouldn't want to be down here looking up if the gate was closed."

Lord Waldheim, a stocky, florid man with blond hair unfashionably long and rather unkempt, strode up as they dismounted. He stood, hands on hips, and regarded them. "So that's the state of the realm, is it? We ask for help, and they send a cripple, a girl and four soldiers."

Marisola withstood his scrutiny. "Jesco and I had a bet on the way here. We both lose. You're more scared than I thought and hiding it worse than he said you would be."

Before the surprised man's mouth could open, Jesco stepped forward with his harsh laugh and laid an arm around the lord's shoulders. "And now you have the measure of the help you've been sent. What we need is a large mug of ale a soft chair, and a bowl of that lamb stew your cooks are famous for. We wore out four horses each coming from Falkengard since noon yesterday, and my butt is sore. I'm too old for this sort of shenanigans."

With a frown back at her, the lord allowed himself to be led into his own castle. She chuckled and followed.

Hmm. Now we send Jesco to be the diplomat and patch things up after you stomp all over everyone.

The sooner he stops thinking of me as a girl, the sooner he will start obeying orders.

And you'll be giving orders, will you?

Only when we need to. At that time, everyone has to jump to obey.

My, my. You are coming along, aren't you?

I have to. We are at war, and you have taught me well.

By this time they were entering Lord Waldheim's informal reception room, and a servant appeared with large mugs of ale.

Jesco grinned. "Someone was listening."

"Stuff and nonsense. Riders approaching on a hot day. Of course there's ale. Cool from the cellar. Stew hot from the kitchen in a moment."

Marisola raised her mug high. "And I, for one, will not quibble about the cause." She nodded to the lord over the rim of the mug and tipped it, swallowing half the contents before slamming it onto the table. "Well! That's good ale, I must say."

How could you tell? You drank it too fast to taste it.

You bet your scruffy tail I drank it fast. I hate the stuff...may I assume that the stories about you keeping people sober were not just stories?

Within limits. And my tail was rather plume-like, as I remember.

Don't worry; I only plan to drink enough to make the proper impression.

She sat and looked up at Waldheim. "So. You need help. What?"

He threw himself into the large, well-used leather chair at the head of the table. "I need an army. I need a hundred knights in full armour, twenty squads of archers, and as many regiments of heavy infantry as can be scraped up in the whole realm. Nice if they'd borrow a thousand or so men from Marida as well."

"Huh! That's not likely to happen, but I'll pass it along as a desperation ploy. What leads you to see a threat of that magnitude?"

The lord pointed a thumb over his shoulder. "Did you look down the valley as you came in?"

"I did. It fades away out into the plains."

"It does. Out where the land disappears in the mist, the mouth is about five leagues across."

"And..."

"And wait for dark. You'll see."

She gave that some thought. "Campfires?"

He nodded. "The whole width of the valley. Farther, for all I can tell. I've lost three scouts, trying to get close enough to get more information."

"We lost at least one on the same mission. There are two others out there somewhere. We plan to rendezvous with them tomorrow before we head in for our own look."

"Four good men dead, but you think you'll do better?"

Marisola smiled. "You did ask for help."

She only let him stew for a moment. "We're having the same problem you are. Our analysis says a nomad breakout from their traditional ranges. An invading army. The Ulaan are a ferocious people, tough and fearless. Only the full strength of Inderjorne can possibly turn them back."

"It's nice to hear someone else say it. Your sources are accurate."

"My source is of the best. But the problem is..."

He nodded. "...to get the rest of those idiots to believe it."

"Exactly. They are too busy with their little squabbles and their dreams of past glory to bother with a mere border skirmish. Both factions are suspicious that the other side has cooked this up as some sort of ploy to put them off guard for a strike from behind."

The lord pounded both fists on the table. "You've nailed it exactly." He stared at her. "You really do know what is happening in the realm, don't you?"

She finished off her mug of ale and crashed it down. "It doesn't take a genius. It's been going on for a hundred years or more. Our task is to change it. For that we need information. Good, eyewitness information from someone with credibility."

A slight grin twisted the lord's mouth. "And that's you?"

She nodded. "My family has the king's ear and the support of the moderates on both sides."

"Ah, yes. Delfontes da Falken. A wise man, your great-grandfather. He is sorely missed when the lords of this area gather. Always had the ear of both sides. No idea how he did it. Probably the only Maridon in the realm who could speak the bare truth in the face of an Inderjornese and get away with it."

"Well, Great-grandfather is gone, and those who follow in his footsteps are back in Falkengard and Koningsholm doing what they do best. Jesco and I have other talents, and we're here to use them."

Waldheim shook his head. "And I'm not the man to stop you." He regarded her from beneath bushy brows. "Worst comes, you'll go up there and never come back, and that will be a powerful message in itself."

Jesco barked a laugh and finished his own mug. "Don't you worry. We'll be back."

The lord frowned at their drinks. "Another?"

Marisola gave her empty mug a shove, and it drifted along the tabletop to stop at the lord's elbow. "I could use a bit more."

Good trick.

I used to practice it at home. Mother hated it when I missed. But I only broke a couple of old pottery mugs.

They toured the castle, discussing methods of attack and defence, then returned to the workroom to talk tactics. The drinking went on until supper, when Marisola switched to wine. The discussion was of wars and battles, and she was able to use Kitten's extensive knowledge to impress the border lord time and again.

When darkness fell they strolled the battlements, gazing out to the north. A ground fog was rising, and far out at the end of the valley the mist glowed from below with an unearthly light. The sight put a damper on socializing, and they strode back inside, where all three immediately took long pulls at their drinks. Jesco set his mug down gently and said nothing for a long time, staring into the fire; Marisola was left to shore up the conversation.

Late in the evening Waldheim had drunk more than he should and Kitten was having trouble keeping her Hand upright. The lord slapped his open hand on the table. "You know too much. What's a young girl like you doing, wasting her time with war?"

Marisola chuckled. "My instructor had the answer and told me frequently. War always comes. We all hope that peace will last forever, but war will return, and there must be someone who is ready. In my family that person turned out to be me. Doesn't matter if I'm a woman. All that matters is that war has come, and I'm ready."

"And a damn good thing you are, my Lady. Don't care if you're a woman, either. Somebody's got to be prepared. I'm ready, for whatever little I can do."

"You can hold the border to the best of your ability as your family has done for generations. The rest is up to the king. Our guess is they'll try your walls, find them too hard and sweep on by, leaving you in enemy territory, besieged but basically intact."

"That's my prediction as well. There are steps I can take to undermine the enemy as long as I have a secure base from which to sortie. As you say, my family has experience with this."

There was a long silence. Both looked into empty glasses, but there was no desire for more.

Jesco had made no attempt to match the lord's alcohol intake, so he was there to escort Marisola to her rooms. Not that she needed it.

"The Cat kept your head clear, did she?"

"Most of this stagger is from stiff legs. I didn't drink that much, either."

"Yes, you did."

"Quite a bit, I admit. The wine was better. A successful evening, though, don't you think?"

"If he remembers half of it when he wakes up. He's very impressed with you." The old swordsman glanced at her. "So am I. Was Kitten feeding you all that?"

"A lot of it. And she's been feeding me the same for about fourteen years. Some of it had to stick." She peered out an arrow slit that looked north, and the glimmer of a thousand campfires washed the misty horizon. Shivering, she went to bed.

* * *

The next morning Marisola was up with the sun, although she was careful not to look too closely at its brightness.

Kitten, can you do something about this headache? I need to be at the top of my wits today.

I thought it better for your social development if you pay for your indiscretions of last night.

She slapped the scabbard. *Forget the social stuff and do your duty. Here comes Lord Waldheim, and he looks even more dishevelled than yesterday.*

"Good morning, my Lord. Going to breakfast?"

He merely nodded and indicated that she should precede him.

Bread and meat were laid out on the table in his workroom, with mugs for tea and a large urn steaming in the corner. She wrenched off a hunk of dark bread and tore at a corner, chewing mightily and washing it down with a swig of tea. "Ah. That feels good. Hard work coming up today." She stripped a chicken leg with her teeth and gestured out the window. "Any advice on how to approach?"

"The scouts I sent lived in the area all their lives. Didn't do them any good." He shrugged. "The hills fade down about three leagues out, but the prairie isn't flat. Just looks that way. Plenty of watercourses and the like, all running north. If it was me, I'd stay away from the main river, but follow a stream north as far as I wanted to go, look around a while, then follow a tributary south again. Keep me off the skyline and put me back in the hills."

She nodded, gnawing another chunk of bread. When her mouth was clear, she spoke. "A good plan. We'll see when we get there."

"My Lady...it's too dangerous. Do you really have to go in there?"

She smiled. "Yes, I do. As we discussed last night, if we don't get first-hand information, nobody will ever believe it's as bad as we say it is."

Kitten chuckled. *You can tell him anything you want about what you said last night. He'll have to pretend he remembers.*

"I bow to your superior knowledge of the politics in the capital. Never could understand it. Correction. Never could stand it. I understand it, all right. Greed and the drive for power. Pah!"

"I have to agree with you. Now, since I've stuffed myself with this marvellous bread, I'm ready for the road."

"Your horses are already saddled, my Lady."

She dropped a curtsey. "Thank you, my Lord. When I prove myself by coming back, you can start to call me Marisola."

"It's a deal. I wish you all the luck my men didn't have."

"I'll take it with thanks.

They started off at a slow trot, saving their mounts for...whatever might happen. A long day loomed ahead, with possible trouble at the outmost end of the journey.

For the first two leagues their route followed a well-maintained road through prosperous farms and extensive woodlots. Later on the woods fell behind, and the farming turned to ranching, with small herds of cattle spread over the thinning grass. Today the stock was held close to the dubious safety of the huge farmhouse-and-barn combinations.

They ate a quick lunch in a gully beside the road, which was now only a cart track.

"It's time we struck out overland."

Jesco nodded. "The road isn't much of an advantage, and it's too exposed." He pointed. "If we follow this gully over to that copse of short trees, we should be able to get on the south slope of that ridge. That will keep us out of sight from the north. Once we get to the end of that, we'll have to see."

"Sounds like a plan. Kitten?"

Definitely a plan. Only way to see if it's a good one is to try it.

And aren't I glad I brought you along. What wisdom!

And now we have our relationship straight. I provide the brains; you give the adulation.

Jesco chuckled, a comfortable contrast to his usual rasping laugh.

"Are you listening to this?"

"Aye." He glanced over his shoulder, to indicate the smiles on the faces of the soldiers.

You're telling everyone!

Good for morale. Also good practice for them.

I'd tell you what I thought of you, but it wouldn't be good for morale, so I'll stay polite.

Oh, don't stop on my behalf.

Shouldn't you be keeping watch, or something?

I am. There is a herd of cows in the next field, a deer in that copse of wood over there, and three cute little bunnies hiding in the hedge to our left...and it's time to get off the path.

All faces serious, they slipped into the shelter of the nearby trees, and Jesco did a quick brush of their tracks.

Who is it?

Nobody I know.

They sat in silence, bows strung, hands on hilts, while a rider trotted up the trail towards them. As he got closer, they could see that he was well armed: sword and dagger at his belt, bow at his knee. From his clothing, a local hunter.

One of Lord Waldheim's lost scouts?

That's my guess.

Shall we let him pass?

Marisola thought about that. *We'll hear his report when we get back. This would be a good time to practise.*

Wind in the trees?

Blow us away.

The Sword took the minds of her troop and blended them together, merging all with her feeling of the growing things around her. The trees, the bushes, the doe and, now that Kitten concentrated, her fawn, blending in his own way with the grass where he lay.

The rider continued down the path, oblivious.

When he was gone, Kitten relaxed her attention. *Well done, children. I'm beginning to get a good feeling about this group.*

"Deer meat for supper?"

Marisola rounded on her uncle, "You will not use Kitten...oh. You're joking." She glanced up at him. "I didn't know you joked."

"You don't know a lot about me. See what happens when you reject someone out of hand because of a few minor flaws?"

"A few minor fla...Fine. I admit it. You have a sense of humour. What a gods-awful time to show it."

She heard the chuckles behind her and turned. "All right, you bunch of comedians. Let's see how funny you feel after bashing cross-country for a candle or so." She led the way into the forest, which soon became brush, then opened up into grassland. Cutting over to the nearest streambed, she followed it down into the lower hills.

For the most part of the afternoon they zigzagged through the ever-decreasing range of hills, trying to find a path out to the plains. Several times Kitten's warning sent them to stillness while a plainsman scout bashed through the brush nearby.

Noisy lot, aren't they?

Marisola shot out the image of a smile. *No practice with trees, I suppose.*

Yes, the prairies are quite deficient in the taller species.

Gradually they made their way closer and closer to the enemy camp. If they had expected to come up against a perimeter with guards and a fence, they were disappointed. In fact, the closest they came to being caught all day was when a trio of little boys thundered down a path above their heads, aiming for a swimming hole in the very creek they were following. Silently, Kitten hiding their presence, they tiptoed their horses away.

As they moved, Marisola took advantage of every high point and lookout to scout the camp and report her vision to Kitten. By sunset, it was quite obvious.

It is time for us to leave. We have what we want.

I'd say so. If you are satisfied, Kitten...?

I am. Frightened, but satisfied. We need to get home, and fast.

I won't ask why you're frightened. Let's get out of here.

They chose the next creek they crossed, moving upstream now, wary of scouts returning from their daily patrols. But Kitten's senses always warned them, and her clouding technique kept anyone from seeing them.

It was midnight before they reached Waldheim, but the lord was still awake. He met Jesco and Marisola in his workroom, generous mugs of ale and tea available. When they were seated, he steepled his fingers and awarded her a wintery smile. "Well, Marisola, you have proved yourself. What new information have you gathered?"

She put down the mug she had been using to warm her hands and stood, moving to the map of his demesne he had hung on the wall. Drawing the Sword, she reached up to point. "I believe we got about to here." She glanced to Jesco. "The double twist in that creek is distinctive."

"Aye, that looks like it."

Waldheim nodded. "That's far enough into their camp to learn more than my men did."

She sighed. "And therein lies the problem. The news is not good."

"I somehow didn't expect that it would be."

"The usual pattern with these nomads is that a war party goes out and sweeps through an area, pillaging and burning. When they have gathered enough booty, they go galloping back to their traditional lands to enjoy their take."

"That is what I expected. Terrible, but survivable. I gather that this is not the case?"

She shook her head slowly. "The reason that the campfires spread so far in all directions is twofold. First, it is a huge group with many warriors.

"Second and worse; this is not the military camp of an invading host. It is a nomad tribe on the move. Children, flocks and even the aged are present in large numbers. They do not intend to loot and depart. They are looking for somewhere to settle...I know. Nomads don't settle. But they do shift their range from time to time, usually because of changing weather patterns or stronger tribes pushing them from their traditional pastures. Whatever the reason, we have a whole tribe of fierce nomads knocking on our door, determined to move in with us."

Lord Waldheim steepled his fingers again and stared at them. "And how does this change things?"

44

She shrugged, her lips turned down. "Not much, I suppose. Our one major advantage — the fact that our backs are to the wall and we are fighting for our homes — is now negated by the fact that they, too, are fighting for survival. We cannot present such a strong front that they give up and go look for easier pickings. They have nowhere to go. The mountains to the east are too high for their flocks and their families to cross.

Northeast is possible, but it is too late in the season.

"They could go back along the foot of the eastern mountains until they reach the end of the chain where they could continue east and south. But it is too late for this year. They would die from the winter on the open steppes.

"They are not patient people. They see us as a ripe crop that they will reap at their pleasure, as they always have."

"So where does that leave us?"

She smiled. "Exactly where we were. I will hotfoot back to Falkengard to warn everyone while you button your people up safely in your castle and hope the nomads haven't learned to make siege engines."

Waldheim allowed his hands to fall to the table. "In that case, we should all try to get what sleep we can. We have a busy time ahead of us."

* * *

They overtook the second scout around noon the next day, halfway back to Falkengard. He had not changed horses, trotting along at a steady pace designed to cover ground, but not quickly. He reined in with fear on his face at their thundering approach, but they were moving too fast for him to duck away.

The four of them pulled up, their dust cloud making his horse sneeze. "Going somewhere, Leof?"

"Lady Marisola! Am I glad to see you." He frowned. "I didn't expect anyone from the north."

She started her mount trotting along, and he followed. "We've just been up to take a look at your Ulaan. Did you get all the way around them?"

He nodded. "It's a huge camp, my Lady. They've spread all over because they need the grazing. They have herds of horses, goats and sheep. Whole families, too. I couldn't get close enough to see, though. There were too many riders scattered around."

"That's what we saw, too, and we were much closer. What happened to Gunter?"

He shrugged miserably. "He didn't make the rendezvous, and I thought my information was important enough that I'd better not wait too long."

"A good decision. Maybe he'll show up later. You keep on coming. We're changing horses up ahead, and your poor mare will never stay with us. They'll still want your whole report when you get in, so go straight to the castle and ask for Lady Caterina."

"Right you are, my Lady."

She nodded and lifted her horse to a canter, and soon he was lost behind them.

7. The Next Battle

Back at Falkengard a new bustle stirred the castle. Crews were cleaning the area outside the battlements, deepening the dry moat and ensuring a good field of fire a bowshot from the walls. The bailey fairly hummed with too many activities to encompass in the quick glance they got as Caterina rushed them straight from the saddle to the meeting room.

It all looks in order.

It had better be.

Marisola stood at the head of the big table, all eyes upon her as she gathered her thoughts. "It's probably the worst news possible." She outlined her observations and Kitten's conclusions. When she had finished, there was silence as everyone took in the situation.

Jandro was the first to speak. "The nomads are dry-plains people. They will not enjoy our mountains and lush valleys. Is there a chance they only want to move into the prairie to the north of us? Will a strong defence of our border persuade them to be good neighbours?"

Kitten had prepared Marisola with an answer for this. "We must divide the two strongest elements of the Ulaan way of life: their herding and their raiding. If they were only herders, your analysis would be correct. However, the young men think of raiding first, herding as a second occupation when they have stolen enough riches to buy a herd. It is probably their intent to clean this valley of anything worth stealing, then make the prairie to the north their new range, where they can drop into Inderjorne for a free market day whenever they feel the urge. They will not be good neighbours, Father."

Inderjorne is no longer resistant to this sort of attack.

Caterina started as the thought intruded into her mind, but she soon recovered. "What do you mean, Kitten?"

In the old days, when Falkengard, Waldheim and the other castles were built, our people were thin on the ground. When attackers came, all could run to the castle with their stock, leaving little for the enemy to steal. Later on, when our population grew, we were able to rally an army strong enough to meet invaders in the field. But always with the option of fleeing to the safety of a fortress.

Now we are far too prosperous a realm to do this. Here at Falkengard we have the castle and Falkenby Village full of townsfolk. Craftsmen, tradesmen. When the enemy comes, what will you do with your sawmill, Ecmund? The tools from your woodwork shop? There is no room in the bailey for the people, let alone their stock or their belongings.

Ecmund nodded. "And we are in the hinterland. Closer to the centre of the kingdom the towns have spread beyond their walls. Think of Hartgast. Completely undefendable."

The Ulaan will find rich pickings in Inderjorne.

Caterina stood and paced the perimeter of the table. "But we have an army. A huge one. That is our advantage. We have been so busy threatening each other that both sides have maintained the kind of standing army usually seen only in time of war."

"If we could get them to stand shoulder to shoulder instead of toe to toe."

Perica has put her finger on it, as usual. What will unite the people of Inderjorne?

Jesco snorted. "The loss of a crucial battle and the advance of the enemy towards Maridon-populated areas."

Ecmund grinned at his cousin. "Thus demonstrating that there is no acceptable military solution to our problem."

Perica shrugged. "At which point more conversation here is useless. This is a task for King Vetrorrillo. Caterina, you have come most recently from the capital. What do you see as the situation there?"

Her daughter-in-law inclined her head in thanks before she spoke.

Why are those two always so polite to each other? The thought came privately to Marisola.

Because it allows them to stay friends.

I suppose that's what good manners are for, aren't they?

My, you have learned something about humans in the last hundred and fifty years.

Be quiet and listen to your mother.

"The situation was such a muddle when I left I knew I would be better off out here finding real information. Now I hope things have settled enough that normal diplomacy can do what it has never accomplished in a century: getting these tribal savages to cooperate. The king has done his best, but he is too old to make any large change."

"What about the queen?" Ecmund glanced at his wife.

Perica's lip twisted. "Cuquita has never been a friend of ours."

Caterina laughed. "She's never been a friend of anyone. Sometimes I wonder if she even likes the king very much. But she's a fanatic about Inderjorne."

"She's a fanatic, all right. You should have seen her when we first met."

Her Majesty is no longer under the influence of the factors that troubled her then. Lady Eirlin and I saw to that. With help from Fang, I must admit.

"Yes, she will aid the king. And with three sons backing her, she is a formidable force."

"If they can keep from bickering among themselves." Jandro shuddered. "Sometimes I wonder how the king puts up with it."

Caterina stopped pacing and laid a hand on her husband's shoulder. "You wouldn't put up with it, would you, dear?"

"Certainly not. I brought my children up to be cooperative." He shot a glance at Marisola, whose face warmed during the laughter that followed.

"All right. You've had your laugh at my expense. This discussion is getting us nowhere. I agree that the king needs good information. I have that information. Mother needs to be at the centre of things where she can use her diplomatic talents," she shot her an evil grin, "to their best effect. Should I go with her?"

Caterina was about to speak but met Marisola's eyes and closed her mouth, glancing at Ecmund.

She knows when to follow the proper chain of command.

He seemed to read a private message. "No, I don't think so. The facts you have given us are unarguable. Their interpretation is best left to those with that sort of skill. You are better use out here where action might be necessary."

"True. Plus the communication aspect." She grinned in the pause that followed.

They are all so surprised that you're being agreeable, they aren't really thinking.

Sword and Hand shared a silent chuckle, then faced the table. "Kitten's abilities. We need her here and Fang in Koningsholm in order to communicate."

Her father frowned. "But surely you could go to the capital with your mother and leave the Sword here to communicate...no. I see that's a bad idea?" He raised his hands in defeat. "I have a lot to learn about magic Swords."

Marisola stared around. "I'm glad we straightened that out so easily." She turned to her mother. "The King's Mail coach will get you to Koningsholm in four days. We'll inform Tyrbrand and Eirlin tonight, and they can prepare everyone for your arrival."

"You make it sound like I'm someone special," Caterina chuckled. "Who needs to prepare for me?"

"Mother, you know they're all terrified of you. They need a few days to quake in their boots, wondering what you'll say."

"I'm not sure whether I should be flattered. Surely I have taught you that fear is a poor way to deal with people."

"You also taught me that with some people, it's the only way to get their attention."

Caterina shrugged. "Life has come to a pretty pass when my daughter can argue with me, insult me, and boot me out on the road." She spun and pointed at the Sword. "And I don't want to hear anything from you!"

Of course not, Lady Skonric.

"And whenever you call me that, I know it's an insult."

Quite the opposite, my Lady. Very few women have had the same effect on me.

"Hmm."

Ecmund sent Perica a private smile, and Marisola wondered what it had been like for her grandmother, having a Hand as a husband. Especially to this Sword.

I'll have you know that Perica and I got along very well.

Stop intruding in my thoughts. You're not supposed to be able to do that unless I invite you.

If you broadcast them on your face, I can't help it.

The meeting broke up with the decision to contact Tyrbrand and Eirlin that evening after supper to pass the bad news. The contact was brief and to the point, and served mainly to prove that the new system worked.

Then everyone went to bed for a worried sleep.

8. For the Future

Marisola appeared in her sitting room after breakfast with a towel and fresh underclothes. "I'm going for a bath."

Whatever you think is best. Swords do not have noses, so I can't help you.

She grinned. "Well, don't get bored while I'm gone."

"Oh, I have a few small details to work out. I'll fill my hours usefully."

"It doesn't take hours for me to bathe."

Maybe that's your problem.

She snapped her towel in Kitten's direction and slipped out, doing a bit of footwork Jesco had taught her as she dodged around the doorjamb.

Somebody's coping well. Now for someone who isn't. Kitten sent out a subtle call. No words, just a suggestion. It wasn't long before Jandro stuck his head in the door. She lay on the table and regarded him.

"Marisola?"

She is not here.

"That's strange. She wanted to see me. I was sure it was in her rooms."

I wanted to see you. I sent the message. Please sit for a moment.

The lord sat, his shoulders slouching. "What did you want to see me about, Sword?"

You are not happy, Jandro.

"My realm is about to be overrun, my demesne will be on the front line of the most important battle, and my daughter will be in the centre of it all. Happiness doesn't enter into it."

You are a good man, Jandro Delfontes da Falken.

"I don't see much place for a good man, these days."

That's where you're wrong. We need all the good men we can get.

"Good men with swords. Fighters."

No, I mean good men. Those with pure thoughts and love in their hearts.

The lord bowed his head into his hands. "I don't find much use for love in this realm right now."

I call false for two reasons. First, your wife. Where do you think she gets the strength to be the leader she is?

"Not from me. I can hardly lend her what I don't have."

Ah, but you lend her what you do have. Your unconditional love and support. Do you think a woman in this time could go out alone and do what she does? I say, no. She can do what she does because she knows her back is safe. You will be there, no matter whether she wins or loses. That is what gives her the strength to extend herself beyond what she otherwise could accomplish. Keep that in your mind.

"I can tell where you're going with this."

Hah! Nobody ever said you were stupid. Where am I going?

"Second will be my daughter. I have given her the unconditional love and support all her life that has made her confident enough to go out and get herself killed."

Again, wrong. She is in mortal danger in any case. I take responsibility for that. Your love and support gives her the confidence to survive. To succeed, even. I will tell you something about Swords and their Hands. The Sword can train the Hand and fortify the Hand in battle. But there comes a point where skill is not enough. Ask Jesco about it. And when that time comes, it is only the strength of spirit of the Hand that will pull us through. You have given your daughter that. You must continue.

"Thank you, Kitten. I suppose you could be right."

I usually am. And come to think of it, there is another reason you are wrong.

A crooked smile crossed the man's face. "I can't wait."

When this is all over, a new situation will exist in Inderjorne. I can see it coming. In the new realm that is forming, a very short window of opportunity will flash by where the people can be changed. Where old prejudices have been disputed and new ideas can grow. That is the time for good men to step up and lead. That is when you will come into your own. Wait for it, watch for it, and do not be afraid, because all those people you have supported will be looking around for someone to tell them what to do.

"How do you know this?"

I only guess. But if it should happen, you must be ready. The time is short before people begin to slip back to the old ways. Be there and be prepared.

Jandro shrugged. "I suppose I can do that. I would like to think I could be of use."

No, no, no. Not, 'I suppose.' Never, 'I would like.' You must approach your time of ascendance with the same determination a Swordsman approaches a battle. Fiercely. With enthusiasm.

"Kitten, I'm not sure I can manage 'fiercely.' It isn't really me. But enthusiasm is well within my grasp, and determination and willpower are my strengths. When the time comes, I will be ready."

Good. And don't forget your present assignment.

"I'm not likely to. My family is my life." The lord rose, looking back once again. "And thank you, Kitten. You give me hope."

Kitten felt his presence dwindle. *Now I have prepared for the future. The tough part is making sure it happens.*

9. Victory!

Kitten, Marisola and Jesco were training in the practice room at the castle. Not a full-on workout; the old swordsman was demonstrating some of the finer moves he had learned in his long career, techniques using either hand, as his handicap forced him to do.

They were in the middle of a quick passage when Kitten felt a distracting pull. All at once Marisola's balance wavered, her head spinning. Kitten hastily re-established contact. *Sorry, Hand. My error.*

Jesco lowered his point, concern on his face. "What's wrong, Marisola? You look..."

She shook it off. "I...I'm fine. But I wasn't. Kitten?"

I apologize if I upset your equilibrium. I received an outside impulse. It was very weak, and I had to use all my powers of concentration to receive it. I suppose I stole some of yours as well. Hence your disorientation.

"What was it? A message?"

I believe so. I had the distinct impression of sunset.

"That's a message?"

That is all we need, considering the circumstances.

"I agree."

"Is it possible that a mere Swordsman might discover what has intruded into my lesson?"

Marisola grinned at Jesco. "Only one person would or could be sending us a message like that. Tyrbrand wants to talk at sunset. Something must have happened. Kitten, did he sound angry or happy?"

Nothing. All I got was an image of the sun setting. No emotion, no words. My Lord Magician is remarkably efficient, as we have noted many times.

She turned to Jesco. "Looks like you're staying to dinner. Do you want to send a messenger to Wynna?"

He grinned. "My wife Listens better than anyone in the demesne. I'm sure she already knows."

Marisola frowned. "Wait a minute. We never thought of that. If we're trying to get messages back and forth, we could use someone who Listens. Kitten?"

Little Sword Lady will be here for supper. I took the liberty of inviting her.

"Well, don't you two get off in a corner talking about needles and point sharpness and the tempering of metal and forget why she's here."

She is one of the more interesting of humans if I wish conversation. Which I don't, at the moment.

Kitten's presence withdrew, and Marisola winked at her old teacher. "Now I've hurt her feelings. Don't worry, she'll come out of it."

"If she doesn't, Wynna will bring her around. Good at cheering people up, my wife."

"Yes, so I hear." Marisola decided to let that go. Jesco never talked about his problems, and she never asked.

They sheathed their weapons and strolled out to inform the rest of the group.

* * *

As the sun sank towards the western hills, they tried to relax in Lady Perica's workroom, after-dinner drinks in their hands. But an underlying tension tainted the air. Darkness approached, people glanced at each other but no one spoke. Time would tell.

So they were rather taken aback when the first seeking tendrils touched their senses. It was clear that it not the cold, precise mind of Tyrbrand that called them. Immediately they all touched Kitten, and the message jumped to clarity.

Good evening, my family. And a very good evening it is.

Eirlin? Is something wrong? Where is Tyrbrand?

Nothing is wrong, Ecmund. My dear husband, Tyrbrand the Great Magician, is sitting beside me, unable to concentrate well enough to control this sending, because he keeps breaking down in helpless laughter. How Fang can concentrate in such a situation, I do not know, but I am thankful his training has progressed so far.

Glances passed around the workroom at Falkengard. Marisola frowned. "Uncle Tyrbrand? Helpless laughter?"

Concentrate, everyone. My Lady Healer, this is very unsettling for all of us at such a sober time. Could you explain, please?

Most certainly, Kitten. I'm sure Tyrbrand will apologize when he puts himself back into a proper frame of mind. But I detect a much clearer message from you. I had thought it would be harder...ah. That explains it. Wynna, my dear. They thought to include you! How intelligent of someone. How are you?

I am well enough, Eirlin, but everyone here is dying with curiosity. What happened?

The clarity of the message boosted again, and the incisive mind of the Magician appeared. *I must tell this story myself. The culmination of all my work for the past forty years just took place in front of my eyes and the eyes of every noble in the realm.*

He paused to concentrate.

But I will control my glee and tell you what you want to know. Yes, we have won. Inderjorne will be drawn, kicking and squirming no doubt, but drawn nevertheless into unity. And all because of two women! How ironic. How appropriate.

This is how it happened.

The King called a meeting of the full Assembly today. He required all members to attend. After the usual beginning, just when everything was starting to disintegrate into the usual verbal brawl, his Majesty intruded into the proceedings and told us that he had invited a special speaker who knew more about the situation than anyone. He was sure, he said, that hearing this information would help people decide the right thing to do.

The speaker, of course, was Caterina Skoenric Delfontes. It was no surprise to us, but you could see the disquiet in the ranks of the fanatics. The rabid Maridons are afraid to offend her in case she throws her weight behind the Inderjornese. The Inderjornese extremists fear that she will discredit them in the eyes of the moderates. At least, that's what they say. I think they are just afraid of her. As they should be.

Lady Caterina started out with the information she brought from Falkengard. Eyewitness reports, facts, numbers, laid out calmly and evenly. Heads nodding all over the chamber. Then she got to Kitten's analysis: the power and intentions of the Ulaan and the need for cooperation. At that point, I could feel her losing them. Mutters in the farther ranks, that sort of thing; you can tell when they're slipping back into their ruts.

And then Cuquita stood! The queen has never, in all our history, addressed the Assembly at any other time than her coronation day. Everyone was shocked, including Caterina, but our family is made of stern stuff. She merely nodded to the queen to take the floor.

There was a pause in which everyone's tension rose while Cuquita scanned the room. Believe me, many faces turned away, afraid to meet her eye. Then she started out. "I hope you are listening to Lady Delfontes. I feel your attention wavering, and I caution you not to fall back into your usual stupor. It would not be to your advantage." And then she stopped. That was it. She nodded gracefully to Caterina and sat down.

So Caterina continued her narrative, but something had changed. Do you remember how Lord da Baneza used the power of his Sword, Ecuas, to entrance his audience? Well, Cuquita started doing the same thing. She was drawing power from me and from all the other Sensitives in the chamber, molding them together into one unified force. As Caterina spoke on, she must have realized that something was working, and she became more impassioned. And then...

... I'd better let Eirlin explain the next part.

Eirlin's calm, sweet presence took over. *"Cuquita looked up to the gallery where I was sitting. Just looked at me. I don't think she has any idea how she does this trick, but she knows that I can do it because I used it on her once. In fact, that's probably how she learned about it. And when she met my eyes, I could feel her drawing on my power and on Fang's.*

For a moment I was unsure what to do, but I soon realized that this was my chance. I nodded once and took over. I used Fang's power to control the situation. Of course, the queen wanted me to boost her ability, but I didn't. I smoothed it all over, softening the raw edges. There were plenty of raw edges, considering from whom the control came. So I added my gentle Healing to the unbridled power of those two, and we led those fractious nobles down a garden path like lambs.

When Caterina finished, Cuquita stood again and thanked them all for listening so well. And then she said she had one point of her own to make. "Lady Caterina, there has been a suggestion that the reluctance of some people to take part in this war is through fear. What do you think?"

And Caterina looked shocked. "Oh, no, your Majesty. Not the valiant lords of Inderjorne."

And the queen nodded. "Well, that's good to hear. Those who are afraid are so tiresome, don't you find?"

Tyrbrand broke in. *And that's when I had to clamp down to keep from laughing. Those two carried on a polite conversation like two ladies at a tea party, dissecting the motivation of anyone who would stand aside when his realm needed him. When they finished, they came to the conclusion that Inderjorne would stand behind the King in whatever way necessary to protect the realm from this terrible threat. And when we walked out of that hall, there was not a man who would dare, even if he desired it, to waver from that goal.*

I tell you, it was wonderful!

The link faltered as people's concentration wavered in their glee and Kitten tried to regain her control. But her fear began to overwhelm her. Old memories of blood and screaming edged into her mind, and she could not chase them away.

Kitten? Kitten, what's wrong?

WHAT'S WRONG? Her blast of anger brought everyone's attention snapping back into the merge. *You are children playing with sharp knives. You are a campfire in a dry forest, spewing sparks in the air. You do not know the powers you trifle with!*

But Kitten, what do you mean?

With an effort, the Cat drew her claws in. *I must make you understand. My Lord Magician, what is the greatest danger posed by all these new Maridon Sensitives?*

It is the fact that they are untrained. Tyrbrand's intensity rose as he moved into a favourite subject. *They have powers that they know little of. Their desire is to learn more, to use those powers, but it takes one...a lifetime of training...*Now the Magician's mind was working.

...to learn to control them on one's own. That is exactly my point. You are worried that some random Sensitive without proper Inderjornese schooling will chance onto a dangerous power and use it for nefarious purposes. I will tell you something far more likely and more dangerous still. Some well-meaning person will chance upon a dangerous power and use it for the good, not realizing what disaster could occur in spite of his or her virtuous intentions.

There was a pause.

...and that is what is happening, here?

It is, my Lord Magician. And that person was me.

Marisola's hand clamped firmer on her hilt. *No, Kitten. It wasn't you that did this!*

Many years ago, before your parents were born, I used this technique to help your grandparents and the king counter a great danger to the realm. In that process, I turned the knowledge of the technique loose in the kingdom, where it has lurked in strange corners looking for a place to burst out. That is what happened today.

Lady Eirlin, I congratulate you on your cool head and presence of mind. If you had done what the queen asked and given her more power, it would have ended with bloody mayhem in that chamber, from which Inderjorne would have emerged, broken and divided, to be plucked like a ripe fruit by these invaders. In doing so, you have proved once again your fitness to be Protector of this realm. But even you are caught up in the glory of this power. You must concentrate on your role.

I see. I will reassess my actions.

I hope you all see. And do you know what the greatest piece of luck is in all this mess? The fact that I have used this technique before and learned the terrible consequences. It assuages my guilt a small amount that the many people who died at that time did not suffer in vain. My experience allows me to see the precipice that yawns before your stumbling feet so I can turn you away before you step ahead into oblivion.

I am not exaggerating. I am also aware of the irony. I am probably making this perfectly clear because of the fact that I am using the technique on you right now as Cuquita did on the Assembly. And I hope that this means you will believe me. This power is to be used with great discretion by those with the proper training – and there are very few of us – and no one else. Remember. Children playing with sharp daggers. Have I made myself clear?

Silence reigned. Finally the Magician took control of the link.

You have made your point very clearly, Ailur, Cloud Cat of the Leute, and the lesson resonates through my soul, reminding me of every teaching I ever held to be true. We will regard this new technique as a double-edged sword and consider its application carefully. May I assume that we will still use it as a method of communication?

Thus putting me in the same quandary as forty years ago. Yes, for the good of the realm we must continue. The chance of a problem is very small with a group so closely allied and separated by such distance. And I will watch and guard.

As will I.

And I'm sure our Lady Protector will be vigilant as well. Fine. And now that we have committed ourselves to the use of this dangerous tool, what should we be saying to each other?

The Magician's presence lost its lighthearted tone. *The king is rallying all levies. The first of our armies will be on the march in your direction within the next few days, led by Prince Guevejar, with the title of Commander-in-Chief. After that the others will take to the road as they arrive here, as they can be armed and supplied. I assess it will be at least ten days before you have a decent army at your disposal, and it will not be nearly enough to defend the border.*

What is your assessment of Guevejar as a commander?

He is well schooled in the arts of war. As long as he keeps his temper, he will be a good leader.

Too much like his mother?

Exactly.

Ecmund's attention wavered towards his wife. *You have spent time with Cuquita over the years. What do you think?*

If he's anything like his mother, he wants to do his duty to the best of his ability. He wants too hard, and when his path is blocked, he takes it badly. I suggest you deal with him, Ecmund. I have heard nothing to indicate that he has a problem with women, but...

...with a mother like that, he probably has not had the best experience with them. Fine. I will use my diplomatic skills as I must. Do you have any orders for us, Tyrbrand?

Keep a very close eye on our visiting friends. I hesitate to suggest it in the light of our recent conversation, but is there any way we can set up a similar communication to this one between Waldheim and Falkengard?

If I take Kitten to the front, as I would be doing anyway, I can at least send messages to Wynna. Jesco will be with me, and he'll want to keep track of what's happening at home.

Marisola smiled at the two, Seamstress and Swordsman, clutching the Sword hilt, their free hands entwined.

All right. We have been talking for too long, and Kitten is flagging. Pass news along when you can. Goodbye all. A good start to a bad time.

They said their farewells and sat back, staring at each other.

Perica grinned. "Who would have thought it. Caterina and Cuquita. Those poor lords didn't know what hit them."

Ecmund shook his head. "I'm worried about this thing with Kitten. I hope we can control it."

The Sword could not find her usual sharp response. *Don't worry, Ecmund. I don't have the energy to do anything evil today.*

The former Hand fixed his granddaughter with a stare. "This is the point where the new Hand learns her responsibility. Kitten has been your teacher and your leader. Now the relationship must balance out, and — yes, she always complains when we say this — you are most needed in the area of morals and proper behaviour.

I am too tired and worried to complain. Listen to him, Hand. He was one of the best I have known. She faded from her Hand's perception.

Marisola faced her grandfather. "You caught her at a weak moment. Don't let it go to your head."

He laid a hand on her shoulder. "I am certain you will be wonderful together. You two are the kind of match that she and I never could be. If there is honour and glory and a Name to be won, this is your chance."

Marisola patted his hand. "And you have taken great pains to teach me that glory and all its trappings are not something you seek. Keep doing your duty, and glory will seek you." She shrugged. "Or not."

Her father came up on her other side. "Well, I have a castle to prepare for war. I'm assuming you'll be headed north?"

"In a few days. But considerably slower than last time, and with better preparation. I want a good horse when I get there."

"Xavier? Please consult with your sister about her mount and supplies. I assume Tariq is in top form?"

"Anxious to be on the road, Father." Chavito turned to Marisola. "The stableboys will thank you for running some of that deviltry out of him. Come down to the kitchens." He put an arm around her shoulders. "The cook and I have some ideas about travel rations I think you'll like."

## 10.	The Twins

War preparations continued, and Marisola began to get a feeling for how complicated it all was. For example, her grandfather pulled her aside two days later as she was headed out of the castle.

"Do you have a moment, Marisola?"

"Of course, Grandfather. After I go to the armoury to check on their progress with the new arrowheads and swing past the stables to see about the horses for the journey...oh, yes, and I got sidetracked by a complaint about that cook we hired. The men say they're feeling sick after meals. I have to figure out if they're getting belly aches or they're just belly-aching like the men always do."

He smiled. "This won't take long. I had a letter from Eirlin today."

"Yes, I know. Why did she write so soon after we talked? How are things going at the capital?"

"About the same as usual. Slow progress, but not much slower than we suspected. There was a note for you, though. She wanted to tell you the Twins are coming."

"The Twins. That's nice. They've always been very good to me, their...what am I...second cousin?"

Ecmund grinned. "Their mother is sister to your grandfather, so it's a bit complicated. Something like that."

She shrugged. "I like them. Sort of. How can you know how you feel about people that are so different? Why are they coming?

"They said they want to help. With the war. They mentioned you specifically."

"Me?"

"They are excellent swordsmen. As a team, unbeatable."

"I never heard that."

"Ask Jesco. He spent a lot of time with them when they were young, when Tyrbrand and Eirlin were busy putting the kingdom back together. Think of two swords directed by one mind."

Marisola regarded him. "Do you want me to look around for a place for them?"

Ecmund shook his head. "It isn't that simple. You can't. And even if you give them a duty, they'll just do something else."

"What do I do, then?"

He shrugged. "Keep in touch with them. Tell them what's going on, what you need. If they think of a way to help, they'll do it. If you're lucky, they may even tell you what they're doing. Usually not, thought."

He turned to face her earnestly. "Whatever they do, it will be for the good of Inderjorne. You can count on that."

Faced with this nebulous reassurance, Marisola smiled. "In that case, I will do as you suggest. You've never sent me wrong yet. I had planned to leave in two days, but I'll wait until I talk to them." Then she had a thought. "How do I tell them apart?"

Her grandfather grinned. "Usually it's not important, but if you really need to know, Divo is right-handed, and Ovid is a leftie. He always stands on the left."

"But those aren't their names. Aren't they Aelfric and Sigyn?"

"No, Aelfric and Sigyn are the names Eirlin and Tyrbrand gave them. They came to their parents when they were about ten years old and told them what their real names were, and that was that. They don't answer to anything else. Don't worry, you'll get used to them. If you ever notice them. They're very self-contained."

"Fair enough. I've got enough to notice at the moment."

"You have." He slapped her shoulder, turning her back towards the door. "Armoury, stables, kitchen. Away you go."

She returned to her duties, but her cousins stayed on her mind.

* * *

They showed up the next day, having almost paced the King's Mail. Their mounts — dark bays but not quite matching — were mud-spattered and tired but in good condition. As were their riders.

Marisola, warned about two warlike strangers approaching, met them outside the castle to escort them into the bailey. They were still on their horses as she came out. *Divo on the right, Ovid on the left. Their right and left, not mine, I suppose. Oh, this is going to be great.*

The moment they saw her they piled off their mounts and strode forward, gathering her in a three-person melee of arms and heads.

"Little Marisola..."

"...how nice to see you."

They regarded each other across the top of her head.

"My, how you..."

"...have grown up."

She looked up at them. Whipcord thin and sleek-muscled, they towered over her, their identical round faces framed by waving blond hair. Dressed in well-worn leather travel gear, they were rather handsome in a dashing way. Long rapiers on opposite hips helped the image. "I don't remember you being that tall."

"Oh, that's just..."

"...our way. We try to seem..."

"...small so we don't..."

"...bother anyone."

She got the vague impression that one of them always spoke first, but it was all too overwhelming to worry about, right now.

"Well, get your packs and we'll turn your horses over to the stable lads. Any worries?"

"No, the horses..."

"...travelled very smoothly."

With quick efficiency they unloaded their gear, and two gawking stable boys came forward to take the reins. The twin on the right — *Divo?* — slapped one boy on the shoulder. "Watch the brown one's heels. He's feisty when he hasn't been fed."

Noting the boy's confusion, she stopped. "They're both brown, Divo."

"Oh, no. Falcon..."

"...is brown. Kestrel..."

"...is browner. Can't you tell?"

The two went off into gales of laughter.

Marisola shook her head and motioned the boy to take the horses. *This is going to be so much fun.*

I think so.

She slapped Kitten's hilt. *Did you think that was funny?*

Well, cats don't see colours like humans do, but I get the joke.

She gave up. "This way, gentlemen." As she led them into the castle and down the hallway to their quarters, she tried to anticipate the conversation. If she said the right thing they would merely smile or nod together, and she didn't have to decipher their strange alternating speech.

Once they were settled and she was going about her other business, she continued the conversation with Kitten.

What did you think about the 'seeming smaller' idea?

Not unusual. You know how my 'wind in the trees' trick works?

Sort of. You make it so people can't see us.

Not really. We can't tell folk what to see, but we can influence what they notice. I learned this long ago when I was forced into the companionship of small forest animals for a few years. If you have the right attitude, you aren't noticed. And if one person doesn't notice you, that helps influence others. The larger the group, the easier to hide from them in plain sight. If the Twins want to seem smaller, they can.

I sort of understand that.

But it means that, Sensitive as each one is, they are more than twice as Sensitive when they join their talents together. They might be very useful.

I'll remember that. But these are the Twins we're talking about.

I have known them all their lives. I will find a way.

11.   New Pet

Later that afternoon Marisola was walking across the bailey when Kitten's warning stopped her.

I think you want to look over in that corner.

She looked. The Twins were kneeling, backs to her, concentrating on something on the ground. She strolled over. *They know we are coming. They always do.*

"What's up, gentlemen?"

They turned, and from between them a half-grown barn-cat leapt, landing in front of her with his claws outstretched. He crouched, his ears flat, eyes slitted, then stalked forward, a rumbling growl stretching his slender throat.

Marisola held firm, and her tiny assailant sidled around her. When he had completed a full circle, he stopped growling, regained a normal mien and turned his back, scratching a scuff of gravel in her direction with one back leg. Then he sauntered back to the Twins, jumped on the shoulder of one of them and curled around his neck, purring.

She regarded their serious faces. "What are you doing with this cat?"

"We thought we might...

...want a pet."

"So you picked the most ferocious kitten in the whole barn."

"Oh, no...

...he's not fierce. Just...

...protective."

Marisola closed her eyes mentally and listened to what her ears told her, ignoring that the voice came from two directions. It helped. "I see."

Communication flashed between them. "May we…

…talk to…

…your Sword?"

"I'd prefer it. This vocal trick complicates things."

"Yes…

…we're sorry…

…it must be disconcerting, but…

…sometimes it's hard to be sure…

…who's thinking…

…and who's talking."

"So it's like you're one brain in two heads."

They grinned. "…something…like that. We can speak separately…Mother says…it's polite. But with family…you don't have to be so polite…do you?"

"I'm getting used to it already. But what do you have to say to Kitten?"

"Can we…talk to her?"

My Hand and I can play the same games. What do you wish to know?

Their voice came clearly now, and Marisola was able to relax and listen.

It's about this cat. One reached over and scratched the ear of the kitten draped over his brother's shoulder.

He's a very nice animal. What about him?

Are some cats special?

Kitten pictured a huge, grey cat, preening her long hair. *I'd like to think I wasn't exactly ordinary.*

Right. That's what we mean. This cat must be very Sensitive or we wouldn't have noticed him. All the other cats wander about with their little minds full of mice and sex and warm places to lie in the sun. This one walks around investigating people's auras. We could hear him, and we came looking.

And what did you find?

He was looking for us. He knew we were here. Cats are curious, and he came looking. Do you think we can keep him?

Marisola grinned. *He's a barn cat. I doubt if you're taking him from any important duties.*

Oh, no. He's an excellent mouser. He always knows where they are.

I'm sure the other cats will take up the slack. Did you want to ask Kitten anything else?

No, not really. We might need assistance with raising him.

Kitten sent them an ironic claw-stretch. *I've never raised a baby — I refuse to count Fang — so I'm not sure I'd be much help, but feel free to ask.*

Thank you, Kitten. We will. Thank you Marisola.

Oh, no problem.

You have more important things to do. We wish we could help.

If I can think of anything, I'll be sure to tell you.

The two faces burst into identical smiles. *Would you? That's wonderful. We would like to help our realm, but it's hard to find a way.*

I know how you feel. Sometimes I have no idea what to do, either.

We are an excellent swordsman.

She grinned. *Do you realize what you just said?*

That is accurate. When we fight together, we fight as one.

I would have expected that.

Yes, we are rather unbeatable. You understand how one swordsman can hold off two enemies by playing their differences and lack of communication against them?

Yes. Can you do that?

When we fight together, we can hold off four enemies and more. In fact, the more there are, the easier it is.

I have experienced that in a way. Interesting.

Yes, we, too, find it interesting. They grinned. *Rather useful as well.*

There was a long pause, and Marisola gathered the conversation was over.

The barn cat undraped itself, hopped to the ground and stalked off. With grins at her over opposite shoulders, the Twins followed.

12.   Company on the Road

The night before Marisola and her group set off they held one last meeting. When she arrived the Twins were there, sitting quietly in the corner of the Work Room, their cat curled on one lap. Since there was no reason for them not to be there, she gave them a pleasant nod and sat at the table.

"What's our situation?"

Ecmund took it upon himself to answer. "Nothing has changed. The king is rallying his levies, but they are coming slowly. We don't know enough about the enemy's movements. If they were coming this way, our scouts would have warned us. That's why you're heading north tomorrow."

Perica leaned forward, and he nodded to her.

"Once you leave, our communications will be weak."

"We have a powerful enough unit to send a simple message in an emergency. If you can't talk back, that's not a serious problem. Father, is there anything you need?"

"More information." Jandro shook his head. "I wish we had more scouts out in other directions. We see the Ulaan as a huge army that will swarm from the north. They have fast horses. What if they send a light contingent roundabout? As we learned that first day, they could take people unawares, and even a small group could overrun a village.

Marisola looked at Jesco. "We don't really need four of us."

He nodded. "We were planning to take Leof and Meir because they are the best stalkers we have, but their stealth will be wasted under Kitten's protection."

Jandro winced. "I don't like to send you out poorly protected."

She shrugged. "I don't like it, either, but if you need good men elsewhere, it makes sense. We won't try to get close again. We're mainly going there to provide communication.

"Will that weaken your merge?"

I'll have to work harder. We will manage. There are Sensitives in Waldheim. Perhaps we can use them.

"We'll go."

All heads turned to the corner. The Twins were smiling, one petting the cat.

"We can go...

...we can help in Kitten's merge."

"You can?"

"Oh, yes...

...we have excellent...

...concentration. We've...

...been practising."

Marisola frowned. "How do you practise?"

"We Listen."

"When we're talking to Koningsholm?

They both nodded, serious now.

Marisola looked around the room. No one had ever figured out how to deal with these two, so she didn't expect any opinions now.

Perica grinned. "What will your mother say?"

They looked at each other. "Well done?"

Kitten. She kept the message very tight. *What do you think?*

They are very powerful in their strange way. I told you.

"Well, if you can fight as you say..."

"Don't worry, they can." For some reason Jesco was smiling. Not his usual wry twist, but a pleasant smile.

She returned it. "Then that's settled. We'll practice on the road and see how our skills fit together."

"Anything else?" Ecmund looked around the group. "In that case, we all have preparations to work on."

Everyone rose, but Marisola sent a message through Kitten, and the Twins and Jesco stayed. When the rest were gone, she motioned the two to join them at the table. They did so, looking at her with interest.

"Are you properly equipped for this trip?"

Both nodded.

"Armed?"

"Sword...buckler...bow...war arrows."

They paused, and one of them spoke alone. "Boot-top dagger."

Marisola feigned surprise. "Just one?"

"Steel knuckles." The other patted his jacket.

They smiled together. "It's fun...to be different...sometimes."

"Hmm. And a surprise for an enemy as well. Fine. We'll be heading out at sunrise. Horses organized?"

They nodded.

"Right. Brown and Browner. Cat carrier?"

They grinned.

She shot an enquiring glance at Jesco, but he gave that big smile again. "I'm glad you're coming, lads."

"We're glad we're coming, too." They both spoke together, then returned to their usual style. "Marisola isn't...but she'll soon...come around."

She had her own opinion about that, which she sent privately to Kitten. *Grandfather always impressed upon me the importance of all the different manifestations of the powers of Inderjorne, and the need to use them all to make the realm function at its best. I will find a way. That is my duty.*

She sent a mental shrug. *Not that I know where to start. They're ten years older than I am and far more experienced in their own way.*

Don't worry. They won't be a problem, and they might be very helpful. I rather like them.

You do? Why? Besides the fact that they like cats.

They're different. Powerful, too. We can use that.

We agree there.

Of course we agree. I am the Sword, and you are my Hand. We always agree.

She winced. *Sooner or later, anyway.*

* * *

The four of them left Falkengard early the next morning.

Six, actually.

I know, I know. Ten if you count the dratted horses. But you and I are a unit, and I'm damned if I'm going to count that kitten as one of my party, no matter how cute he is.

He is more than cute. He is Sensitive.

Another element about which I have even less idea how it might be used.

They saluted the guards at the top of the town wall as they galloped past Falconby and hit the northerly road.

They were taking it easy on their mounts, with several long days' ride ahead of them and a fight possible at any moment. For travel in familiar territory Jesco and Marisola led. The Twins followed behind, Falcon and Kestrel — *I wonder which is which, or if they switch back and forth —* side by side, a wicker cage behind the saddle on the left, although the cat spent equal time crawling over both men and horses and tearing around on the ground.

Don't worry, Dear One. It is all part of his training.

They made good time in fine weather over hard roads, staying at manor houses on the way. Marisola watched her little party to ensure they caused and received no trouble. The kitten was the most likely victim, but a pattern soon emerged.

When they approached any village or manor, the cat would jump down and scamper ahead, rubbing against the legs of anyone who came out to meet them. He would then range wider until he inevitably ran up against one of the local dogs, usually the leader. There would be a brief standoff, during which both animals stood perfectly still. Then the dog would seem to shrug his shoulders and stroll off, and his pack would follow him.

In the stables it was different. There, he would make cute with the lead cat, rolling on his back and batting with soft paws at the animal's nose when it came to check him over, and soon the two would be strolling around like the local lord showing an honoured guest the premises.

The Twins likewise made themselves inconspicuous, chatting in a friendly way with anyone they met.

Did you notice that only one of them ever speaks to strangers?

What?

Ovid talks. Divo nods and smiles at all the right places while his brother rambles on. They seek not to bother people with their strange ways.

Marisola chuckled. *They are a mixture of their mother and father. As unbending in their pursuits as Tyrbrand, but as considerate of others as Eirlin.*

That is a very astute observation, Hand. Your training progresses.

She slapped Kitten's hilt. *I didn't learn that from you, Sword.*

I didn't say you did.

One lunchtime they were resting while the horses grazed, and the kitten was having a great time batting at leaves and wrestling with them to the amusement of the humans. Marisola thought to ask what its name was.

They looked at her, surprise on both faces. "We don't...have a name for him. He is..." and they sent her a flash of...*something*...that identified the little creature fully in less than a heartbeat.

"That's an interesting way to give a name. It certainly works."

"When you are...talking to Kitten...do you give people names?"

She considered. "I suppose I don't. It's hardly necessary, because we always know who we're talking about."

"Exactly...you're doing...the same thing."

"Yes. But we need a name for the little guy for when we're talking to other people."

There was a brief burst of mental activity that even Kitten couldn't follow, during which the cat froze in position, staring at the brothers. Then they burst into laughter. The kitten turned and stalked away and was soon lost in the undergrowth.

The Twins stifled their hilarity. "We made...a mistake...we shouldn't have laughed...his feelings are hurt."

"What does he want his name to be?"

"Ambassador."

"Ambassador? Of whom? To What?"

"That's the...funny part...Ambassador of Lions."

Highly appropriate, I would say.

"My experience with Kitten tells me to take this seriously."

They shrugged.

"Wait a minute. He always leads when we enter a town. So that means he's our ambassador. So who are the lions?"

They smiled.

"You are! You think of yourselves as lions."

"And Kitten is...a Cloud Cat."

"This is interesting. So, what do I think of myself as? Some sort of cat?"

"No, you are more complicated." The two exchanged glances.

"And more simple."

"Say, are you two disagreeing on something?"

The one on the left — *Divo?* — answered. "We find it amusing and good for our mental acuity. I consider you very complex. You think of yourself as a different person depending on whom you are speaking to. I suppose all humans do this to some degree. It is not strange at all."

"I can see that. I speak differently to Grandfather or Jesco than I would to Tyrbrand."

"Yes. Unlike Uncle Jesco."

"Why am I unlike her? Except for all the obvious reasons."

"There are only two of you. Your greatest weakness is that you are always fighting between what you know is right and where your past drives you."

The old swordsman nodded grimly. "It's not fun."

"You're saying I do it, but everybody does it." Marisola threw up her hands. "What does that mean?"

The twin on the right leaned forward. "But that is the surface. Inside, you are the simplest person we know, except Ecmund, of course. Deep inside you are Marisola. That is all."

"I suppose that makes things easy for me."

"Exactly. It is your greatest power. You are never divided against yourself."

"Yes." The twin on the left joined in. "Kitten, you think a lot about Names. You are proud of those you have earned. You wonder what others might come."

I do. They are important to me. Less than they used to be.

The left-hand brother nodded. "Marisola, what names do you dream for yourself?"

She frowned and thought about it. "I don't waste time with that sort of thing."

The brothers grinned at each other and reached out to slap hands. "Exactly."

"So in the end you agree on that, too."

"We do not...disagree. We...look from...different angles."

"A good practice."

"Our use to you...is to look from...different angles...because you focus...on one. That is...why we are here."

"Oh. That does explain a lot, I suppose. Thank you. Now I know what to expect from you."

The one on the left chuckled. "Not really."

The other nodded. "Expect the unexpected. That is why we are here."

She nodded. "I can handle that. I never expected anything different."

This time only Jesco laughed.

13.   A Meeting of Minds

They reached Waldenheim on the afternoon of the fourth day and slipped back into their old quarters with little fuss.

Until the middle of the next morning. Marisola was striding across the bailey when Kitten was distracted by a faint feeling of worry. She concentrated and caught a flavour of Ecmund.

Marisola, we have a message coming in. I told them to wait a moment.

You could talk to them?

In a manner of speaking. The Twins are in the stable.

She adjusted her course. *Let's go.*

Soon they were sitting in the sunlight in the stable yard, and Kitten reached out to the south. *All right, everyone. Marisola and I will control the merge. She speaks. The rest of you concentrate. We get the best use from focused minds.*

They joined hands on her hilt, and the message from Falkengard came through clear but faint. *There has been another raid.*

Oh, no! Where? How big?

Her father's presence took over, calm and practical. *To the west. A party similar to the one you met. Sounds like the same leader. They did not try to overrun closed farmsteads, but killed anyone they found outside and ran off all the stock they could find.*

Foraging.

It looks like it.

They will be heading back north with their booty, then. Taking the most open paths because of the herd.

Yes. They are avoiding the Demesne of the Falcon, so their best path would be past Pieterburen and Visgard, then up the Aelsund road.

The feeling of a chuckle ran through the merge, and Ecmund's placid presence permeated the bond. *Where Jesco saved Eirlin, many years ago.*

As if she needed any saving. I didn't come out much of a hero, as I recall.

Kitten gave a short hiss of disdain. *I can think of six men who might argue with that, except they can't because they're dead. But no time for old folks to relive old battles. We have a new one to work on. Fifty of their best on fast horses?*

Then we must move fast as well.

Just a scouting mission, Marisola. It is not the moment for a battle.

Yes, Grandfather. Force of arms will not win. Fear is our greatest asset.

And be careful.

It's war, Grandfather. Kitten and I are always careful.

Kitten reached in a talonned paw. *Until the time not to be careful.*

Marisola swatted the Sword and returned her attention to the merge. *If there is nothing else, we must get on the trail. We want to cut their path as soon as possible.*

There was nothing more except mutual well-wishing and several admonishments to take care which she pretended not to hear.

The moment they were clear of the merge they broke into action with no need for discussion. The Twins sprinted into the stable, Jesco moved at his own economical pace to the arms store and Marisola went to inform their host of the latest development.

"How many men do you want?"

"None, my Lord. This is scouting, and the smaller party the better."

"But you said they have fifty."

"How long will it take you to organize an equivalent force, mounted and fully armed, with supplies for three days? I want to be gone within the candle."

"I see. Is there anything else?"

She grinned. "Perhaps you could send a party west tomorrow morning. There may be cattle to retrieve."

"You're going out there to scout them and steal the stock back?"

"Depends how the bones fall. Now, I hear horses' hooves in the yard."

He rose. "By all means, my Lady."

When she got to the bailey, her little troop waited in the saddle. Receiving her travel pack and bedroll from a servant and a new sheaf of arrows from the armourer's apprentice, she mounted. Her gear settled around her, she nodded to Lord Waldheim and they turned their mounts out the castle gate.

This time there was no holding back. They had only a few leagues to go, and she was determined to get there first.

Two hours of gallop-and-trot brought them to the Aelsund Road, and they approached cautiously. It was apparent that no herd of cattle, let alone fifty horsemen, had passed here. She turned to Jesco. "Either they haven't got here, yet, or they're farther west. Ideas?"

He frowned, thinking.

Kitten sent out an image. *There's a mountain trail about an hour west.*

The swordsman nodded. "They don't know the area, so if they missed this road, they might have taken the trail."

Marisola glanced back at the Twins, who shrugged and regarded the sky. "Right. We have about three candles of daylight left. We can go there, come back, and still search to the south if they haven't been cooperative and shown up."

She heeled Tariq into a trot, and away they went.

When they reached the smaller trail, nothing moved, and the carpet of last fall's leaves was untouched since that rain a week ago. "Now what?"

Jesco looked down the trail, winding out of sight among the low hills they were crossing. "Do we assume they are south of us somewhere?"

"I think that's safe."

"Then why don't we cut south for a league or so on this trail. There are small paths between the two routes once in a while. We'll either run into the raiders as we go down, or cut across and come in behind them after they pass on Aelsund Road."

"There are high points along this crest with good views. A herd of cattle will put up dust."

Jesco nodded and took the lead. It was a narrow trail, and as the country became rougher, it twisted and turned even more. After a while the slanting sunlight began to fade, and Marisola felt uneasy. She stopped.

"We could come around a corner and meet an outrider. We need more information." She glanced at the Twins and pointed. "Could one of you cut up to the top of that ridge and get a wider look?" She had a thought. "Or do must you go together?"

The one riding in front shook his head. "We are quite capable of independent action."

The other's voice drifted up from behind. "Better if I stay here. With Kitten's help we can communicate over short distances."

"Fine. We'll keep moving, taking more precautions, so when you come back down farther along you'll be able to catch up to us."

The front twin nodded and turned his horse up the hill.

Jesco listened to him crash away through the dry underbrush. "Nobody's going to sneak up on anyone in this forest."

She slapped Kitten's hilt. "Not without help."

She nodded to Jesco, and he started out at a walk now, every sense alert.

They meandered among the low ridges for almost a candle, but nothing disturbed their progress.

Kitten was concentrating so hard on the trail ahead that she barely heard it. *Hold. Message coming.*

Marisola motioned her two companions to come up on either side, and they all touched the Sword.

Found. Aelsund Road. North.

The voice was indistinct, so Marisola merely sent the feeling that they were waiting, and they broke contact.

"They've passed us going up Aelsund. We'll wait for..." She grinned. "...whichever twin to catch up, and then we'll cut over and come up behind them."

Jesco pointed a thumb back over his shoulder. "We passed a side trail back there. It'll probably get us across."

"We'll be waiting a while? The Ambassador would like to get down."

"Until your brother gets here."

The twin opened the crate, and the kitten shot out, took a running start along the horse's rump and hit the ground at a mad tear. He scrambled around the horses' feet, lost his balance and rolled over in a cloud of dried leaves. Then he got up, shook himself, strutted over to a nearby bush and sprayed it.

"What's he doing?"

"Marking this spot so he can find it again."

Marisola laughed. "After these horses have stood here for this long, it would be hard to lose it."

"Hmm. But after a rain?"

Rider approaching.

They all froze, including the kitten, and soon hoofbeats could be heard coming down the trail from the north. The Ambassador took another running leap, caught the outside of the rider's leg and scrambled up to his box.

"Bet you're glad you have heavy pants on."

"He's very careful."

Marisola kneed Tariq up the trail, and soon they reached where the small path led off to the east. She turned in, and when their scout pulled up they were already filing ahead. Kitten contacted him mentally to keep from talking.

He says they're half a league north of us.

Sun's down. They'll camp.

There was nothing more to say, and they trotted their horses in silence.

Soon their route levelled off, and Marisola slowed to a walk. The light had been dim as they twisted lower down the hillside, but once they reached the flatter valley bottom and the trees began to open up the path became visible again.

After half a candle they smelled dust in the air, and soon they hit the road. They sat their horses in a half circle regarding the churned dirt.

"Not much doubt."

Jesco nodded. "Can't hide that trail."

"We'll follow carefully. Either Kitten will warn us or we'll hear the cattle."

"Cattle will be tired..."

"...Don't count on them."

"Fair enough. Jesco and I will watch ahead. You two take the sides and behind."

They nodded in unison, and she gave them a tight grin and moved out.

It is still quite light. A mixed blessing.

Marisola pulled up. "If we can see this well, so can they."

"Aye." Jesco glanced south. "If they're expecting trouble, it will be on their backtrail."

"Time for the wind in the trees, Kitten?"

Certainly. It is done.

That easily?

This group is coming together. The practice in communicating this afternoon helped.

"All right. Let's move quietly."

They walked their mounts now, stopping at any sound from the forest, all senses alert.

Rider behind.

They pulled off the road, and soon a tired horse galloped past, its sides flecked with sweat, the rider looking just as worn. They were paying no attention to anything but the path ahead of them, and Marisola grinned at Jesco as the hoofbeats faded. "If that's their tail sweep, he's not much use."

"Probably a long-range scout left behind to watch for pursuit. There won't be any, so his news will be good. Good for us as well. They'll relax."

She nodded and pushed ahead.

They have stopped.

How do you know?

I can feel a group that size a long way off. Now they are closer.

How close?

Around that next bend, then the same distance farther.

She reined in, and Jesco slid up beside her, the Twins pushing tightly behind.

"How should we do this? Slip right in and surprise them?"

"Perhaps we...shouldn't reveal...all our skills."

"I'm in agreement there." Jesco grinned, his usual twist of the lip. "I don't want to face fifty surprised Ulaan. It only takes one of them deciding he's mad about it."

Marisola considered. "So we should use Kitten's shield to get past the outermost sentries. Then we can show ourselves. How would visitors normally approach a camp, do you think?"

Jesco shrugged. "If you dismount it shows confidence. As if you aren't worried you'll have to run. Of course, it's also harder if you have to run."

"I'll work with that. Everybody ready?"

The Twins lifted their scabbards from their saddles, belting them at their waists.

Marisola started forward again.

Sentry. Mounted.

To their left a rider appeared, patrolling the perimeter. They faded against some bushes, and he crossed the road ahead of them and disappeared into the dusk.

Again they paced ahead.

Around the bend you will be in sight.

It is dim enough their fires will blind them. Let's go farther.

They edged around the corner and found themselves in full sight of the camp. Marisola continued until she could see individual faces in the firelight. *All right, Kitten. Show us to them.*

Nothing happened.

I guess it's darker than we thought. Let's continur.

Someone has seen us. He is unsure.

She put two fingers to her mouth and blew a sharp whistle blast. "Hello! The camp!"

Heads came up, and every man in sight reached for his sword. As they started to gather in her direction, Marisola dismounted and led Tariq to meet them, her other hand on Kitten's hilt.

Radiate calm and confidence, please.

How could I do otherwise? We are all calm and confident.

Glad you think so.

The ones in front are young and uncertain.

The warriors were nearing, but Marisola did not stop. She smiled and continued to stride ahead. Seeing her intent, the Ulaan stepped aside, and her little party was engulfed by the growing crowd.

Finally they came up against someone with enough authority to make a decision. An older warrior stood in the path between the tents, his hand on his sword as well.

Marisola stopped and gave him a respectful nod. "We would greet your War Leader."

"Who are you, and what do you want?"

It's working. I can understand him.

Of course it's working.

Can he understand me?

He is marginally sensitive. He gets the general idea.

I'll give him the general idea.

"I am the Hand that wields the Sword. I will tell your War Leader what I want."

Recognition dawned on his face. "Ah. The Shield Maiden of Inderjorne. Our War Leader will be happy to speak with you."

He turned to lead the way further into the camp. They ground-tied their horses and followed.

"Well, that was easy."

90

Jesco raised his eyebrows. "It seems your reputation precedes you."

"I hope that's a good thing. We didn't exactly part as friends."

"Show strength...you have lions...at your back."

There was a lilt of laughter in the Twins' voices, belying their stern visages.

Marisola glanced at the ragged, fierce men pacing her party: sheepskin coats with the wool out, leather armour studded with iron plates, conical helmets with wide ear flaps, braided beards. "Then keep this pack of hyenas in its place."

The tents on either side were made of strips of woven cloth about an arm's length wide, in varying shades of red, brown and grey. Multiple ridgepoles held them aloft, tied down by a complicated system of ropes, pegs and rocks. Warriors stood or sat in the doorways regarding this parade with curiosity but little antagonism, from what Kitten could pick up.

They are very confident. This is some kind of elite group.

The warrior led them to a larger tent with an awning on the front. In its shade a simple carpet was rolled out, and there sat Marisola's former opponent in a hide-upholstered chair.

She stopped in front of him and afforded him a polite nod.

He stared at her, but did not rise or respond.

"So, besides being cowards, the Ulaan have no manners, either." She swung around and sat on the carpet beside his chair, gesturing the Twins to stand behind her, and Jesco to sit at her other side. "I suppose you must be the barbarians we thought you were."

She sat, looking around with interest. "I like your tents. You weave them on a handloom, I suspect. No, I take that back. Your women weave them. They look too complicated for men's clumsy fingers."

She watched him out of the corner of her eye. He, too, kept facing forwards.

This one is much more Sensitive. About the same as Jesco. And he is thinking furiously. He knows something is going on, but he doesn't know what, and that makes him cautious.

"It is good to be cautious in an unfamiliar situation. Many a hotheaded young leader fails to learn that. Some day you will be a fine War Leader for your people."

"I am Husam al Din, the Sword of the Faith, War Leader of my people."

"I am Marisola da Falken, Sword Hand to the Cloud Cat of the Leute. I assumed you were the War Leader. And some day you will be a good one."

He broke his pose and looked down at her. "You are determined to test my patience. Is this a courting ritual of Inderjorne?"

"If this is courting, you seem to have attained a very large dowry of our stock. I suppose it's going to be a huge wedding, so you'll need a lot of cattle to feed everyone."

"Let's not rush into things. I have not decided if you are worthy of my attention."

"And I have pretty much decided that you are too rude to be worth mine. Perhaps we should stick to diplomacy for the moment. That has a better chance of success."

"Diplomacy? What do you hope to accomplish? Special treatment for your family once we have overrun your land?"

"My family can take care of itself."

"That remains to be seen. But when the war is over, should you survive, I would be happy to accept you as my shield maiden."

She pretended to consider. "I'm not sure I like the sound of that. A shield maiden would be someone with a shield who stands in front of the hero in battle to keep him from the threat of a common soldier with a bit of luck."

"That is fairly accurate."

"In case you hadn't noticed, I rarely use a shield. I have other methods." She drew Kitten and laid her across her palms.

Be careful, Marisola. He is...

Like a darting snake, his hand shot out and snatched Kitten from her. He jumped to his feet and slid back into garde.

... very quick.

A double "snick" as two swords jumped from their scabbards behind her, followed in half a heartbeat by the longer sing of Jesco's draw. She had her own boot-top dagger out before the agonizing loss hit her.

Don't worry. It is more difficult than that to steal a magic Sword.

"I have the Sword. Now I will be the greatest War Leader our tribes have ever seen."

Do the glissade like last time.

This better work...

Marisola reached out to contact the tip of Kitten's blade with her dagger, pressing lightly. "You will find it is not that easy to steal a magic Sword." She moved forward. As her dagger slid down towards his breast, the veins in his neck bulged, and his arm shook. But the pressure of her knife forced the Sword out of line until her point touched his chest armour.

"That was a very brave try, though." She raised her dagger and laid the point on his cheek. With a feather-light touch, she drew it down and off the tip of his chin. "Yes, some day you will make a very good War Leader. But not with this." She took Kitten from his motionless hand and resheathed her.

"Now! It is time to stop this silly posing and talk." She spun and pointed to a warrior standing nearby. "Please pick up your War Leader's chair. You! Yes you, with the big fuzzy vest. Bring me another chair if you will, and one for my swordsman. My lions prefer to stand."

Soon she had everything ordered to her satisfaction, and she sat and made a flowing gesture with her hand. "Please, sir. Do join me."

He sat, regarding her.

"See? This is the way we do things down in civilization. It is so much more pleasant, don't you find?"

"And this gibberish is what you call 'good manners'?"

"Yes. Don't you see how it allows us time to assess the situation and the opposition? So much information can be given through gesture and tone of voice. For example, right now, you need time to recover from a very unsettling experience. I can't imagine what it must be like to have someone else completely in control of your body. Very unpleasant, I'm sure."

She relaxed back in her chair. "But you are an intelligent and hardy person. Even now you are recovering. You have already suppressed your desire to call on your men to chop me to bits." She rewarded him with a smile. "Because you would be the first to die. Hardly the action of one who wants to become the greatest War Leader his tribe has ever known."

He sighed. "I'm beginning to have second thoughts about the courting. I doubt if I could stand to be married to someone who talks as much as you do."

He does recover quickly.

Yes. He seems intelligent.

He never expected to succeed. He is relieved that you didn't kill him.

I'll take that into account.

She shrugged. "Well, you'll have to speak your share, and it will all even out. So tell me. We have never in our history seen such a movement of the nomad people. Raiding parties, yes. We have not found it difficult to handle those. But this is special. What is happening, up there on the prairies?"

"The Ulaan are nomads. We come and go. As we please and where we please. It has never pleased us to move in this direction, but now we do. There is no puzzle."

"And now that you have had your share of time for empty speech, you may answer the question. I am an educated person, and your culture was a subject of my studies. The nomads move with the seasons as they must, to find water and grazing for their flocks. It takes a cataclysmic disturbance of politics or climate to affect patterns developed over centuries."

There was a pause as he regarded her again.

Now we get the truth.

"Well, Sword Maiden of Inderjorne, you are intelligent as well as beautiful and brave...right." He held up open hands. "Answers, not empty flattery. You are correct. I am sorry to say that our situation is not so free as I wished to show. As you suspect, both the climate and other peoples have forced us from our traditional patterns."

"I am sorry to hear this, and not only because of the effect on my own people."

"Thank you. The weather has changed. Waterholes once full are now parched. Pastures once green are sere and barren, and the soil blows away on fierce, hot winds we have rarely felt. This means that our herds and flocks need larger areas to survive."

"I can see that. And are others finding the same problem?"

His shoulders slumped. "You may be surprised to find that there is another group of nomads who are more numerous and perhaps even more fierce than the Ulaan. We

95

are nomads always and raiders when we choose. They are raiders first and nomads second. Their lives are consumed with warfare. We cannot stand against these raiders and tend our flocks as well."

"I understand your difficulty. Farmers can wall themselves up in castles and keep you from stealing their stock. You have no such defences."

"Exactly. So we have no choice but to move away, to look for wetter climes. Thus, here we are."

"Ah, but here we are as well. And we have been here longer. We know how to live in these climes. You do not."

"Then we will change. We have no choice."

"And so ends diplomacy."

"That is the case. I am not a violent man. I enjoy a peaceful day tending my flocks, and a pleasant evening with my hunting eagle, Fahad. But I do not shirk the duties of my position. I am War Leader of a people who must win a war."

She rose. "I am glad we have had this time to speak. In future I hold you no ill will, and that will ease my conscience."

"Must you leave? We have a nice, young heifer already on the spit."

"One of ours, I note. No, I do not think it appropriate to sit and dine with a man I will probably kill when next we meet. That is taking diplomacy to a ridiculous extreme."

He looked up at her. "I have great respect for you and your Sword. But you cannot protect all of your land and all of your people with one Weapon. Likewise, killing me will not stop my people. Once my warriors have beaten yours down and you stand alone against me, there will no longer be any use in us fighting. At that point, perhaps we will speak again. I could use a shield maiden...no, a sword maiden to help me rule this new realm I will own."

She afforded him a pleasant smile. "You have missed one small point, War Leader. I represent the people of Inderjorne, and no one in Inderjorne is ever alone. So when this war is over and your people are fleeing back into the plains where they belong, perhaps I will come and help you hold the place you rightfully own against those who would take it from you."

She gave him her usual courtesy, rose with dignity and strode out between the tents, Jesco at her side and the Twins following. Unchallenged, they mounted their horses and rode away.

They had only gone a few bowshots when Jesco pulled his horse alongside her. "We're letting them take the herd?"

She rode along for a while. "Do you have an idea?"

"No, no, I just wondered."

"Since you are my most loyal supporter, I will give you a straight answer. I never thought there was much chance of taking the herd back. A few cattle are a cheap price to pay for the information I have received today."

"I have to agree. Their desperation makes the Ulaan even more dangerous."

"Exactly. And it makes it that much more important to get our armies together and out here to confront the attack that is sure to come."

We are all agreed on that.

She wasn't sure which "all" Kitten was talking about, but a glance at the Twins assured her of their support.

14.   New Vision

For the next two days Kitten and her troop covered the countryside between Waldheim and the Ulaan camp, learning the terrain and trying to find a way to get more information. They encountered many nomad scouts and amused themselves by practising their skills. Sometimes the scout was dispatched with a well-aimed arrow, sometimes he moved on, oblivious to the death that had brushed its wing past him.

They even captured a few for questioning, but never got anything out of them. When one died at the hands of frustrated guards and one grabbed a dagger and slit his own throat, they stopped.

As they rode back to the castle that evening, Marisola pulled in beside Jesco. "I don't think there's any use trying to get closer. We can't find out anything anyway."

He nodded. "Once we get down in those creek valleys, we can see less, not more."

"And when we find a hilltop that overlooks their camp, we're too far away to see anything.

"I don't understand it. The Ulaan are ready to move, but for some reason they are holding back."

I would have to agree.

She grinned. "I can't say that I'm unhappy about it, the way our army is not showing up..."

"...but when your enemy doesn't do what you expect, you always suspect he has a reason."

And not one you will like when you find out.

Marisola snorted. "Isn't it nice when we all agree."

They rode the rest of the way to the castle in glum silence.

As they sat around after supper, Lord Waldheim slapped his hands on the table "They aren't coming."

Marisola looked at Lord Waldheim. "They are not."

"Why not? Everything we know about the Ulaan tells us that they will attack. They move fast and strike without warning. Surprise is their main advantage. And now they camp and stay. Why give us time to prepare?"

She shook her head. "But they cannot stay. They are nomads with their flocks. They are camped in an area that is more fertile than they are used to, but sooner or later they will use up the forage, and then they will be forced to move. I do not understand it, either."

They have a problem. I have no idea what it is, but something is holding them from doing what their usual patterns dictate.

The lord glanced at Kitten. "More than the invasion the War Leader told you about?"

"Must be. We need more information."

Then we go and get it.

"I'm not sure how. We have been in and out along their perimeter. We'll never get close enough to the centre of their camp without literally stumbling over someone, whether he can see us or not."

I confess that I have no other solution.

Marisola grinned. "Then we do what good little Inderjornese always do."

"Consult?"

"Time for a meeting. Do you want to join us, my Lord?"

He waved a big hand in negation. "All I get is a buzzing, with too many voices going on at once to understand. You just tell me what you come up with."

It didn't take long to get their small group together, hands on Kitten's hilt. She sent out a searching, using Jesco's sharp memory to seek out Wynna. Almost immediately she received a positive response.

Meet?

Another positive, then the woman's presence was gone.

When the connection was broken, Jesco glanced around at the group. "Almost like she was waiting. I guess she can't really answer us."

Wynna is open to you at all times, Jesco. She cannot answer by herself, but she will gather the Falcongard Sensitives.

Jesco and Marisola chatted about supplies and practical matters while they waited. The Twins were either playing with the Ambassador or teaching him some obscure game. Kitten kept them in her subconscious, aware that anything they were doing might have use at a future time.

Soon there was a stronger questing.

Here they are. Join me.

Hands touched her hilt, and she opened to the familiar brush of Ecmund's mind.

What's going on, Kitten?

Not much, Ecmund.

You mean that.

Exactly. The Ulaan are doing nothing. I don't understand it, and I don't like it.

Well, let's not complain about a benefit. It gives us more time to gather our forces.

How is that going?

The old lord's spirit took on a wry tinge. *About as expected. Rapidly by any standard other than our need to be even faster. We now have a small army camped in the fields around Falconby, and a faster-growing camp of refugees a few bowshots south. I'm not sure which is more bother.*

I see. Any other news?

Most definitely. It's good you made contact. You're about to receive visitors.

Pleasant ones, I hope.

That depends on your point of view. Prince Guevejar left here this morning with twenty knights and thirty lancers, headed in your direction.

Marisola broke in. *Guevejar!*

Yes. I don't think you know him well.

I've met him formally a few times. I doubt if he knows who I am.

Oh, he's very aware of who you are, now. He has strict instructions from the Queen herself to treat you like royalty. At least, that's the impression I got. He doesn't like it much, but he's a good son, and he loves his mother.

Is that supposed to be a joke?

Not really. He is totally loyal to the present monarch. Not an illogical philosophy for the heir to the throne to take, if you think about it.

Kitten was beginning to feel the strain. *I have known him all his life. He will be a good general. He comes to see for himself. Leads from the front. Is there anything else?*

Sorry, Kitten. You're carrying the weight of this sending. We have nothing that the prince will not tell you when he gets there in three or four days.

We were wondering what to do, but there is no point in making plans when our general is approaching. We must go.

Fair enough. Thank you, Kitten. Goodbye, Marisola. Wynna would send her love to Jesco if she could.

He knows. He has a silly grin on his face.

The contact slowly faded. Everyone in the room turned to look at Jesco, who rearranged his features, his cheeks red. "So. Prince Guevejar himself. That takes the onus off us to come up with something."

Marisola shook her head. "No, it means we have three days to gather enough good information for him to make a proper decision."

"Four days...at least."

"Why do you say that?"

"Twenty knights...thirty lancers...the general's staff...and their baggage? Maybe...five."

"Fine. Let's make plans. Ideas?"

Jesco shook his head. "We can't get any closer. I don't think there's any point trying."

"I agree."

"Perhaps we...are looking at this...from the wrong angle."

"Well, that's what you two are here for. What angle should we be looking at it from?"

"We don't know...a different one."

"Easy to say, hard to do. What do we need?"

Jesco snorted. "To be a hawk and fly over that camp, way up out of bowshot."

Marisola pictured it clearly in her mind. *What do you think, Kitten? Can you look through a hawk's eyes?"*

I can experience another animal's senses, yes. Close up. I cannot do it from very far away, and if it came to directing the bird's flight at the same time, I doubt it very much. Unless somebody has a Sensitive bird of prey somewhere?"

Marisola shrugged. "Well, I suppose we could wander through Lord Waldheim's falconry and see what you find. But it's a long shot. Anything else?"

"Seeing...is the problem. We need a...viewpoint from...higher up."

"That's the problem. There are good lookouts in the hills, but the high ones are too far away. By the time we get close enough, it's all low hills and we can't see anything."

"But seeing...is the problem, then."

"Kitten, you can make me see better."

A little. Jesco has keener eyes than you.

"Let's try." She led the way out onto the battlements. "See those workers in the field over there? I can just make out that they're people, and that's about all. Jesco?"

"I can sort of see their arms moving. I can see separate legs."

All right, Marisola, concentrate and open your mind as much as you can. What do you see, now?

"It's definitely better. I can see arms and legs. Movement."

Jesco?

The old swordsman stared out. "About the same. Clear arms and legs."

That is to be expected. Marisola is more Sensitive, so I can help her more.

"And where does that leave us?"

It leaves us with the lions. We have proved that Sensitivity is more important than visual ability.

"So the Twins, by combining their ability..."

We can only try. Gentlemen?

The Twins stepped up to the balcony and took identical poses. Kitten stayed ready, noting the interplay of their minds.

"We can see arms...legs...faces. The...two by the haystack...are women. The man...on the wagon...has a beard."

I have it. Put your hands on my hilt. She began to feed power into their merge. *Jesco, Marisola, help us.*

As the other two joined in, a picture formed in their minds. Two women looking up at a man on a wagon. His lips were moving, and they were smiling at him.

Then one of the women frowned, staring around. The others turned to her, and she shook her head, wiping a hand across her brow.

Kitten sent a feeling of peace and happiness to her. At once she stood straighter and smiled, speaking to her concerned friends with reassuring gestures.

Kitten broke the merge. *We have intruded enough into their lives today.*

"That woman was Sensitive. She must have felt someone spying on her."

"We were...can you imagine? We...could see their lips moving."

Jesco stared out at the faraway figures. "And from here they look like posts."

But we don't know how much that picture was helped by the Sensitive person at the other end.

"That doesn't matter." Marisola grinned. "Some Ulaan are Sensitive. They'll help us whether they like it or not."

Jesco shook his head. "But they'll feel they're being watched."

And we'll be so far away they won't be able to see from where. That'll put the shivers into them.

Marisola nodded. "We have always said that fear will be our best weapon." She sheathed Kitten. "Let's go talk to Lord Waldheim about the best overlook to use."

* * *

The next afternoon they stood beside a craggy outcropping on a barren knoll that thrust above the lower hills at the approach to the plains. The Ulaan camp was spread before them, dim in the distance, fading out towards the horizon as usual.

Jesco pointed. "Dust over there."

The Twins concentrated. "Herd...moving. Sheep...and goats."

Marisola was scanning the nearer tents, following the largest creek to the centre of the camp. "There. I can see glints of light and splashes of colour. That's their headquarters."

"Yes. Larger...tents and...armed guards."

"All right. We've proved that we can't see anything from here that the other scouts haven't reported. Kitten?"

All of you look at the same time. Let's start with the main tent. Once we get good at it, I will be able to guide us all to look at different things. For the moment, one hand on my hilt, and concentrate on that tent...yes, the one with the red stripes and the golden tassels on the awning. There is a standard outside the door...a large bird, I believe. No, it just spread its wings. It's a real bird.

"I can see someone..."

Concentrate, Marisola. If you speak you break the merge. Yes there is someone coming out the door. He is sitting in the chair. Well, we know who that is. Wait. Can you see it? There's another chair beside the War Leader's. Yes, the man who followed is sitting at his right hand. The rest of the group is standing in formation behind him. This is some kind of rite. See, a lot of people with fancy helmets are sitting on the ground in front. Now the Leader speaks. Don't we wish we knew what he is saying?

Now the other man speaks, but only briefly...now the leader again. He stands. They all stand, waving their weapons. Watch how they break...no, they go in all directions. If they all moved in one direction, I would be worried. Yes, the two leaders are going back into the tent, the second one following.

Have we seen enough? Good.

They took their hands away, and Kitten was alone again.

Now, wasn't that interesting.

"Yes. Our handsome War Leader has a second-in-command who also gets to speak, but not much. My big friend speaks first and last. We don't know what he was talking about, but his people liked it, so I don't. What do you think? Preparing them to attack in the morning?"

Let us watch for action in the camp in general. I have had a brief rest, and I would like to practise moving our attention from place to place.

"There's something about this I don't like."

"What's that, Jesco?"

"When we're looking out there, our attention is out there. Who is watching our feet?"

I will scan the area...no, there are no large animals nearby. Unless you want to take a few turkeys back for supper.

"Maybe we'll do that to prove we aren't completely useless. For now, let's concentrate on our duties. Kitten, where would you like to start?"

The Hand speaks, and we all obey. Connect up, my children, and let's start out at the centre tents and move down towards the closer foothills. We don't need to focus in, but to see a wider stretch of their camp. Let's follow that open path. See it...there?

They scanned the whole near side of the camp, but nowhere could they find any excess of movement. As the sun slid down and the shadows lengthened, they could distinguish less and less detail, so they stopped and went down to their horses.

"I don't think there's any attack imminent."

Jesco nodded. "Which puts us back where we were this morning."

"But we can get more information this way. I want to come back tomorrow and get a better picture of what normal life looks like, so if there's any change, we can tell."

"We should...find the horse herds."

"Yes, any attack will start with preparing the horses. Lots of dust and group movement."

And when we come back, we will bring a few non-Sensitive guards who can concentrate on our protection with no distractions.

"And post a lookout here permanently."

15.   General Guevejar

For the next three days they watched the Ulaan camp, building a picture of its routines and geography. The horse herds were downwind to the east of the camp and easy to spot.

But for three days, nothing happened. The nomads cooked, ate, moved their flocks, trained, and relaxed. The same late-afternoon meeting happened every day, with the same weapon waving and cheering at the end.

The fourth day the watchers stayed at the castle because the prince and his entourage were expected. Marisola made sure that her little troop was arrayed at their ceremonial best, except for the Ambassador, who needed no adornment. He sat on top of his crate, grooming himself to perfection.

Kitten and Marisola had decided, with the agreement of Lord Waldheim, that they would go out and escort the prince for the last league or so. It was good manners and also useful, as there was no guarantee that the enemy hadn't infiltrated the area.

And we have no idea what state of readiness our general has achieved.

So when the scouts said the prince was approaching, the foursome trotted their freshly curried horses slowly out of the castle gate to meet him.

This close to the castle the road was wide enough to ride four abreast, and Marisola glanced at her allies. "Should we give Prince Guevejar a little surprise, plus a demonstration of our abilities?"

Jesco spat into the road. "I don't recall the prince being the type to appreciate surprises."

"That's one good reason to do it. I'm sure he's a good leader and well educated in conducting a war and all that, but he's never fought in one. The sooner the unpredictable nature of his occupation hits him, the sooner he will become the general we need."

"This is an...interesting development."

"What is?"

"Two huge...traditional forces...meeting on the battlefield...and each one with...a young, untried leader."

"Do you consider Husam al Din to be young and inexperienced?"

"You cannot...get the experience...to become a...great leader in the time...he has ridden this earth. That...is why your...jibes about becoming...a great leader...bother him so much."

"Let's talk about how much we plan to bother our own leader. I don't want to alienate him, just tune his strings in a higher key."

Slip through his advance scouts, sit by the road and wait for him to pass, then join in as if we were always there.

"I like that, Kitten. Let's do it."

In that case, let us slide over into those trees, there. She cast her pall over the four of them, and they watched an overdressed lancer trot straight up the middle of the road past them, looking neither left nor right.

Once he was gone, they regained the road. "If that's an example of how useful his army is, I'm not enthused."

Let us see. Oh. Here comes the next bunch. Three this time.

Again they regarded the ceremonial parade, shaking their heads.

No reason to continue. That copse is close enough to the road.

Now they could hear the clopping of many hooves. As the prince's party came into view an order rang out, and they all dropped from a trot into a walk. Kitten had an idea.

Is our Ambassador free?

He is ready to do his duty at any time.

Fine. Concentrate very hard. We will let them get very close.

Six knights in all their panoply, two by two, paced past them on shining destriers. Following that was a single knight in more serviceable gear, and then Guevejar himself, flanked by two overdressed older men. When this trio was right beside them, Kitten made her move.

First the distraction. Ambassador, take his Majesty our greetings.

The cat scampered away and took a flying leap, digging his claws into the skirt of the Prince's war-horse and clambering up to the front of his saddle. Guevejar looked down to see the little face mewing up at him. He grinned and removed a gauntlet to ruffle the Ambassador's ears. "Now, where did you come from, little fellow?"

And now the magic. Let's go.

She pushed Tariq forward, and they blended into the procession: Marisola parallel to the prince on his left, Jesco at her outside shoulder, the Twins close behind.

Guevejar lifted his attention from the kitten and did a comical take when he realized he had company.

"You have met my ambassador, your Majesty," She bowed in the saddle. "Marisola Delfontes da Falken, at your service."

The prince's start had jerked the reins, and his destrier skittered a few steps, calming to his master's unconscious control. The prince's head came up, and he stared around, his helmet swivelling. Seeing no danger, he looked down at her. "Is this some kind of joke?"

"No, your Majesty. It is some kind of demonstration."

"I see. And what are you demonstrating?"

"The abilities of my troop. Any other lessons I am sure you will draw on your own accord."

"I certainly will." The prince glanced ahead, to where the well-armed knight was sending emphatic gestures to several lancers, who peeled away from the procession at a gallop.

They rode in silence, while the various members of the Prince's escort dealt with the new situation, each in his own way. Most of them did nothing, because that was the only option available.

Guevejar turned again to regard his new escort. "Calicasas."

"Yes, your Majesty?" The attendant who had been pushed back by Marisola's arrival moved his horse ahead again.

"Put Lady Marisola's guard and the Ostersund lords in the procession here behind us. The lady will stay beside me."

"At once, your Majesty."

Jesco flashed her his sardonic grin and faded into line with the Twins.

"Will your ambassador wish to return to his quarters?"

This man misses nothing.

Yes, he handled this all very well.

"He pretty much goes where he wishes, your Majesty. At the moment, he seems content with his location."

The kitten had perched himself on the high cantle of the prince's saddle and was staring around with interest.

"So, besides coming out to show off your tricks, did you have any other reason for joining me early? A word in my ear about something important?"

"No, your Majesty. All is as you have been led to believe. Lord Waldheim is prepared and competent. If only our foe would act in their traditional manner, all would be in order."

The prince snorted. "First lesson of war. The foe is not there to cooperate. Please explain."

"As I am sure Lord Ecmund informed you, we have information from a direct source that this is not the usual raiding party. Drought and the incursion of a more violent people have driven this tribe to change their grazing areas permanently. Where they wish to locate is here. So they are not moving in their usual patterns.

"Direct source? How direct?"

"I spoke to Husam the War Leader himself."

"You are on speaking terms with their War Leader?"

She grinned. "Yes, he has offered me a position of shield maiden once he has taken over my realm. I declined, suggesting I wanted more."

"You are in marriage negotiations with the leader of an invading army. And why should I not have you executed for treason?"

"Mostly because it would be a waste of a powerful resource, your Majesty. See it from his point of view. I have twice surprised him, the second time in a similar way to today's stunt. He needs a way of dealing with what would otherwise be a great loss of face. So we spar with words. Hence he gives me information that I could not obtain any other way."

"I see. And you have no reason to believe anything else?"

"It was too candid an answer, and too likely to be true. However, there must be other factors. The Ulaan are not the best fighters in the world, but they have superb tactics, One of their first rules is to strike first, strike hard and move on before retaliation has time to form. The War Leader is young, but seems intelligent and competent. He is not making a mistake. I am hoping that it is circumstance that has forced him from his traditional tactics."

"And hoping it is not a superior tactic that we have not considered that is causing the departure from their usual style."

"Exactly. That is why I am so glad you are here. I have plenty of training, and Lord Waldheim is experienced, but

112

another trained mind will give us a better chance of figuring this out."

To her surprise, the prince laughed.

"What did I say that was so funny, your Majesty?"

"Because my mother warned me. She told me exactly what to expect from your family, and here you are, exposing your hand before I have even reached the battle zone."

"Hmm. And in what way am I true to form?"

"She said you would automatically assume that you were equals in the process. As the leader of the Falcons on the ground in the battle zone you would be there ahead of me, would have superior information, and would take it for granted that I will accept your conclusions as from an equal."

"That may all be true, your Majesty, except for two things."

"Yes?"

"First, I assume that you will accept my information on the basis of your own independent analysis, not my position. I have confidence my facts are correct, but their use is certainly up to you, as Heir to the Throne and General of the Armies of the Realm. And second, if you noticed, I have no conclusions to offer, which is why I am so glad to see you."

Again he laughed. "And are you still so glad to see me, now that I have been forewarned?"

She considered, as their horses clopped along the sunny forest road. "I do not know her Majesty personally, but my family has close connections with her, as does my Sword. I have no reason to believe that anything she told you about us was false or malicious in intent. If I may be so bold, Queen Cuquita's reputation at Falkengard is of the highest, and her loyalty and her desire for the good of the Realm are her most cherished traits."

"So you attempt to get around me by flattering my mother?"

She grinned. "Your Majesty, this is rather ironic. My way of dealing with Husam al Din of the Ulaan is to keep him off balance by a series of spurious accusations. And here you are playing the same trick on me."

This is fascinating. Are you planning to marry one of them? What?

"Is something wrong my Lady? You look thunderstruck."

"Oh...no, I'm sorry your Majesty. My Sword just made a particularly strange comment."

"And may I know what that comment was?"

"Definitely not. It was personal, and it had nothing to do with the present situation."

And you are a liar. And to the prince himself.

"The military situation, at least."

A smile quirked one corner of his mouth. "A lady may have her secrets."

"Thank you. Are we now past whatever hurdle we were fighting to surmount so we can get on with planning this war?"

"I believe we can. I'm glad we had this time together alone before the situation becomes complicated. It's good to know that I have one element of my battle array already in place."

"Hmm. You've heard what happens when your battle plan gets into battle."

He laughed. "I accept your warning. How far are we from Waldheim Castle?"

"Just around the next corner, your Majesty."

"Then we could start our entrance. Trumpeter! Sound the Trot, please."

He had hardly raised his voice, but at once a series of notes rang out, and the whole party picked up the pace.

"Is it your intention to ride in with me?"

"I hadn't thought about it, your Majesty. I don't want to steal any of your glory."

"I'm sure I have enough to go around."

She considered their conversation. "In fact, I think it unwise to be seen with your procession. I would not like anyone to think I am toadying up to royalty. With your permission, I will pull aside from the parade and follow at a respectful distance."

He rode for a moment, thinking, then nodded. "You wish to preserve yourself as an independent unit, as that maintains your freedom, which bolsters your power. Again, I have taken the best advice on the use of your Sword in this situation, and all agree that independence is your best tactic. Much though it bothers my personal sense of neatness." He grinned over at her and waved a hand in dismissal.

The Ambassador made a flying leap to her knee, digging in painfully, and clawed up to her shoulder. She pulled aside with her attendants and allowed the prince's party to parade past, pennants flying, in a brave show of colour and armed might.

With an internal snort, she followed.

16.   Movement

The evening was wasted, in Kitten's opinion. In Marisola's as well. They sat at the head table in the Great Hall, observing.

Why must we have all this panoply? We need a meeting. We need to be training. We need to figure out what we need to be doing.

Calmly, Dear One. Humans must gather their allies around them to give solace before the fighting starts.

This human would rather be better prepared for battle.

All right, then. Let us prepare. This prince is aware of power politics. He has seen through all the tricks you tried on him.

They weren't tricks!

Exactly. You have played the trump card in his game: the truth. But still, we must consider how he thinks.

Fine. So what do we do?

We plan our tactics.

But I don't have a plan.

Our plan is to persuade Prince Guevejar to make the right plan.

In that case...he needs to see our source of information himself.

I assume you don't mean taking him out and introducing him to Husam al Din.

She giggled. *I can imagine the results. Unfortunately, neither side would find the loss of their leader a reason to stop. No, let's get him out to the lookout, put him in the merge and show him the enemy. I assume he's Sensitive enough to catch the picture?*

That is a good short-range plan. He is Sensitive enough to help the process.

And long-range?

I hesitate to confess defeat, but our best chance is to watch the Ulaan and react. It is not the best tactic, but sometimes in defensive warfare there is no choice.

You forgot the part about watching to see what mistakes our new General is about to make and somehow stopping him before he makes them.

Between waiting for that and waiting for the Ulaan to act, I'm not sure which worries me the most.

* * *

The next morning, festivity seemed the last thing on the General's mind. He was dressed for a sortie in light half-armour, and his destrier had no frills or flounces, only business-like gear. Once the Twins had taken handfuls of mud to the shiny bits, he was ready for the trail.

As they dismounted at the bottom of the hill, Marisola thought of some final instructions. "Your Majesty, when we get to the top of this ridge we will be visible to the enemy camp. They have not yet discovered this post, and we prefer that they don't. Could your people stay below the skyline?"

Guevejar raised his eyebrows at his Guard Captain, who nodded and started pointing out assignments to the ten men who had followed them.

They took their time, allowing the General to understand the scope of the scene before him: the size of the camp, the distances involved, the difficulty of approach. Finally he declared himself satisfied. "I can see how hard it is to get information on a group this large. I assume you have a solution?"

"Yes. It involves joining a merge with Kitten, who then combines our visual acuity to give us a much better picture of what we see."

"Ah. Like my mother does, except with vision instead of listening."

"You are aware of that trick."

He smiled. "The queen has prepared me well for my duties."

Marisola's hand clamped firmly on Kitten's hilt. *Do this my way.*

"Has she also told you what a danger it is?"

"Lord Tyrbrand has taught that lesson so many times we are getting tired of it."

"Fair enough. Let us wait until you have had the experience, and then we may talk further."

"What do I do?"

"Put your hand on Kitten's hilt along with the rest of us. There. Now look at that red blob in the centre of the camp and open your mind."

Kitten eased into the merge slowly this time, giving the General's mind a chance to get used to the event. Soon the man's exultation over the effect had him completely involved, and she boosted the power. Nobody said anything so as to keep the merge as clean as possible.

Finally the king nodded. "I have seen enough for the moment. What do we do to get out of this?"

Kitten gradually slid away, and the others removed their hands.

"I begin to see the power of your Sword, lady Marisola. What an advantage!"

"But you also understand the obstacle we face. Yes, we can see when the enemy collects its army to attack. But from this distance, we have no idea why they do what they do."

"But you can also sneak in on them, like you did to me yesterday."

"Which we have done. But we can only get so close and then we will be noticed. We have not tried to move right in because it is too dangerous."

"Yes, we mustn't risk such a valuable weapon."

She smiled. "Thank you, General."

"You know what I mean." He stared once more out into the enemy camp. "And what do you have planned, now?"

"I was waiting for you to suggest the next move, your Highness. Our present plan is to monitor the camp for several hours each day. Every time we watch, we learn something new. Nothing useful so far, but knowing our enemy is the best we can do at this moment."

"I begin to understand your limitations. However, that does nothing to solve the problems facing us back in the rest of the realm, and specifically facing me as the General of such a disordered army. But this is not the place for that discussion. I suggest you stay here and continue your reconnaissance. I will return to the castle and consult with Lord Waldheim on my plans for the defence of this area. We will meet late this afternoon, before dinner. Does that suit you?"

She smiled. "Whether it did or not, that is your plan, and we will be there."

"Thank you. I appreciate what you are doing. I begin to see what my mother meant."

"I'll take that as a positive comment."

"Please do."

The prince turned away and motioned to his Guard Captain. No words were needed. The royal party crept down the hill, mounted and disappeared in the trees.

"Well, that went as well as we could have expected."

I'm not so sure.

"Kitten, it was not the time for you to lay down the law to him about the merge. He is too new to the situation to have anyone ordering him about. First we need to get you involved with him in a positive light. Once he is used to you, then you decide when to discuss serious matters with him. We are not in a rush. He can hardly misuse your power when all you have to do is refuse to use it.

"As long as...the Ulaan...do not move, we...have all the time...in the world."

"There you go. We have our orders, and like good little soldiers, let us obey them."

We should track the streams to see where they're getting their drinking water.

The four humans touched Kitten's hilt and stared out into the enemy camp.

* * *

The meeting that afternoon started out bad and got worse. When they arrived in Lord Waldheim's workroom Prince Guevejar was parked at the head of the table, up to his elbows in papers and documents. His two aides stood, one at either shoulder.

He is back in his element.

Afraid so. I'm glad we got through to him first.

He looked up as they entered. "Come in, come it." He waved a hand. "Pull up a chair. I won't be a moment."

They sat and watched as he worked through documents with quick efficiency, scanning, noting and signing. As soon as one was whisked away by the left-hand aide, the right-hand man laid another in its place.

Finally the left hand was empty, and the prince leaned back, interlaced his fingers and cracked his knuckles. "There.

Got that out of the way." He looked at them. "Anything important happen this afternoon?"

"Nothing. We made some interesting..."

That was as far as she got. "No, no, as long as they aren't moving, that's all we need." He tapped his fingers on the table. "We have more pressing matters to attend to."

Marisola couldn't think of anything to say, so she tried to look interested. Kitten read what she could from the surface of the man's emotions.

This isn't going to be good.

Which is what he just said.

"Here is the situation. You have mobilized the whole nation on very sketchy information. Now, I happen to believe you. But what I choose to believe makes very little difference. For that matter, even what my father the king chooses to believe doesn't matter that much. All that matters is that we have, by whatever means, dragged the whole realm into support for this war. A good number of those participants required a lot of dragging and are actively looking for any excuse to withdraw their support."

He bent his elbows and stared at them over his folded hands. "I have come specifically to see for myself, hoping to calm the fears of the reluctant, to give the king a reason to mold this realm into unity to face a terrible threat. And now that threat is faltering."

He paused, inviting comment.

Marisola shrugged. "A wise man reminded me recently not to expect the enemy to collaborate."

"Correct, but of no consequence. We are fighting a battle, not of facts or arms, but of conceptions and desires. The radicals on both sides are experts at, 'I need to believe this, therefore it must be true.' I have to take them something better than your Sword's analysis. Many of Maridon descent don't believe she even exists. We need more."

Is he going to go home and tell them to forget the whole situation?

I don't think so. He's being honest. Let's listen.

"You're not suggesting we instigate a battle, create an incident to prove the danger."

"No, I am not, and I see no martyrs poking up their hands to volunteer. Besides, I only have fifty men. That is the number this Hassam al Din wanders our realm with, is it not?"

"By my rough count. An elite guard."

"So I don't see myself creating enough of a stir to make a difference."

"I believe that you believe."

"That is not the same as believing it is true."

"You are correct, your Majesty."

"I have seen nothing definite to answer the naysayers, and I will not lie to my people. The consequences of dishonesty could be worse than the effect of the next battle." He raised a hand to still her protest. "Right. The next battle could be Inderjorne's last. But our people have not attained their present position by allowing our principles to be compromised by convenience."

Marisola let out a huge gust of air. "And that is the argument I cannot fight, because I believe it, too."

"Right. So I have made up my mind. Unless we get other information – either from the front lines or the backward demesnes of Inderjorne – I will stay here three days. Then I go back to the capital and advise my father to move to a wait-and-see mode of war."

Marisola was thinking furiously. "Four more days here. It will take you eight to get to Koningsholm. That means eleven days for the Ulaan to make their move." She met the king's eyes. "I can deal with that. If, in ten days, the nomads have not done something significant, I will be forced to agree with you that the situation is different. I will support whatever you decide."

"Ten days. But you said eleven."

"Yes, but if nothing has happened after ten days, I'm going to ride down into that camp and take Husam al Din by the scruff of the neck and demand some answers."

"Thus giving me the incident I need to continue the mobilization of the army?"

"I don't think so. The only reason I can think of for the nomads not attacking is that somehow they are not strong enough. Having seen the size of their encampment and the number of warriors riding around, I find that very difficult to believe, but nonetheless..."

The prince laughed. "Here's a thought for you. Do you think we are the only ones with a divided realm? These nomads have been forcibly tossed from their usual routines, the same as we have. Maybe unresolved feuds are causing them the same problems as well."

Marisola frowned, but then a smile lit her face. "They are not a peaceful people, and they are not here by choice."

I wouldn't count on it, but who knows?

Marisola straightened in her chair. "Your Majesty, if you are set on this path, then we have little more to discuss. May I introduce another matter?"

"Of course."

"My Sword."

"Ah, yes. The famous Cloud Cat of the Leute. The Cat With Many Claws as well. A beast of many facets, I gather. I am certainly seeing how useful she is."

"You have not seen half of it, your Majesty. I have been keeping her apart from you because she has an unsettling effect on people, and I did not wish to taint your first days here with any distractions. Now that your mind is made up..."

"...you intend to distract me."

"Meeting Kitten has been a worthwhile distraction for those who have achieved it, your Majesty."

The prince's jocularity disappeared. "I am well aware that your family, your Sword and your magic are one of the main reasons my father still sits on the throne. If I am to be afforded the same benefits both my parents have enjoyed, I will be the last one to object. What do you suggest?

"Kitten swore allegiance to your father many years ago. As General of the Army and Heir apparent, it would not be out of line to ask her to swear to you now. The added advantage is that it will create a bond between you. She can communicate more clearly with you and hear you and know your needs from a farther distance."

"What ceremony is required?"

"A simple one, your Majesty." She knelt and held out the Sword.

I will amend the ceremony as is fit.

I'm sure you will do it properly.

"Now touch her hilt, your Majesty."

The prince placed his hand on Kitten's pommel. Once again, the words were there in her mind. *I, Ailur, Cloud Cat of the Leute, Cat with Many Claws, do swear my fealty to the issue of King Vetrorrillo da Inderjorne, and swear to use my powers in every way possible to aid in the proper ruling of this realm and the winning of this battle.*

The prince's glance leaped to Marisola. "What...?"

She smiled. "I, Prince Guevejar of Inderjorne do accept your fealty..."

The prince frowned in concentration "I, Prince Guevejar of Inderjorne do accept your fealty..."

"And do swear to use your powers only for the good of this realm."

"And do swear to use your powers...only for the good of this realm."

Kitten could feel the rightness of the moment and relaxed into the red glow of heat that shone her Names onto their faces. *That is it, your Majesty. You now come under my protection like your father before you.*

"Under your protection. Wasn't I before?"

It is not the same. Before it was only the loyalty of my Hand that made it so. Now it is personal.

"Well, we have a few days together, and perhaps we can explore the meaning of this bond." He turned a not-too-serious frown on Marisola. "And is this another one of your clever methods of gleaning support for your cause? I warn you, it will not affect my impartiality."

"That is all I wish for, your Majesty. Since you always seem to see through my pathetic attempts to manipulate the situation, I'm sure you are already aware that this could also be seen as a method of forging the partnerships that Inderjorne needs to confront this threat."

"Please remember that I have been schooled in the arts of diplomacy, the tactful and the not-so-pleasant, by a mistress of the discipline."

"In that case, should you ever suspect another interpretation of my actions, I need to inform you that a magic Sword can never be Joined to a king, overlord or army general. It would put too much power in one set of weak hands. I'm sure that rule applies to queens as well."

The prince burst into laughter. "Now I see how you stymied poor Husam the War Leader. I have only known you for one day, and already you refuse to marry me. The blow to my self-respect is devastating." He pointed a finger at her. "Aha! I have discovered your nefarious plot. You are going to antagonize the two of us so much that some day when we sit at a negotiating table, we will have so much in common to talk about that we will make peace in order to protect each other from you."

She shrugged. "You have been well schooled by an expert. Who am I, a mere country swordswoman, to contradict you?"

This is not diplomacy as I have ever seen it practised. Nor courting, come to think of it.

17.   False Alarm

The next day was a dull one. Guevejar joined them at the lookout, but nothing happened. The prince observed the afternoon speeches at the War Leader's tent, but other than the fact that the second-in-command spoke for much longer, all remained the same.

The third day was different. Just after sunup a panting messenger from the lookout threw himself off his horse and staggered up the steps into the castle. Waldheim and Marisola, forewarned by Kitten, met him in the great hall, and Prince Guevejar soon arrived.

"What's happening, man?"

"The nomad camp is all astir, my Lord, starting at daybreak. The horse pastures especially. We can't see what's going on, but we thought you'd want to know."

"We most certainly do. Any idea which direction they're moving?"

"We couldn't tell. Don't think they've started out yet, my Lord. They were swirling around like they couldn't get organized."

The prince grinned. "You've never seen an army mobilize, lad. It seems to be a swirling mess, then suddenly they snap into line and off they go. And these are nomads. I doubt if they'll be forming ranks."

He looked at the others. "I must go there and see what's happening. Genille," he pointed to his Guard Captain, "get everyone packing. If that army is moving our way, I want to be ahead of it. Lady Marisola, your troop is with me at the lookout. We need the best information we can get. Waldheim, if I were you, I'd start to button up. You know how to go about it."

"I do, your Majesty. If they try my walls, they'll get an example of the might of Inderjorne."

"Unfortunately, I doubt if they will attack. Best guess by the experts," he put his hand on Marisola's shoulder and started her moving, "is they ride right on by and set their teeth into the softer towns to the south."

Servants scrambled, and very soon the party was on the road north, the crumbs from hasty breakfast of bread and cheese spotting their mail shirts, a sack of watered wine passing from hand to hand as they galloped.

They reached the lookout just in time. A soldier ran to meet them. "They're pulling out, your Majesty. Look!"

They rushed forward, Marisola drawing Kitten.

You too, your Majesty. Put your hand on my hilt and look out with them. It will be even clearer this time.

As they stared down through the dust thrown up by many hooves, a pattern began to emerge. There was little order, but a steady stream of riders flowed out of the pastures at the eastern side of the camp and wheeled to the right.

"This is it. They're heading south."

Calmly, your Majesty. There is a junction in the trail. Move your glance slowly to the right. Everyone follow. There. See the stream that comes in from the east? There is a trail there. Wait until...

They waited, controlling their panting breath. The first riders, galloping hard, reached the joining...

"East! They've turned east!"

The connection was broken, and they looked at each other.

"Are they trying to get around us? They're riding hard. We need to get down to the castle and get moving to stay ahead of them."

"No, your Majesty. We have scouted that route. It goes east, and the mountains close around it. They're going into the mountains."

Jesco's soft curse interrupted her. "The Leute."

"They're going to attack the Leute. Why would they do that?"

The prince shrugged. "They're doing everything else backwards. Why not?"

We have to warn them. We can contact Polvijarvi.

Jesco shook his head. "He was an old man. He'll be dead by now..." He paused. "Ah. The Champion. Karvilanti. Kitten and I will know his mind anywhere."

As long as he isn't dead, too. But we have to try.

Marisola was staring down at the torrent of riders. Suddenly her head shot up. "Numbers. Divo and Ovid. The leaders are still in sight. Start counting!"

Kitten merged with the Twins, and they began to tot up the numbers.

Silence descended on the ridge. The prince was pacing, his hands behind his back, his face tight. Finally he stopped in front of Marisola. "What do you think?"

She shook her head. "This changes nothing. The nomads are still not doing what we expected them to. All right, they are attacking. But why the Leute? I'm afraid they've got one more day to make a definite move, and then you're off down the road to start a hide-and-seek war until they finally get back together and smash us."

He nodded grimly. "My feeling exactly. We should wait and get a count. Then we might as well go down and tell everyone to relax."

"But not too much. The Ulaan are on the move. Something's going to happen.

Marisola...

She turned. The Twins were no longer counting.

"What's wrong?"

"That's all, Marisola... about twelve hundred, we think...hard to tell...they refuse to...line up properly. Dratted foe...won't cooperate." The two chuckled to each other.

The prince nodded. "Perfect. That tells us precisely nothing. Not enough to be an invasion. But it takes enough strength away that there probably won't be an invasion. No, that doesn't help us at all."

He spun to Marisola. "Is that enough to take on the Leute?"

She shrugged. "Nobody knows how many Leute there are. Nobody knows how they fight. The only sure fact is that no one has ever beaten them. They fold up their tents, slip back into the mountains and disappear."

"So this looks like another mistake."

"It does, and the last thing we want to do is start thinking the enemy is stupid."

They aren't. This I know.

"I'll come back to see the meeting this afternoon. It will be important if Husam has gone with them."

"That will be the only piece of information that might be of use. I should get back and stop our travel preparation. Let's go."

Marisola looked east again. The mountains were grey and foreboding, and a bank of dark cloud hovered low along the peaks. She shuddered. "I wouldn't want to be going up there."

And our Ulaan friends are about to find out why.

You don't sound worried.

I know the Leute. Kitten felt no need to say more. She had loved her time with the mountain people, but it had left a bitter feeling, like a sour drink after a pleasant meal. She put the thought away.

They walked down to their horses and took a leisurely time getting back to the castle. Marisola was uncharacteristically silent, and Kitten opened her mind to her Hand. *You are not speaking.*

I hope I didn't offend anyone.

No, but you are not usually this quiet.

Isn't a girl allowed a moment to think?

I don't see thinking. I see thoughts swirling around like mud in a pigsty.

If that was meant to joke me out of my mood, it's not working.

Worth a try. Don't worry. This is progress. After all, wouldn't we like to be wrong?

What?

What if the nomads never do attack? What then if some nobles duck out of an army we don't need? The Crown Prince has witnessed the size of the enemy camp. No one can say we exaggerated the danger.

Yes, you're right. Thank you, Kitten. I mustn't become so attached to my idea that I forget to be logical about it.

Correct. Clinging to a disproven theory is dangerous.

As opposed to not giving in under pressure, which is a strength.

And knowing which one is which is called wisdom. Of which I have a great deal.

And that means, in this case?

We aren't out of the woods yet.

And even if we are, it wouldn't hurt to stay alert.

Now, tell his Majesty that.

She glanced up at the stern look on the General's face. *I don't think he's given up, either.*

* * *

131

"Lady Marisola, could I speak to you in private?"

"You have only to give the order, your Majesty."

Shooting her a crooked smile, he turned back into the castle, leaving his men mounting for their departure to the south. "Oh, certainly. And I recall a certain turn of phrase in the Sword's oath. 'Only for the good of Inderjorne.'" He chuckled. "My father prepared me for that one."

"It seems to be the way the realm works."

"And I fully support it. But that is why I wish to speak to you. Please sit."

He took a chair facing her. "I am about to give you information that goes no further. I have no doubt as to your discretion."

He sat back, steepling his fingers. "First, please understand I have no fear of magic. A healthy respect, yes. However, I am restricted by my position from seeming to be under its influence."

"Of course."

Where is he going with this?

Kitten yawned. *They always start out with the philosophical stuff when they're about to tell you something you don't want to hear.*

"You are wondering what that has to do with the present situation. You have played several very clever ploys in the past few days, and they have all worked, to a greater or lesser extent. The fact that I know they were planned makes no difference because I also know that they were intended for the good of Inderjorne." He shot her a direct glance. "That blade cuts on both sides, too."

"As it should."

"The oath of allegiance was a very clever move, and I admit to its effects on me. It is probably why I am having this conversation with a minor scion of a backwoods house.

132

But I agree with my father the king on the cooperative nature of the ruling of this realm, and I deem your cooperation might be key in averting this great calamity which might befall us."

Note the 'might.' He is still not convinced.

"I agree, your Majesty. I am not so blinded by my belief that I don't see the possibility that this will all somehow fade away. I'm just very doubtful."

"We agree on that. However, others will not."

"Mostly the more traditional of the Maridons."

"But not only them." He took a deep breath. "You have a brother."

What?

"Xavier. I had assumed you met him."

"I did. A very correct and accomplished young man. Did anyone ever accuse you of taking a contrary stand simply because it allowed you to exert your individuality? Did they tell you that many of the things you did had more to do with the things he didn't do?"

She burst into laughter. "Oh. I see what you're getting at. Yes, my brother is the staid and serious one, always doing what he is told, living up to the expectations of Lady Perica and my father, who represent the line of Falken. I was the tomboy who was always running off in pants to watch the soldiers practise and listen to their stories."

"Then my point is made."

He is talking about Prince Tahal

"You have two younger brothers. Are they both like that?"

"No, just Tahal. He is, like all of us, completely supportive of the throne, but he chooses to show his support in his own personal ways."

"Which often have a lot to do with what you do not do? Or think?"

"Exactly."

"And he has decided, what? That this supposed attack could backfire, be interpreted as a hoax perpetrated by the king to dominate the lords. Thus, when nothing comes of it, there will be a backlash of rampant individualism and continued internal conflict."

A crooked frown wrinkled the prince's brow. "You state it so well. That is the nub of the problem. He does not side with the Maridons. Quite the opposite. But he chooses to be sensitive to their opinions…"

"…perhaps because it gives him a chance to disagree with yours?"

"The thought had crossed my mind."

Kitten replayed the conversation in her mind. *And he wants…what?*

"I appreciate your candour, your Majesty, but why are you telling me this?"

"I'm not exactly sure. One of the reasons I came here was to ascertain that the threat was real. Now I have first hand arguments to counter my brother's vague charges.

"I also wanted to assess our defences. I find Lord Waldheim thorough and competent, his position firm. I also find the king has agents in place who are powerful, useful, and loyal. And, in keeping with my father's philosophies, I want to bind those agents to me, to ensure their cooperation on top of their loyalties."

He will be a very good king some day.

He feels the temper of his people and can work with it.

"So I am conscripted into his Majesty's army, am I?"

"I would prefer to consider you a willing volunteer."

"You may do so."

"Good." He stood. "And now I must go back to where the real battle seems to be, leaving you to keep track of this imaginary threat which covers several leagues of our realm."

She stood as well. "Are we still on the same timeline?"

"Yes. Husam al Din has now only six days to return to his traditional habits, quaking the whole time at what you will do to him should he decide not to cooperate."

"If that still fits your battle plan, your Majesty."

He clapped her on the shoulder. "I will not hold you to the method by which you assist my efforts. If this war changes in nature, your information will become even more important, and I urge you to do whatever you can without getting killed. I need you and your troop more than I need heroes."

"I understand, your Majesty."

"Oh," he turned back. "And I am now not your prince but your commanding officer. 'Sir,' will be enough."

She tossed him a stiff, formal salute. "Yes, sir!"

He grinned at her, but then his face fell into grimmer lines. Stiffening his shoulders, he spun and strode out into the sunlight.

His escort was waiting, and he mounted and spurred his horse away without fanfare.

Jesco had stood outside. Now he slid in beside her. "This visit has had another good outcome."

"In what way?"

The Twins chuckled from behind. "What came down the road was...a parade of popinjays. What...just left was a...squad of fighters...prepared for war."

Jesco nodded. "Only essential pennons flying. Not a bright colour to be seen."

She grinned. "Except the knights' shields and helmets. Some traditions are impossible to break."

Those identifiers have their uses on the field of battle.

"Stop pontificating, Kitten. I listened to my lessons."

Just don't forget any of them. In battle, you can be killed even if you don't make any mistakes.

She elbowed Jesco. "And now our commanding Cat places us on a war footing. No jocularity. A war to win."

The old swordsman did not smile. He moved a step closer, and she could feel the presence of her lions at her back.

"Then let's get out there and win it. First priority. We must warn the Leute."

They probably already know. Still, it would be a courtesy to contact our allies.

She turned inside, making for their chambers. "How do we contact them? If both Polvijarvi and the swordsman Jesco fought are dead, who do we send to?"

Kitten sent a cat's version of a chuckle. *You don't contact a Leute. You contact the Leute.*

Marisola sat and laid the Sword on the table. "I'm sure that bit of obfuscation will become clear soon. Come. Join hands and let's see what the Leute are doing."

The now-familiar feeling settled over them, but Kitten did not send immediately. Instead, she nurtured the bonds between each of them, smoothing out any irregular thoughts, tightening each member's focus. When she felt that her merge was a firm weapon, pulsing with power, she brought up the image of the army of Ulaan riders, streaming off to the east.

You have all seen this. Hold it in your minds.

Then Kitten reached back into her memory, pushing aside the horrors that tried to intrude, and sought the feeling she remembered. When she found it, she injected it into her merge and pictured sending Horde image eastward to the rocks and the mountains, to the entity that resided there.

It took no time at all. The sense of a gathering storm chilled their souls, and a crushing weight of stone loomed over them. A vast power reached out and accepted her offering, regarded it closely, indicated gratitude, then withdrew. That was it.

A stunned silence filled the room, and Kitten gradually eased her people away from the merge. They took their hands back and sat, staring at each other.

Marisola rubbed her arms as if she was cold. "I think...they already knew?"

I never thought they wouldn't. I have felt their presence several times since we got here. They have been scouting the Ulaan, keeping their distance.

"But what was that...entity...we contacted? I have never experienced anyone...anything with magic so powerful."

That was the combined Sensitivity of a nation of people welded together by tradition, belief and sacrifice. As you are probably now aware, I was part of the sacrificial part, a deed I am not proud of. That is why I fear the use of this power I wield. The Leute have taken my gift and molded it into a positive force. What if it were turned to evil?

Marisola shuddered. "I can't imagine having that...whatever it was...turned against me. I felt insignificant enough when it was friendly."

Jesco rubbed his hands over his face, then snapped them away, as if removing water drops. "This is all very well, but the Leute live in small villages. How will it help them against twelve hundred fighting men?"

It won't. The Leute will resort to their usual defences: the mountains. They use trails horses cannot follow. They have hidden fortresses, and their paths are riddled with traps, deadfalls and rockslides. A foray of this sort will have no success in the short term. Whether the Leute could hold out past one year, if they were unable to return to their villages to plant their crops, is another matter.

"Hope that this war is over long before planting time."

Let us hope.

"So we expect the Ulaan to come stumbling back out of the mountains in a few days, sadder but wiser?"

Jesco snorted. "More likely madder."

"Is there another...way to leave the mountains...further south?"

Yes, there is an easy road out through Oliveres and Quentar to Falconby.

"Then we send a message by conventional means to Lord Oliveres, telling him to push his scouts north and east and keep us informed. Anything else?"

There was no response.

"So, back to the lookout this afternoon. I want to see whether that second leader is at the evening meeting."

Are you thinking what I'm thinking?

"Silly question. I'm always doing that."

It would explain a lot.

"We'll head out after the noon meal, then.

"

18.   Reinforcements

Sure enough, as the sun slanted west and Husam the War Leader greeted his lieutenants, he sat alone under the awning.

Jesco turned to Marisola as they took their hands from the Sword's hilt. "So he shares power."

"He cannot override the wishes of his co-Leader, but he doesn't have to support him. He lets him go. That's what one would expect of a society like the Ulaan."

"Sounds like...family." The Twins grinned at each other.

That is not so funny. I wish we knew the power structure of the Ulaan better. Perhaps co-rulership is a normal situation.

They stopped their observations for a drink and a bite to eat while they tossed around ideas, but they could add little to their conclusions.

As they returned to the castle, Kitten assessed her allies as Eirlin had taught her. *Amazing how useful a Healer can be.* All traces of jocularity left her mind as she read their emotions. *From frustration to defeat and everything in between. We need a training exercise. Better still, we need a mission where we experience success.*

Nothing came to her.

I will spend the night thinking while they waste their time in sleep.

* * *

The night brought no new ideas, and she met the humans the following morning with no solutions. *Well, in the true*

139

spirit of Inderjorne, there is a solution. They are the ones that need help. I will ask them.

After breakfast they met to plan the day, and she bided her time, looking for the right moment. *After all, maybe one of them has a solution.*

From Lord Waldheim's tone, it didn't sound good. "I'm really caught, here. My people have put their lives in limbo, waiting for an attack that does not come. The first few days they occupied themselves with preparations.

"Now, their fear subsides somewhat, and they want to be useful. They cannot go back to their duties, because their stock is sequestered, their farming tools are hidden, and they cannot spread out across the demesne for fear of a sortie." He scrubbed a hand across his face. "Keeping troops ready for battle is hard. With the civilians it's worse."

As he spoke, Kitten's senses picked up an approaching mind. Not too sensitive, but radiating such urgency that its presence spread.

Marisola nodded. "We are all feeling it. We need some action..."

Be careful what you ask for.

"What?"

Rider coming. It is one of the guards from the lookout. He has urgent news.

Their interest rising, they crowded out the door and down into the bailey as the panicked rider galloped in, jumping down before his horse was fully stopped.

"More Ulaan, my Lord! A whole army of them!"

The lord grabbed the messenger by the arm to freeze him in place. "Where? Are they attacking?"

"No attack, my Lord. They are streaming in from the northeast. A huge mob of them. I came before the count was finished, but from the look, it will be thousands!"

Marisola glanced at her troop. "We need to be up there now!"

She gave no further orders. Within heartbeats they were springing into the saddle. Marisola looked down at Lord Waldheim. "This doesn't look like an attack. Yet. We will send word the moment we see movement in this direction. Otherwise, consider this a little gift from the enemy to keep your people interested in the war."

With a cold smile, she spun Tariq and led her troop out of the gate.

When they reached the lookout, the influx seemed to be over, although a huge dust cloud at the horse pastures gave testimony to the number of animals milling there.

The soldier in charge met them as they dismounted. "In the range of two thousand, ma'am, maybe less, because many of the horses were riderless. No other details, I'm afraid. Too far away. But we couldn't see any pack animals, so it must be a war party.

Marisola nodded and handed him her reins. "We'll take a closer look."

With their added power, they could see little more.

Lots of horses in the pasture, but they have settled quickly. Possibly they were tired? More movement on the paths between the tents. Look down there. See that group moving slowly? Focus on them. Do you see bandages? Yes, check their postures. The people on the outside are helping wounded.

Now that they knew what to look for, there were many such groups, escorting bandaged warriors to their tents. In front of Husam's tent a mob swirled. Then the War Leader himself appeared, waving an arm in command. The group stilled, then sat.

He's getting them all in order. Aha! This is interesting. See the taller one who does not sit? Look at his posture. He considers himself a leader. Now the chairs are brought.

Sure enough, The Husam sat, the new arrival to his right.

I have a feeling the number two man will be sorry he wasn't here to take advantage of his rival's loss of face.

Marisola struggled to speak and keep her focus at the same time. "Loss of face?"

We can assume that this army has been off fighting someone else, probably their original enemy. From the look of it, they were not successful. If there is rivalry between the leaders, then this man is a step down at the moment. There seems to be a lot of nothing happening. Shall we speak?

They broke the merge and stood looking at one another. "Kitten, you have the most knowledge of these people. What are you thinking?

We are assuming rivalry. The second leader has taken his troops off to a battle he thinks he can win, thus raising his status. It seems the third leader has done the same thing, but has not been successful. I didn't see any "Hail the conquering hero" in that reception. Husam was not bending to his rival in any way.

"So we have to wait for the outcome of the raid against the Leute."

"Ovid and Divo, can you add anything?"

The brothers glanced at each other, and the one on the left, probably Divo, spoke alone. "We are of two minds about this. If the Leute attack succeeds, the winner might consolidate his win by moving his people into the foothills. He would then have to keep his troops because of the continuous counterattacks the Leute will indulge in. This would lessen Husam's numbers."

"But if he loses, or if he returns to the horde triumphant, it gets more interesting."

"Yes, if he has won and thus gained more power, there will be more conflict in the leadership...His rival will then have to find a way...to prove himself, either by...taking on another foray...or by throwing his support behind Husam."

Marisola threw up her hands. "But that assumes rivalry. If there is no rivalry, once the Leute attackers return, the whole Ulaan horde, with reinforcements, is still knocking on our door. This leaves us absolutely nowhere. We still have no idea what the Ulaan are going to do."

The Twins shrugged "So we will wait with great interest for the next move. And watch even more carefully."

Marisola ran her fingertips up and down her forehead. "Jesco, please send a messenger to Lord Waldheim to tell him what we just said. We'll be waiting and watching until the evening meeting is over."

"Aye, ma'am." Jesco turned away.

"And Kitten, if you aren't too tired, let's the four of us take a look at the horse lines and see if we can find anything useful."

I am not tired. This group becomes easier and easier to work with.

"Great. Maybe we can fill our time trying to make a count."

"If we can figure out...how many horses are...in each pasture, maybe we... could estimate..."

"You're serious?"

"Were you?"

"Half."

"Well, since you...have half the brains...we do, that's...about right."

She ignored their chuckles. "Come on, Kitten. It seems we have our orders."

19.   Moving Out

They watched all that day and all the next, and their frustration grew as nothing happened in the Ulaan camp. Conversations went on longer at the evening meetings, and it was clear that this third leader did not have the same relationship with Husam that the other man did. There was confrontation and arm waving although never a move towards weapons.

Still the watchers persevered, and the following morning their patience was rewarded. As they approached the top of the ridge, an excited soldier met them.

"Glad you're here, ma'am. We were about to send a messenger. Action at the horse lines."

"An attack forming?"

"Too early to tell."

Once again, the merge was not needed; the stir of dust would have obscured any details. Huge numbers of horses were preparing to move out, and Kitten could feel the intensity of her humans rise.

Calmly, now. Watch and wait.

"Easy for you to say, lady Nerves-of-Steel. This could be the attack."

So far it hasn't been. Our forces are ready, our plans are complete. We have plenty of time to give warning.

Marisola kept her sending private. *And we know what happens when the plan hits the battle.*

And we have further plans to cope with that. The wait before the action is always the hardest part, and the uncertainty makes it harder. Relax as well as you can and prepare your mind for whatever happens.

"Look!" Jesco was pointing. "They're moving."

"Which way?" Marisola's eyes rose to the dust cloud. "I don't see anything different."

"That's because you're looking in the wrong place. Not down here towards us. Far out at the western edge."

"Let's take a closer look. Everybody here."

They formed the merge and zeroed in where Jesco indicated. Marisola's heart jumped as they made out a tight formation of horses, tiny flags flying, circling out around the camp, headed towards the west. Streaming out of the dust cloud behind them came a seething mass of horsemen, too far away to see individuals, even with the merge's enhanced vision.

Marisola pulled her hand from Kitten's hilt, and everyone reeled at the sudden return to normal sight. "We don't have a plan for this. Think fast."

First question. Where are they going?

"West? Are they moving on like we hoped they would?"

"Ignore that...idea. If they...are leaving we...have nothing to do."

Marisola nodded. "Kitten, what about the geography...?"

Another mountain range blocks the southwest. The only other possibility is the Batkhaan Valley.

"Which leads south. But that's even drier than the plains. There's nothing for them there."

"Except a straight route to Marida."

"They're attacking Marida? Why?"

A double chuckle behind her. "You are asking why...the Ulaan do anything?"

"Right. Useless. We must focus on action, and we have no plan. Ideas?"

Are we in any hurry?

"Of course we are! If they're attacking Merida...oh. I see. It will take them several days to get there."

A well-made plan now..."

"I know, I know. Saves time later. Why do you have to choose now for a lesson?"

Because this is war, the greatest teacher of lessons.

"Don't give me that...you're trying to distract me and calm me down, aren't you?"

Is it working?

"I am calm. We aren't in a hurry." She thought a moment. "We have two objectives. We must find out the number of the enemy headed south. We must warn General Guevejar about the attack.

"Priorities. First, time. We need people in place at the corner to see if they turn. That would also be the best place for a count. Should we go there to get the best information? No, the other priority is the warning. That is more important. If we go into danger and don't get the message out...a poor message is better than none at all."

That is logical. So?

Marisola raised her eyes to her expectant troops. "Sergeant Hreb, lead seven men hotfoot to the west, staying well in the foothills. Find a safe lookout at the edge of the Batkhaan Valley where you can get a rough count of the enemy forces."

"Aye, ma'am."

"And Sergeant, safety is most important. Keep a close eye for enemy outriders. Don't try to kill them unless you have to. We don't need heroes. We need the information you will be carrying. As soon as you have a number, split into two groups and take different routes back to Waldheim. Got it?"

"Aye, ma'am. That will leave only two men here."

"Not important. Your mission is."

He saluted and strode off, calling names and orders.

Did I miss anything?

Nothing I could think of. I would have told you.

Thanks.

She gathered her small troop. "Now, us. Is there any reason to stay here?"

"It depends on the...timing. If we wait until...the army has departed...that is good information."

"And if we go now, we will have a warning, but no facts to go with it."

"Consider the General's...problem."

"What's that...? Right. A warning with no information will not be believed." She shrugged. "I don't agree, but that's the situation we are forced into. We will stay. If only part of the Horde leaves, we can head out fairly soon. If all of them are going, it will take all day. We'll have a pretty good guess in a couple of candles. For the moment, let's amuse ourselves by checking around. Who knows what we'll come up with?"

They formed the merge and scanned the camp. Nothing seemed different. The meeting-place in front of Husam's tent was empty. Horses were still forming up and streaming out of the pastures.

But the cloud is less, now. See? The wind carries it away, but more is not rising. We can make out horses in the lower pastures where before it was all dust. Grazing horses. Many grazing horses. Perhaps this is only another raid.

They watched further, and it became apparent that only a portion of the Horde was on the march; the rest were staying put. They returned their watch to Husam's tent and were rewarded by the War Leader striding back from the direction of the horse lines, throwing himself into his chair and slouching there, his aides and officers making a wide circle around him.

I think the noble Husam is angry. Have we seen enough?

The troop showed their agreement by removing their minds from the merge and their hands from the Sword.

Marisola sheathed Kitten. "Let's get moving." She strode over to the two soldiers left on the hilltop.

"I have an assignment for you."

"Yes, ma'am."

"You too exposed here for such a small party. Our sentries have killed several Ulaan outriders who came to investigate. I want you to clean up this site as well as you can to disguise that fact that many people have spent a lot of time here. Shovel in the latrine and cover it with brush. Pick up anything lying around and sweep the dirt with a branch. Then conceal your horses back in the rocks and move up into the crag and continue watching the Ulaan camp. If you see something important, one man comes to report. That's risky as well, but we need to keep a presence here as long as we can. Any questions?"

"No, ma'am."

"We'll send relief as soon as we hit the castle, and we may come back for the evening meeting, down there. But you're on your own the rest of the day."

"Got it, ma'am. You can count on us."

"I'm sure I can. Now, give us a hand with the saddles. We are officially in a hurry."

Her troop was soon headed towards the castle, and when they hit the open road, they moved up to a lope, Jesco riding point. Marisola used her time to consider all the possibilities of this new situation.

"Marisola?"

She glanced around and slowed her horse as the Twins rode up on either side of her.

"It is good...that you handle the...details so well."

She could not stop the heat that rose in her cheeks. "Umm...thank you...

"It leaves us...free to think...of other things."

She grinned, left, then right. "That was our plan, as I recall. What other things?"

"Politics," came from her left.

"Geography," from her right.

Her mind spun. "Politics. The Maridons in Inderjorne will want to help Marida. Of course. That will strain any alliances our people have managed to form. Geography...?"

"There are several open passes from Marida into southwestern Inderjorne..."

"...that the victorious Ulaan might use to attack Inderjorne's Maridon holdings which are concentrated in that area. They will use those excuses to pull out of any agreements the king has forged."

"Such were...our thoughts."

After one panicked moment, Marisola took hold of herself. "But that is not our problem. We fulfill our role by passing along the information we have discovered. Those more adept at the political side of things will deal with it as they know how."

She was always a good student.

"What do you mean by that?"

Laughter came from the minds on either side of her. "You have taken a...very mature stance." They chuckled aloud. "You must forgive...us. We can't...help but see you...as our little cousin Marisola...who was so cute, playing...with her toy swords."

She faked a growl. "I'll show you toy swords."

"That's a good...idea. Once we have...passed on our message...then we will have...little to do but...prepare for war."

"We did speak of working together, but I've been too busy to think about it. Jesco?"

149

The swordsman, riding ahead of them, twisted in the saddle. "I can always tell when the troops are plotting mutiny. What have you cooked up?"

"Sword practice."

"Sounds better than rebellion. When?"

* * *

They stayed at the castle the following day and had their promised workout on the practice field. As expected, nobody could get close to the Twins, no matter how many soldiers they recruited to help.

Marisola had just decided to try them against Kitten and herself when a cry rang out from the highest watchtower.

"Rider from the north. Fast."

They broke off and headed towards the castle gate. It was one of the soldiers from the lookout, and he rode straight up to Marisola, falling from his gasping horse. "They're coming back, my Lady. The ones who attacked the Leute."

She seized his arm, holding him up. "How do they look?"

"Not good. Spread out, moving slow, many wounded."

Marisola glanced at her troop and they sprinted for the horses. "Thank you, soldier. We'll get out there and take a peek."

By the time they got to the lookout, the retreating army was in full flow.

"If you can call it a flow. More of a drift." The condition of the Ulaan who stumbled out of the mountains was visible to the naked eye, even at this distance. Each horse moving at its own pace, some wandering as if their riders were not paying attention. By the men's huddled postures, they probably weren't.

Behind them, the mountains appeared even taller, closer, their flanks speckled by stabbing shafts of sunlight and the sweeping shadows of the ever-present clouds.

Let us take a closer look.

Once they combined their powers, the details were visible. Empty quivers. Empty sleeves. Rough bandages, blood seeping through. While they watched, a slumped rider tumbled from his mount, lay in the road for a while, then dragged himself to his feet. Another stopped to help him remount, and his horse wandered on.

They broke from the merge, then stood staring down at the pathetic scene, half in sympathy, half in joy at seeing their enemy brought low.

"There don't seem to be any seriously wounded. What kind of fighting ends up like that?"

The Leute women see to the seriously wounded.

"That's nice of them, considering they're enemies."

It isn't nice at all.

"You mean...?"

That's right. The women go onto the battlefield when the fighting is over and give mercy to any who cannot leave under their own power. Their belief is that the enemy pays for his transgression by enriching the soil with his blood.

Marisola turned to the soldier who stood nearby. "Have you been keeping count?"

"Yes, ma'am. We're at seven hundred now."

"It looks to me like the flow is lessening."

"It looks that way, too, ma'am."

"Tell me when you have close to a final count. From the look of them, they'll be trickling in for hours."

"I'll do that, ma'am."

"Thank you."

She turned to her troop. "So. What does this mean?"

The Twins regarded the returning Ulaan. "It means the...second leader is...discredited."

"More power to Husam, then."

"And he is the one...who wants to attack us."

"So the outcome of the battle for Marida is crucial. If the Ulaan succeed, he will have to attack us with his reduced army."

"Bolstered by...the remains of...this one."

"But if the Ulaan are turned back, then their leader will also lose power, and Husam will finally have the whole horde at his back, slightly reduced but united."

Jesco's harsh laugh broke in. "Never thought I'd be saying this, but I find myself wishing the Ulaan good hunting."

20. A Different Visitor

Which goes to show how strange our chances in life are.

Marisola looked up from her reading and frowned at her Sword. "What do you mean by that?"

Come out to the battlements.

As they left the tower, a sweating horse pulled up inside the bailey, the rider tumbling off in his haste. "Ready the drawbridge. Riders coming!"

This sounds familiar.

They raised their eyes to the surrounding forest where a cloud of dust rose above the trees.

"That's quite a large party."

Listen.

Lord Waldheim strode into the bailey, strapping on his sword. "Calm down, man. What riders? How many?"

"Fifty or more my lord. No idea who. Lancers dressed for battle, I would guess by the gleam of armour. As soon as I saw them, I turned and hurried back."

"A good choice." The lord looked around, then up at Marisola's group on the wall. "Anything in sight, yet?"

"It's a large dust cloud. Just before the last bend, I'd say."

And you'd be right. Probably Inderjornese, by the feeling...or perhaps Maridon. Hard to tell. Strange

"Yes, you'll see them soon," she called down. "Kitten says they're probably our people."

"Probably?"

"A mixed group of Inderjornese and Maridon, if you can credit that."

The lord looked around at the soldiers at the drawbridge windlass, the men swarming up the stairs to the battlements. "Right. We'll be ready for whatever."

Let's have a quick glance as they come around the corner.

The Twins joined Marisola, and they concentrated. When the first rider came into sight, she relaxed and broke the group. "Friends, my Lord. Royal pennant."

"Just a moment." She put her hand back on her hilt and they peered down the road. "Not the king or Guevejar. I don't know all the flags. Prince Tahal, perhaps?"

"Thank you, my Lady." Waldheim started snapping out orders. Those hurrying to defensive positions reversed their steps, and by the time the formation of panting, sweating horses and grim, well-armed riders approached the castle, a similarly warlike reception was formed up in greeting.

Aha. Prince Tahal. I wonder what brings him here?

"I'm sure we'll soon find out." She followed the retreating soldiers down the outside staircase to the bailey.

The leader, a dark-haired, upright figure who rode directly behind his pennant, swung down from the saddle and strode up to Waldheim, who bowed.

"Greetings, your Majesty. We did not expect to see you here,"

The prince grinned. "I make it a practice to move fast and show up where and when I'm least expected." He looked around the bailey and up at the soldiers on the battlements. "I thought I would not catch Waldheim Castle unawares. You look well-prepared."

The lord's back straightened. "Waldheim has always been ready for the defence of the kingdom, your Majesty." Then he relaxed and gave a twisted grin. "And when our enemy is good enough to give us this much warning, it helps a lot."

"Yes, and that's one of the reasons I'm here." He turned his attention to Kitten's little group, standing a polite distance away. "And you will be Marisola of the formidable daFalken/Skonric alliance, Hand to the Cat with Many Claws." He stepped forward and bowed over her hand. "It is an honour to meet you."

Hmm. A very smooth one. Shall I add him to the list?

*Umm...*She bowed to the prince and retrieved her hand. *...perhaps not.*

Getting picky, are we?

Just a feeling.

"A pleasure to see you again, your Majesty." She eyed the horses. "You have made a great effort to get here."

He laughed. "As I suspected. Come," he turned her towards Waldheim. "Get me some ale to cut the dust in my throat and I will answer your questions — asked," He glanced at Marisola," — and unasked."

As they followed Prince Tahal's lead, Marisola sized him up.

As handsome, strong and active as his brother. Not very Sensitive, though. Less than Jesco, I'd say.

And a little too smooth for my liking.

Prefer your rustic War Leader, do you?

As a leader, definitely. Other than that? We'll have to see.

Quite right. No hurried judgements.

Waldheim led them to an alcove off the main hall. When the prince was seated at the head of the table with a large mug in his hands, the others took their smaller drinks and sat as well, although Jesco remained in the archway and the Twins stood at her shoulders as usual. After slaking his thirst, Tahal regarded the group, nodding. "Yes, I see you are unified and prepared for battle. A pleasant change, I might add."

"How goes the levy, your Majesty?"

The prince raised a hand in protest. "I have no pretensions to the throne nor military position. 'My Lord' is sufficient." He used his fingers to smooth the dark, straight hair along the side of his head. "The levy is going exactly as we expected, although the Maridon sector has perked up rather quickly."

Waldheim nodded. "Not surprising. And what is the general feeling?"

Tahal shrugged. "Divided, as you might expect. The more ardent supporters of our Maridon heritage want to raise an army and go and aid our brothers. The more paranoid are afraid to leave their demesnes, lest the Inderjornese or the Ulaan take advantage of the situation to attack their holdings." He shook his head and grinned. "It must be a difficult life, always fearful."

He laid his hands flat on the table. "But we are at war, and we have little time for pleasantries. Why am I here?" He shrugged. "For the same reason I have requested no position in the army. Freedom. I'm sure Lady Marisola knows what I mean. His Majesty the King has plenty of soldiers, motivated or not, to do all the usual things as they are ordered. It is my practice to stay outside the chain of command so I am not tied in any place or position. I am more use to my father that way."

He looked at them. "Please, my friends. Do not hesitate because of my position. Ask what questions you would. For example, what should I expect to find here?"

Marisola grinned. "My lord, I have been wondering. What do you expect to accomplish by this little four-day jaunt at high speed?"

He laughed. "And thus my patronizing is answered." Then his face became serious. "In the first place, I expect to find exactly what my brother did. I may interpret the facts differently, but I do not doubt either those furnishing the information," here he nodded at Marisola, "or my brother's honesty in reporting.

"However, I do reserve the right to form my own opinions. Which I will then communicate with my father. That is why I am here."

Do you notice how much of his conversation is about himself?

He seeks acceptance, but on his own terms.

Marisola laced her fingers together on the table. "So you wish us to show you what we showed General Guevejar."

"I do. I have heard his full report, but I want to see for myself. I am very interested in your Sword's ability to enhance our vision."

Kitten, can you do that? Is he Sensitive enough?

Not as sharp, but I can use him in the merge.

"Then tomorrow first thing we will go to our usual viewing point and show you the enemy."

Tahal sat back, a look of satisfaction on his face. "Good. My men and horses need a rest. Please provide me with a fresh mount tomorrow, in case of the need for speed. My Safiy has carried me well, as he always does."

"A fine animal, my Lord. I'll be sure my stable hands give him the best of treatment."

"Yes, a quiet night under cover will do him good."

Can't fault a man who treats his horse well.

I'm sure Husam al Din treats his horse well, too.

Kitten, I am not running a competition, here.

No, your role is to sit by looking coy while they fight over you.

Me? Coy? You have rust between your ears.

If I had ears, you would be justified in that opinion.

* * *

157

At dinner that night, Tahal proved himself to be a genial guest, with good stories of all sorts and carefully considered opinions on many topics. He waxed more loquacious as the evening progressed, but Marisola wasn't fooled.

He's not drinking that much, is he?

Well noted, Hand. But then, neither are you.

And he will probably notice that, too.

Which is to the good. We are allies, after all, and his good opinion is valuable to us.

I hope it stays that way.

Marisola...

I am being cautious. It's not as if I dislike him. I'm just...cautious.

As you should be.

Do you feel it, too?

Nothing wrong with him that the proper circumstances couldn't turn into a major disaster.

My thoughts exactly. Other than that, nothing wrong with him. Let's enjoy the evening. Work tomorrow.

I cannot relax when I am keeping you sober.

Then I'll stay sober.

And I will not relax.

Then all is as it should be. We are on guard for our liege lords, the king and the general.

"Lady Marisola, you are pensive. Communing with your inner self? Or with your Sword?"

She shot him a glance, trying not to look surprised.

"Come, now," he laughed. "My family is all well-versed in your Sword's abilities. My mother especially."

She smiled. "My Sword is flattered. Your brother told us all about her reputation."

His smile disappeared. "Good. Then you know what we know." He shifted in his seat. "Tell me about this Husam al Din, this War Leader."

She raised her eyebrows. "He's a leader, all right. For a barbarian, a surprisingly complex man. He is a leader in war who says he likes a quiet afternoon with his flocks. He is unquestionably brave and quite clever. Whether he has a good command of battle tactics is something we will learn when it's probably too late."

"You know a lot about him."

"I have met him twice, as I'm sure you have been told. Once at sword point, once in conference."

"And so your Sword has his measure as well."

An astute observation.

"She does."

"And what is her opinion?"

Is now a good time, Kitten?

My opinion is not something easily put into words.

"My lord, sooner or later you will have to communicate with my Sword. This would be a good opportunity, because she does not always use words, and her impressions of this man will come across more clearly with a mental connection."

The prince looked around. "Should we do it here?"

"It is an unpredictable experience. Perhaps in private...?"

With a glance to Lord Waldheim, Tahal led the way back to the workroom and sat in the chair at the head of the table. "How do we do this?"

I will need his touch.

Marisola pulled up a chair, drew Kitten and laid her on the corner of the table. "You simply touch her hilt, my Lord. She will do the rest."

Instead of a mere touch, Tahal grasped Kitten and raised her, swinging a few quick arcs above the table. "She is very light and well-balanced. Could I fight with her?"

Don't worry. I am giving him nothing.

I hope not. What nerve!

He has always been a prince. It's a normal amount of nerve.

This is not a normal situation.

She controlled her reaction. "It is forbidden for anyone of your stature to be a Hand because of the uncontrolled power you would wield. Only in an emergency would you be allowed to fight with her."

"As my father did when he killed Fuentes da Baneza."

"Exactly."

"So, how do I talk to her?"

"You lay her back on the table. Husam the Ulaan Warleader picked her up without my permission, and he had a considerably less pleasant experience. You only need to touch her hilt. She will do the rest."

He regarded her a moment.

He got the message. He is re-evaluating you.

As he should.

Reluctantly, the prince did as she suggested.

Kitten did not try for conversation. Instead she sent a feeling of welcome through the contact. As his emotions settled, she sent an image of Husam, taking care to make it as detailed as her memory could. Once he seemed satisfied with that, she slowly and gently inundated his mind with her impressions of the War Leader, trying not to overwhelm him with the complexity of her understanding. When she felt that he had received enough she faded away, leaving him with a sense of satisfaction.

For a long while, the prince sat staring at the Sword. Then he removed his hand and looked at Marisola. "That was a fascinating experience."

"I'm sure it was, my Lord. Do you have a good picture of War Leader Husam?"

"I'm not completely sure. There was a tumble of images, some too fast for me to pick them up properly."

"She requires time to get used to communicating with a new person. It is not something she was created to do, but a talent she has developed lately. Perhaps your mind will sort through those images and make more sense of them as time goes by."

Tahal nodded. "Perhaps. At least I have a better idea of the enemy. Is there anything else I should meet with her about?"

Again no conversation was necessary. Both of them were completely in agreement.

"No, my lord. That was enough for the first time. Probably too much." She grinned. "I hope your dreams are not full of Husam al Din tonight."

He nodded, with some disappointment tempered by relief, Kitten thought. "I already have spent more time than I would like thinking about him and his people."

"As has the rest of the realm."

"And now I am feeling my day in the saddle. About when, tomorrow?"

"We usually rise after sunup, have breakfast, and leave soon after."

"Then I bid you good night," he bowed over her hand. "And sweet dreams."

She returned only a polite smile. "The same to you, my Lord."

* * *

The experience at the hilltop the next morning was very similar to the one eight days ago with his brother. Once the novelty of the experience had worn off, the prince looked at everything they showed him, absorbed it all and, for a change, inserted few of his own comments.

On the ride back to the castle he was deep in thought, and they did not disturb him.

As they dismounted, though, his mood seemed to be over. He met Marisola's eyes and faced her. "Thank you for a very interesting experience. It confirms many ideas in my mind. I have a few tactics of my own to add."

"We would be glad of any guidance, my Lord."

"Good." He slapped her on the shoulder, turning her towards the main hall. "We will speak over the noon meal."

Once they were settled at the table, Tahal regarded Marisola and Waldheim until he was sure they were listening. "I received good information this morning, but nothing new. I have an idea for getting more." He sat back with a smile.

He wants you to ask him.

Ah. "We'd be glad of fresh thoughts, my Lord."

"How difficult would it be to pick up one of their riders? A scout, for example."

"Not difficult at all, my lord. There are many around, and they are not good woodsmen. We took three of them just after Marisola got here."

"And what information did you get from them?"

"None. In the first place, none of them speak our language. In the second, they are incredibly tough."

"What happened to them?"

"One committed suicide, one escaped, one died."

"Died?"

"My men are not experienced at this sort of thing, my Lord. They were getting frustrated, and they were...overenthusiastic, I suppose."

"Nonetheless. Marisola, you have spoken to this Husam fellow. How?"

"My Sword understands their language. She puts our words into each other's heads. It only works with people who are Sensitive."

"And with those who are not?"

She shrugged. "Images, emotions, little more."

"Fine. It's worth a try. How long until we can find a subject?"

"It's hard to say, my Lord. We have not captured one for some time, and they are getting rather sloppy. Perhaps even this afternoon, if we're lucky."

"Well, give our luck a little help and put several patrols out. I'm getting bored with this lack of information."

"Yes, my Lord." Waldheim began to rise, but the prince's hand on his arm stopped him.

"No, no, wait until you have finished eating. We aren't in that much rush."

And now we see the real prince.

The one he's been practising all his life to become.

It shows.

Late that afternoon one of the search parties showed up at the castle gate, a small pony in their midst, a battered nomad tied to the saddle.

Tahal was the first one there, and the soldiers dragged the man off his horse and pushed him to the ground at the prince's feet. He knelt there, staring at the dirt.

"Tie him to the hitching rack in the stable yard."

As the soldiers complied, the prince turned to Marisola. "I'm sorry to bring you into this, my Lady, but we will need the services of your Sword."

She nodded, her face grim. "I expected that."

"Good." He faced the prisoner. "How do we work this?"

163

"You speak. My Sword will put the proper words in his mind, and his words into yours."

"Oh. Good." He turned again to the Ulaan. "Now, you listen here, my man. We have you, and don't think you'll get away. You've had a taste of what awaits you if you don't cooperate." He turned to look at Marisola.

He hears.

"He has heard. He has nothing to say."

Tahal smiled and laid a hand on the nomad's shoulder. "But if you cooperate, and the war is averted, then there will be no need for us to be enemies, will there? We will send you and your horse back to your people, and all will be well." Once again the questioning glance.

Marisola shook her head.

The prince nodded to the soldiers, and they moved in on the victim, punching him repeatedly about the face and body.

Marisola gritted her teeth and looked straight ahead.

This is what war is like, except much, much worse. It is a good experience for you, if any good could come of it. Which it won't.

Can't they see he's resigned to death? None of this means anything to him.

You are right. As far as he is concerned, the more they hurt him, the sooner it will be over.

The prince motioned the soldiers to stop. "Well? Are you ready to talk to us?"

Again Marisola shook her head.

Tahal, shook his head in disgust. "What do we do? As far as I can tell, we could beat him to death and he'd never tell us anything."

"My Sword says he thinks of himself as already dead. He welcomes if it is sooner."

"Pah! What do we do now?"

"Do you mind if I have a try?"

The prince's head came around. "You?"

"Yes. Give me some time with him. Perhaps I can talk him around."

"Aha! The direct way. Yes, yes, by all means. Have a try."

"Good. Untie him and put him on that bench over there."

"No, no. Have your Sword go into his head and take the information we want."

She froze, staring up at him. "What do you want me to do?"

"Use your powers. He has a simple, weak mind. Surely with the ability of your sword…"

I never expected this. What do I do now?

A lot of thinking. Not that I didn't expect it, humans being what they are. Be honest. Are you so surprised?

No, I suppose not. I think a bit of training is in order.

I will watch my student with interest as she becomes a teacher.

Don't distract me with inanity. This is serious.

This is war.

She took the prince by his arm. "Walk aside with me a moment, will you my Lord?"

He complied, frowning.

"My Sword has too many talents and too much power to be turned loose on humans without some controls."

"I can see the wisdom of that."

"And most of her controls are the same ones humans have. Morals. Ethics. Even a conscience."

"Really?"

"Yes. Did you enjoy torturing that poor man?"

"It made my stomach heave, but sometimes we must act for the good of the realm."

165

"Perhaps. But in the end, it is up to each of us to decide what is best for us to do."

"Oh, yes. The oath she swore to my father and my brother. 'For the good of the realm of Inderjorne.' That is what the oath says. This information could save the realm from invasion. How can gaining it not be for our good?"

"My Lord, I have an exercise for you. Pretend that you were a citizen of Inderjorne, but not one of the royal family."

"My father does this all the time. All right. What?"

"How would you like to live in a realm where the king could pry into your head at will to find out what you are thinking?"

"I...but this...oh."

"That's right. There are some powers that should never be used, no matter what, because of the damage they may do." She raised a hand. "I am not saying that there is no circumstance where this power might be needed. But this is not one of them. We could go through all this bother and find out that he has nothing of use to us. It isn't worth it. Besides, you must consider another factor."

"What is that?"

"This discussion is useless. My Sword will not do what you ask. Simply will not do it. I cannot persuade her. I cannot force her. She has morals, a conscience, and a sense of honour tempered into her very steel, and she will not do it."

He stood silent, a vein throbbing in his forehead. Finally his face and body relaxed. "Well, if she won't do it, then she won't. What is your plan?"

She smiled to hide her relief. "I will use my womanly wiles on him. I'm going to sweet-talk the information out of him."

He stared at her for a long moment. Finally, a grin twisting his lips, he turned back to his soldiers, who were looking doubtfully at their leader. "Do what she says."

Glancing at each other, they obeyed.

"Now, I'd like everybody to leave."

"Everybody? Is that wise?"

She shrugged and drew her Sword. "He's not going to do me any damage. I'll have Jesco stay at the corner, over there."

"We will...stay as well. The...safety of our cousin...is our duty."

For the first time the prince regarded the Twins directly, taking in their size, their swords. He seemed surprised. "Oh. Yes, by all means." He waved his men to follow him and stalked out of the stable yard.

Marisola approached the rider, slouched on the bench.

"You were very brave."

He did not look up.

"What is your name? Your people will want to hear how brave you were, even in the face of death."

A hoarse croak came from the man's throat.

His name is Wafiyah. It means 'faithful' in their language.

"Wafiyah. Faithful. You are well named, Wafiyah. I'm sure your family and your War Leader will be proud of you. Do you follow Husam al Din?"

Now his head came up. "All the Ulaan follow the great Husam al Din." He coughed, then spoke more firmly. "He is our Leader in war and peace."

"I have spoken to him. Perhaps you have heard of me?"

He glanced up at her through swollen eyelids. "All know of the Sword Maiden."

"Good. But you follow Husam, not his brothers?"

An astute guess. It can do us no harm.

167

The bleeding head came even more erect. "I follow the True Leader. His brothers do not have his wisdom and cunning. They do not follow the proper precepts of our people. They would divide our might." He coughed, and his head fell, exhausted by this final show of spirit.

She nodded and laid a hand on his shoulder, hoping for an unbruised part. "Fine, Wafiyah. Now, you can do something for me."

"One refuses the Sword Maiden at the peril of his soul. What may I do for you?"

"I don't think your soul is in much danger, but will you take a message to Husam al Din for me?"

"Willingly."

She grinned. "Mostly because it means you have to go home to deliver it. Tell him that this area is under my protection. I do not appreciate his raids and foraging, and I suggest that they stop. Do you have that? Suggest. That is all. This is not a threat."

"I understand, Sword Maiden. The strong have no need to threaten the strong."

"Exactly. Now, I'll get you a drink of water and have them bring your horse around. Can you ride?"

The little man stood, tottering, then straightened, one arm falling at his side, one knee quivering at the strain. "I might need help to mount, but once a Ulaan is in the saddle he can ride forever."

The Twins and Jesco have been Listening. It will take but a moment.

While this conversation was going on, the Twins closed in on him from either side, and a soldier brought his horse. After he had drunk from the bottle that also appeared, they made it look as if he had mounted unaided, and Marisola led them out of the stable yard.

Where they were met by the prince and several of his men.

Send them caution, Kitten. I will not be gainsaid on this.

Kitten did not answer, merely directing her thoughts towards the angry mind of the prince. For a moment the man stared at Marisola. Then the stiffness left his posture.

Marisola nodded her approval. "Do you have any message for Husam al Din?"

"Tell him he interferes with Inderjorne at his own risk. The might of Inderjorne is on its way to crush him. He will not escape."

"I will do so." She turned to the ragged man on the pony. "Did you get all that?"

A grin stretched the battered lips. "Yes, Sword Maiden. I heard the usual words the young men utter before they prove their weakness and inexperience."

She hid her grin and nodded to him. He shifted his weight and, with no further instruction, the horse walked away.

The prince stood beside her, glaring. "What did you tell him that made him smile?"

"Nothing. He received your threats, and he will pass them along faithfully. I doubt if they'll have much effect."

"What was your message for the Ulaan Leader?"

"I sent him what he expected to hear."

"What he expected."

"Yes. I have no message to send to Husam that will make the slightest bit of difference to this war. So I sent him what you did. He expected me to demand protection for my people, and you to utter more general empty threats. Thus we give him absolutely nothing except the message that we can pick up one of his men at will, wrest information from him and set him free, simply to demonstrate our power."

"You have a subtle diplomatic mind."

"I had the best teachers."

"And what did you get from the captive? Anything worthwhile?"

She led the prince over to where Lord Waldheim and the rest of her troop were waiting. "Oh, yes. We have learned that our guess was correct. The horde is led by three brothers who don't get along very well. The older one cannot order the younger two to do anything, and so they are running off to assuage their own pride at the expense of the welfare of the tribe." She met the prince's eyes. "Is there a message there?"

He decided to laugh. "Except that my father the king still rules the land of Inderjorne, and for his sons, his word is law."

"My grandfather taught me that there is the word of the law, the letter of the law and the intent of the law, and one must be truly wise to decide which one to follow at any given time."

"Your grandfather is a wise man. Now, let us move to other things."

She glanced up at him.

"Yes. Your message was subtle and diplomatic, but these are nomad barbarians we are dealing with. What affects the leader will mean nothing to his people. So I suggest we take your fine, sharp nail, and drive it in with a very large hammer."

Oh, no. What's he going to do?

Prove his weakness and inexperience?

She presented a calm face. "What do you have in mind?"

"I agree with my brother. All of this messing around is the prelude to a real battle, which needs all of Inderjorne behind one banner. My father's banner. But this raid into Merida has provided another distraction. You discussed an incident that would spur everyone to action."

"And decided against it. We have to consider the outside possibility that the nomads will give up and move on. I would not be the one to start a war that might not otherwise have happened."

He shook his head. "You are falling into the trap that all peaceful people must beware. The enemy assumes war will happen. The peace lover hopes too strongly that it will not. And thus the enemy has an edge.

And here we have my favourite argument used against us.

You don't think we should do this?

Let's see what he wants us to do. Probably a lighting raid that makes a big fuss and accomplishes nothing but what it is intended to create: more antagonism.

"What do you intend to do, my Lord?"

"We have a force that is strong, focused, and highly mobile. We can make a lighting raid deep into the enemy camp before they have any chance of raising a response."

Having predicted this gives me no pleasure.

Do you see any way of dissuading him?

They are his men to do with as he will.

But he will expect you to provide cover. We must go.

Yes, and I will cover him until you are in danger. Then I will give our group the far greater cover we can create alone and get us out of there.

I don't like it.

We could do better.

The horse pastures?

Yes.

She nodded to the prince. "We have attempted nothing like that in the past. They would certainly be surprised."

"So you approve?"

"As a matter of fact, I'm not enthused, but if we're going to do it, let's at least make it useful."

"What do you mean?"

"You haven't been down in the camp. It is far too spread out and hilly for a decent attack, and all you'll do is kill a bunch of innocents. The horse pastures, however..."

It took a moment for the idea to sink in. "The horses!"

"Yes, the land is flatter out there, and we could spread farther apart, sweep up a huge number of horses and simply drive them out into the plains. From what my Sword tells me, most of the Ulaan steeds are only partly tamed. It could take half a month to gather them together again."

"The horse pastures are much farther out."

"I can disguise our troop for most of the way. By the time we attack, we will be moving away from the centre of the camp. We can circle wide and come back in safety."

"I like it. Tomorrow at dawn?"

"Exactly what they will be expecting. This afternoon while the leaders are all at their usual meeting. We can disappear in the dust cloud caused by the stampede. My Sword can keep our men aware of where our centre is, and they can form up on us, even in the dark. I notice that half your men are of Maridon blood."

"Yes, it allows me access to many places I would otherwise be denied."

"Your group is to be complimented for working together. How many of them are Sensitive?"

"I have no idea. How do we find out? Ask them?"

Sixteen.

"No, we ask my Sword. There are sixteen. Form your men up in trios, each with a Sensitive. That will help."

The prince beamed. "This is going to be wonderful. We will strike a blow for Inderjorne that will seriously hinder our enemies and hearten our people."

"And incidentally give us an excuse why the enemy isn't attacking. They're out horse hunting."

"Perfect! I'm beginning to see why my parents are so intent on keeping your family as our allies."

She wanted to say, "A lot of people are learning that," but Kitten bit the comment off before she formed it.

Now is not the time.

She sighed, but only to Kitten. *I have serious trouble working with this man. The idea of him becoming king makes my blood chill. Is there any chance we can get him killed, sort of by mistake?*

Marisola!

I know, I know. We don't act like that, either. And even if we did, now is not the time. The best we can do is wait until this finally comes to a battle and then make sure that Guevejara lives through it.

It would help if we won the war as well.

I though that went without saying.

21.   Horse Hunting

They formed up in front of the castle, fifty men in helmets and light breastplates, armed with sabres and lances meant for charging, not throwing. Waldheim scouts sat their horses nearby.

Tahal nodded to Marisola. He had been cued that Kitten would select the Sensitives.

Her technique was very simple. *Take three steps forward.*

Sixteen men strode out of the ranks, looking rather confused. Most were Inderjornese, but three dark complexions stood out.

Jesco chuckled. "The smart soldier never volunteers. These poor guys can't figure out what just happened or how."

Marisola stepped forward. "Listen, now. We will be fighting in heavy dust and may be coming home after dark. These men will always know where our standard is. Don't worry about how. Form yourselves up with them and stay with them for the duration. Groups of three. Do it."

There was a fair bit of shuffling, but finally the men were properly arranged, with two rather forlornly left over.

The prince stepped forward. "You two are with me. Now you sixteen, for the whole foray, you must keep concentrating on the image of Marisola, here. Keep her in your mind when we're riding and when we're fighting."

There was a mutter of, "That won't be hard." Followed by a chuckle.

The prince glanced at Marisola's red face, then swept his hand up. "To horse!"

With that they were away, Marisola's group in the centre of the column. As they travelled, Kitten connected each of

174

the Sensitive soldiers to their merge, getting their minds used to the image of Marisola that she used as their rallying point.

If I lose my Sword, this will all fall apart very quickly.

If you lose me, more than this raid is at risk. You are well protected. Do not seek battle. Do you three hear that?

Three mental images responded positively.

Kitten, will it be hard for you to keep this up for so long?

Until more is needed, I will not use more power than is provided by the group. I will only have real work to do once the battle starts.

Unless we can avoid a battle.

The Ulaan take good care of their horses. Even with my talents, they will respond.

At first they travelled straight up the road, their scouts killing the three outriders Kitten showed them. As they neared the camp, however, the road looked far too busy ahead, so they cut east and went roundabout.

So it worked out that just as the sun was angling down and the leader's meeting was about to start out in the middle of the camp, Kitten and her little army sat behind the crest of a hillock overlooking the horse pastures. She made a merge with her own troop and Tahal to scan the target area.

I never expected there to be so much clutter. Marisola stared in dismay at the tangles of training rings, corrals and light fences in front of them.

Jesco pushed their gaze higher. *Those are only in close to camp, where there aren't many horses, anyway. That's our target.*

Farther out, swarms of horses lazed about, swirling in slow coils as they munched their way over the short grass. A few boys on horseback circled even farther away, and a group of colts frolicked around their mothers: a tranquil scene.

The trios need to spread out and hit the herd in a line, screaming and whooping for all they're worth. Noise is the only way to do the trick. Once we get the herds moving, we move into the dust cloud for safety.

Noise will bring defenders down on us.

Can't be avoided.

They broke the merge and passed the information to the troops.

Marisola glanced over at Tahal. "Well? Here we are. The orders have been given, the army prepared."

The prince licked his lips. "Anything you can think of we've forgotten?"

He's nervous. Not afraid. Nervous.

"This your first battle?"

He nodded.

"My second."

My two hundred and fifty-first. Let's get going.

Two hundred and fifty?

I have no idea. Somebody start this thing.

Maybe he'll chicken out.

I hope he does, but I hope he doesn't.

Me, too.

The prince raised his voice, but not too loud. "All right, men, we're trying to stay hidden until the last moment, so don't start yelling until I do. Ready? Move out."

They burst over the top of the rise and stampeded down upon the peaceful herd. Once they were through the pens and fences they spread out in a long line. The herd boys looked up, frozen in terror, then spurred their horses towards the centre of camp, yelling in fright.

This brought heads up in the herd, and Prince Tahal shouted. Soon his men picked up the call, and they thundered forward.

Marisola glanced at Jesco, galloping beside her. "Why aren't they moving?"

"It takes a while for the message to get out, I guess."

Maybe I should help. The soldiers can do their duty without me. Kitten dropped her concentration on the Sensitive riders. She gathered the power offered by her troop and created a huge, screaming Cloud Cat, claws reaching, and jammed it into the mass of placid, grass-chewing little minds before her.

As far as Kitten's mind could reach, every head came up, ears flat, eyes goggling in terror. Now the herd began to move, at first uncertainly, but then the shouting of the riders to the south made their impact. The Sensitives in their army caught the echoes of Kitten's sending and raised their voices into falsetto screams as well.

Slowly, and then with increasing power, the Ulaan horse herd formed into one heaving, straining merge of horses and minds, each animal with one objective: to get away from the wild feline that threatened to tear out its throat. Once again Kitten felt the heady power of the mass of emotions that churned around her. This time there was no holding back, no conscience to keep her from the glory of the charge.

The dust boiled up, and her riders stormed into the herd, slapping rumps with the flats of their sabres. Mayhem spread.

Kitten?

Kitten!

KITTEN!

...Yes, Hand.

That's enough. We don't want them killing each other in terror.

Oh. Yes...I suppose.

You suppose right. I could hardly get your attention.

All that power is very intoxicating. It's good they were only horses.

You mean you can do that to people?

A cold rush of reality blew the tendrils of satisfaction from Kitten's mind. *Yes, I certainly can.*

I'm beginning to understand.

Good. Kitten went back to her duties, contacting the Sensitives, showing them where Marisola rode, an oasis of stillness in the midst of chaos.

I am so glad that wasn't people.

They rode for miles before the raw terror in the herd began to calm. *Have we driven them far enough?*

We have to get ourselves home, and our own horses were not unaffected.

Fine. Let's pull to the east.

She sent out the call, and her army began to swing towards her. They wove their way among the running horses, sliding between individual animals and avoiding clumps. Soon they gathered together, watching the remnants of the herd go by.

Company. Kitten put up the masking, and two Ulaan on spent mounts galloped past, their attention on the departing herd.

Marisola pulled Tariq up beside the prince's horse. "A satisfactory incident?"

"Oh, yes." He glanced down at the Sword, hanging innocently at the Hand's belt.

"Time to go home, my Lord?"

"I believe so. It was your plan. You set the course."

Kitten located her position in the vast open space and brought her troops into formation, trotting slowly through the foothills that stretched down to the plains. There were no scouts out, every mounted Ulaan having other work to occupy him, and they made the trip home in peace.

178

As they regained the road to Waldheim, Tahal pulled his horse alongside Tariq again. "My Lady Marisola?"

Watch out when he gets polite.

"Yes, my Lord Tahal?"

"My brother told me about the Swearing of the Sword."

"A very important ritual."

"It occurred to me to wonder, me being the next prince in line..."

"If she would swear to you, as well."

"That's it. Do you think she would?"

This means a lot to him.

I can imagine why. He's thinking of all the power it would give him.

"I will ask her, but I wouldn't be optimistic."

"Why not?"

"Because Swearing to Guevejar was nothing more than acknowledging that he was the heir to the throne she was already sworn to protect. Also giving loyalty to the General of the army she was part of. Your chosen path...well, you understand."

"My choice to have no official capacity precludes me from her power...I mean her protection?"

"Because she swears to the person holding the position. She doesn't swear to the person himself. If you have no appropriate position, you have nothing for her to swear to. It may sound simplistic, my Lord, but there it is. Her rules were laid down a couple of hundred years ago to deal with the situation in the realm as it existed at that time. The realm may have changed, but she hasn't."

"I see."

"I understand your disappointment, my Lord."

He slashed a negating gesture with his free hand "No, no. I am grateful for her support. It has given our people their first real victory over the Ulaan, and I must be satisfied with that."

They rode along in silence, and she allowed his horse to move ahead of Tariq.

'The realm may have changed, but she hasn't.' What kind of nonsense is that?

The kind he will accept?

Ah. Human diplomacy again. You are doing well, my Hand.

As are you, my Sword.

22.   Last Look at the Enemy

The following morning Tahal and his men were on the road. All he would give as explanation was, "I have better uses for my talents."

Marisola nodded. "The Aelsund Road is the fastest way to the south and follows the western border all the way down. There are trails that access the Batkhaan Valley. The nomads must sweep farther out to miss the mountains."

"I had considered that. Thanks again, Lady Marisola. Perhaps we can catch up and keep an eye on them." Then he mounted his horse, thanked his host for his hospitality, and trotted out of the castle, his men forming up behind him.

Marisola glanced over at Lord Waldheim, who gave a wry chuckle. "Go where the action is. Glory to be won."

"I hope he shadows that mob of nomads and makes sure they don't make a quick stab at the centre of the realm. The western border is poorly defended."

"But access to the realm is limited. I think we're safe in assuming the nomads will stay out of heavily treed mountains and take the longer path to easy pickings."

She shook her head. "He's three days behind them. I hope he doesn't rush his men so hard they have no energy to fight once they get there."

The Ulaan will have a tough slog down the Batkhaan Valley. He takes a shorter path with easier travel and will reach the battle in better shape, especially if Husam's third brother pushes his men hard.

"And we are assuming Third Brother will try Marida first. If he is repulsed, then he will turn against our southern border. If he doesn't try Marida, he will get to our borders sooner."

And then we have war on two fronts.

Marisola glanced at her group. "Which means we had better be on our guard for movement in the main camp. Back to the lookout tomorrow."

"And perhaps a wider sweep...Husam knows about the Aelsund Road...and that trail we took as well."

She nodded to the Twins in thanks. "I didn't think of that."

They grinned, one petting the cat on the other's shoulder. "That's why we came."

Marisola turned to Waldheim. "If Husam is attacking with two armies, he needs to coordinate. No sense letting his messengers stroll down an easy road."

The lord nodded. "If we're sure there's no attack coming, I could free up a few men for patrols out west. Push their envoys out into Batkhaan Valley."

She shrugged. "Nobody's sure about anything the Ulaan do. But we'll have warning if they start to move."

"I'll see to it."

"And we'll see to the Ulaan camp."

Now Marisola and her band were on the hunt all day, every day. They spent a few hours each morning and evening spying from the lookout, and the rest of the time harassing the enemy scouts, pushing them farther and farther back into their camp.

This is a good idea. It gives Husam the impression that we're up to something.

Even if we're not.

We are up to all sorts of things. This just helps keep him off balance.

Perhaps there is something we should be up to. Let's contact Grandfather tonight and see how the battle is going in the south.

They did not have to wait for evening. Kitten heard the call as they trotted down the road towards the castle.

Ecmund has made contact.

What did he say?

I told him to wait a candle.

Soon they were huddled around the Sword in Waldheim's workroom, and Ecmund's voice came through, loud and cheerful. *The Maridons have prevailed.*

Is that good news?

Not sure. The better news is that the Ulaan then made a strike to cross the border into Inderjorne. Tahal showed up with reinforcements at just the right time, and the nomads backed off. They have turned back up the Batkhaan Valley.

Carrying their wounded, with few supplies.

That's the picture. If they started with the 1,800 your men reported, they lost about a third of their forces.

That's pretty bad.

Yes, their leader seems the type to throw his troops into battle with heedless abandon and little regard for their lives.

If you win, it's a great tactic.

If you lose, it's a slaughter. He also shows no respect for the etiquette of war. His men attacked from the rear at the same time as he was conferring with the Maridons at the front.

Marisola snorted. *This is the commander the Ulaan need. Husam is not a great War Leader. He has already lost one war, or he wouldn't be knocking on our door. He might be a great peace leader, though.*

Kitten let out a low growl. *younger brother must not take over. I have seen this type of leader in action. If he commands, the number of dead will double, both ours and theirs, no matter who wins.*

Ecmund laughed. *There you go, Marisola. Add it to your assignment. Keep the enemy leader alive.*

The Hand did not disagree, only paused, thoughtful. *When the final battle comes, we will be on the same field. It is possible, I suppose, that I could protect him.*

If the final battle comes.

Kitten arched her back and spat.

I know, I know. Ecmund pictured his hands held up defensively. *You keep telling us.*

Do you have any other news? Is Tahal a great hero, now?

In his own opinion, probably, but no one is certain, because he has disappeared.

Disappeared? Where to?

I believe the whole concept of disappearing involves no one knowing where you went.

Yes, yes. It's easy to tell, anyway. He's headed back up the Aelsund Road, following the retreating army to make sure they come all the way north again.

That would be wise.

So both we and Husam should expect our problematic little brothers to show up here in three days or so. Maybe they'll meet each other on the way and solve all our problems for us.

We will not be that lucky.

Anything else? Or have you given us enough bad news.

That's all we could come up with. If there's more, you can be sure we'll pass it along.

Thank you, Grandfather. It's nice that you're thinking of us, suffering from all this boredom up here.

Then get back to work.

After a general exchange of goodbyes, Kitten cut the link.

Marisola regarded her troop. "Any thoughts?"

The Twins glanced at each other. "In about two days...Husam the War Leader will...know what has happened. He...will start to take steps."

"I'm afraid he will. Back to the lookout tomorrow."

* * *

184

Marisola turned to look back at her party, jogging along the trail to the lookout at an easy trot, alert and ready for any action. She sent Kitten a private thought. *We have a good troop, here.*

Yes, you are coming together nicely. All this practice is forming stronger and stronger bonds of all sorts. Do you notice how much easier it is to talk mentally?

Divo was a long way out, yesterday, and it was like talking to him across the room.

Did you notice something else?

What?

How could you tell that was Divo?

She frowned. *No idea. I just knew.*

Exactly. You have been able to distinguish their minds one from the other for some time, now, but you didn't notice. I found it quite amusing.

Glad to be of entertainment value.

Oh, you have other value than that. We have yet to see how much.

That sounds ominous.

As it should. Let us not forget...

...that we are at war. I never forget that.

I know you don't, Dear One. And I hope you are ready now. Kitten spread her voice to all four of them. *Because we are riding into a trap.*

Marisola's head jerked erect, and she stared around. They were just approaching the lookout, the trees thinning as they climbed.

"What kind of trap?"

It is very difficult to say. I noticed someone out there, but I am not getting a clear picture.

"How many? Should we make a run for it?"

Again, I am not getting clear numbers, but they are far enough away that there is no worry. Just a moment...yes, they are holding position.

A jab of fear shot through Marisola's mind. "Waiting for us."

That would be the logical conclusion. Well, that is to our advantage. We have spotted them, so we can prepare to defend ourselves or leave, depending on how the situation develops.

They trotted up to the horse lines. Seven mounts were tied to trees by hackamores, their saddle girths loose, bridles slung across their withers. The guard saluted, eyes alert.

"Trouble coming. Get the horses ready to ride. I'll send help back." She turned to Jesco. "Better if you stay with our horses. I don't want any mistakes."

At his nod she dismounted, handing him her reins. Then she strode to the ridge top. "Trouble coming, men. Gather yourselves together and get back to the horses. Hygelac, send word to the lookout on top to lower his gaze. There are enemy troops..." she consulted the picture Kitten sent her, "...that way and that way. Close."

The officer in charge nodded to a soldier who sped away, and the rest slipped off the knoll and down to the horses.

Now they are moving in. Slowly. No attack yet.

She turned to the Hygelac. "They're coming now, but not fast."

"Any idea how many?" His eyes were scanning, his hand on his sword hilt.

"No, my Sword is having trouble reading them. That's reason to be more worried."

Kitten, help the Twins look around. I have to keep my wits and eyes up and out.

I will do so.

The Twins stepped forward and stood peering into the undergrowth that surrounded the bare knoll.

Marisola took a moment to look back. "Hygelac, the moment we have an idea of their numbers, we'll decide whether to run for it or hole up in the cleft where we hide the mounts. Be prepared for either. *Kitten, is there any chance they're behind us, too?*

We have to assume so...yes, they are circling to entrap us.

"There we have it. Move slowly. If they think we don't see them, we might have more time to get ready. Move the horses into the cleft, a man with a bow on the rim, and everyone else ready to fight.

Ah. There we are.

Men on foot began to show between the trees, moving slowly up the mountain, weapons still sheathed. A lot of men.

"Thirty that we can see...probably more behind us."

"All right, let's back down towards the cleft. There doesn't seem to be any rush. This is getting interesting."

"All we need is Husam to show up. You can't spy him?"

...I'm not sure. I get a feeling...

"There!"

The unmistakable form of the War Leader strode from the forest, pacing up the hill towards them.

I see him through your eyes, but I cannot read his presence clearly. Something is stopping me.

Now Husam had reached the crest of the knoll and looked down at them, a pleased smile on his face. "Aha! The Sword has not availed you today, Sword Maiden."

Marisola nodded in greeting. "I admit to being rather surprised."

His head came up. "We Ulaan are not without our shamans. When we discover a problem, we fix it." He reached into his fish-scale mail shirt and pulled out a

187

talisman. It was a series of cords, knotted in a stiff circle with small, colourful stones or beads threaded on them.

He tucked it back inside and patted the spot where it lay.

What is it?

Kitten sent a shrug. *A bunch of cords and stones, from what I can sense.*

How does it work?

It does nothing. The power is in his mind.

Ah. He believes, so it works.

That's about it. And his men believe in him...

She nodded. "But now that I can see you, Husam the War Leader, it no longer functions."

"Oh, no, Sword Maiden. It does much more than that."

"Perhaps. So, what are you after this fine morning?"

"Many things, as befits the War Leader of a mighty people. I would like you to stop using this ridge to spy on me. I also do not enjoy your interference with my folk. I have come to tell you that story as well. And perhaps, if I am very lucky, I might return to camp with a hostage who would be worth a great deal to me."

She shrugged, caressing Kitten's hilt. "Perhaps you could stop us from using this lookout. All it would take would be about..." *How many, Kitten?*

Fifty, as usual.

"...your usual escort of fifty men. As far as your luck is concerned, my Sword and my men might have something to say about that."

He nodded and drew his weapon. "Then let us find out. This will not be the same as the last time we crossed blades."

Kitten jumped to Marisola's hand, and she went to garde, backing slowly to her position in the defensive line in front of the cleft. An arrow arced towards them, and she batted it aside. Then the enemy closed, and there were no more arrows.

Husam attacked with a strong series of cuts, and Kitten parried them easily, starting her song of battle, her yowl stretching upward and gaining in volume...

It's not affecting him.

A grin twitched the corners of Husam's mouth. "I hear your song, Cloud Cat, but I am protected by the magic of my people."

Marisola's riposte rattled a stroke off his helmet. "I doubt if your little twist of rope will be much defence against a sharp blade."

His face lost its smile, and he bored in again, attempting to use his superior weight and length of arm, but Kitten was a match for any normal sword. While she helped Marisola hold him off, she scanned the rest of the battle.

The Twins held position at Marisola's shoulders, Jesco behind her. The old Swordsman fought little, only jumping in where aid was needed. Instead, he watched the shape of the battle, his fifty years of fighting experience far more valuable than any man's blade. There was room for a couple of Hygelac's troops on either side, with a reserve of two men to step in at need. The scout from the crag had come across the top and was trying to make use of his bow.

As they fought, Kitten became aware of a feeling of power creeping over her. Her four moved tighter together, merging their battle skills into one smooth-running machine. Ulaan soldiers surged forward in a mass, but the flashing swords carved into them, and they fell back in confusion or down in death.

She concentrated more on the Ulaan leader, who was sweating, now, his strokes not so sure or heavy as before.

Shall we kill him?

And have his treacherous brother take over? We don't dare even humble him too much, in case he loses face.

We fight with the weight of politics hanging on your arm.

But that doesn't keep us from doing maximum damage to his men, who are not so adept. Marisola darted sideways in concert with Ovid, and between them they took his opponent down. Then she was back with Husam again, foiling his attack and pressing home one of her own.

Unfortunately, the same is true for our soldiers.

One of Hygelac's men was down and another wounded. The officer had a cut on his cheek and was favouring one leg, a dark stain on his thigh.

Back in and spread out. We can cover more of the front.

This worked, but still there was no sense of winning.

This cannot go on. Tell the men to mount.

At her command, the soldiers slipped back into the cleft one by one and mounted, until Marisola and her men were alone on the ground. Now her horsemen pushed in on either side, their steeds lashing out with steel-shod hooves. This drove the Ulaan back, and Jesco and the Twins mounted as well, leaving Kitten and her Hand to face Husam.

Now I can concentrate on this fight. She poured strength into Marisola's arm, breath into her lungs, and a fierce desire to win into her heart. They lunged forward, striking and feinting and striking again.

With blood showing from gashes on shoulder and thigh, the Ulaan leader gave ground, but Marisola refused to follow and finish the job.

The battle faded down around them, and they stood, breathing heavily, staring at each other.

Marisola flicked her Sword in a quick pattern. "Well? Not so keen on fighting any more?"

He shrugged. "I am not like my brother. I will not throw my men away in the faint hope they might prevail." He gestured towards the bodies with his free hand. "Once again I prove my argument. Your group is unbeatable, Sword

Maiden, but you cannot protect those around you. There is nothing to prove by pushing this further. You may leave, but do not return."

Her head and Sword point came up. "I make no promises."

"Nonetheless. You are denied the use of this hill."

"Then I will find other ways to make your life miserable." She grinned. "Perhaps I will join your side in the battle. I might do you more damage that way."

He bowed with a graceful sweep of his hand. "I have my hands full with my brothers. If the Sword Maiden would be so kind, she will stay with my enemy where I can keep track of her."

"For the moment, I think that best, as well."

He stepped closer and spoke in a low voice. "You could have killed me." He gestured to his amulet. "This is no protection against the Cat when her claws are out."

She nodded. "As we have discussed, the death of either of us would make no difference to the great movement of peoples that has caused this clash. And I would prefer to fight against an honourable enemy." She turned and mounted Tariq. "Who might some day make a good ally."

Husam motioned his men away, and Marisola led her troop down the path, moving slowly in deference to the wounded.

23.   End and Beginning

Despite Husam's warning, or perhaps in spite of it, Marisola and her friends were on the road north early the next morning, though they did not push through as far as the usual hilltop. Waldheim had shown her a higher outlook farther back, and she was headed there to get a look at the bigger picture.

They were still deep in Inderjorne, so they took no extra precautions, dismounting on the hill in plain sight. Soon they were in the merge, straining their senses while Kitten organized the search.

There is the old lookout. If he wants to deny us that area, his patrols will push south. There! A troop of horses. Six or seven. Heading west.

They searched farther, following the path of the riders they had seen.

Yes, another troop on the same line, headed east. And another, farther over.

After a short time, Marisola broke the merge. "It's easy to see. He has set up a line. No one crosses into his territory."

Jesco grinned. "Let's surprise him and not try."

"I agree. It's not as if there is any news to be attained. He will wait for his brother's tatters of an army return and then start his advance."

"An active leader would...begin to advance... before his brother gets back...to take the full initiative."

"But Husam is not that sort of leader, and we don't know the relationships between the brothers or the rules of their culture. So this is his compromise."

So let us watch for whatever scraps of information we can glean.

As the day progressed, a pattern evolved. The patrols came more regularly, and groups of riders began setting up small camps close inside their track. As the sun dropped to the western mountains, the nomads had a battle line across the whole valley.

Husam is staking his territory.

They returned to Waldheim with this news, which they passed on to Falkengard, but no one could give any opinion. Only one point was clear: the Ulaan were starting their move.

Ecmund signed off with a promise to pass the information along to Koningsholm, and Marisola stated her intent to watch what happened on the morrow, when Husam was sure to get news of his brother's defeat in the south.

* * *

When they reached their hilltop the next morning, it became apparent that Husam had received his message.

Marisola looked out over the valley. "There's our answer. He has moved his line at least half a mile closer. I can see the riders without Kitten's help."

The Twins stared, shoulder to shoulder. "There are more...men camped behind...the line as well."

We cannot let this development pass without a response.

"We can hardly drive them back."

No, but we need a line of our own. They must not see weakness. Let us figure the size of the patrols and send groups of our own to counter them.

"As soon as we can?"

"If we see no other movement, this lookout is no longer useful."

They joined the merge and searched the far bulk of the nomad camp, concentrating on the horse pastures, but there was no notable movement. Just a slow, menacing percolation of men and animals towards the south.

As they trotted back to Waldheim, Marisola pondered the situation.

"What do you think he has in mind?"

The main problem an attacking army has is supply lines. If they outstrip their support, they soon run out of food, weapons, and medical help. The nomads usually solve this by living off the land.

"But they can't do that, because we are stripping the crops from the fields in front of them, and all the animals are safe in the castles or driven south with the people."

It is the closest we can come to a scorched earth policy.

"Scorched earth? Is that what it sounds like?"

In time of dire emergency, a retreating army will destroy everything to deny the invaders sustenance. It has been effective.

"Usually used by armies who do not have to come back and live in the area."

As I said. Dire emergency. Which we do not have quite yet.

The unified thoughts of the Twins interjected. *We thus have a very slow race going on: the Inderjornese to raise an army, the Ulaan to get their army to the chosen battleground.*

That is correct. And our advantage is that we get to choose that battleground.

"Which is not ours to choose." Marisola put her heels to Tariq's ribs and lifted him to a gallop. "It is time to pass this conversation on to those with a broader view of the situation."

Yes, the initiative will soon be torn from our hands. Larger masses of people and more powerful actors loom.

"So we will become but a small cog in the machine of the army."

I have never been a great friend of machinery, although the image is apt. While an individual part of the assembly rarely gets to make an outstanding contribution, a single small failure can throw the whole machine into confusion.

"And speaking of those with the power to cause confusion, I wonder when Tahal will arrive?"

"Some time tomorrow...is the best guess. He...made it there...in three days."

* * *

The next morning they returned towards their second lookout, but were stalled by the number of scouting parties of Ulaan that crisscrossed the terrain. Large groups: twenty men and more.

Marisola changed their focus, now sliding behind the most advanced troops to see in what condition they were leaving the land. All the farms were empty, and the nomads seemed to be ignoring them.

She shook her head as they regarded an abandoned farmstead, the wind blowing wisps of straw across the empty barnyard, a broken wagon askew by the wall, a few lonely birds flitting through the fruit trees. "Hard to say what it will look like after the whole horde has been through."

She reined Tariq around and they headed back to the castle, sliding easily past the two large groups of riders they encountered, but taking little pleasure in the skill.

When they reached Waldheim, she reported the new position of the nomad line – now only two hours ride away – and returned to her rooms, where her troop waited for instructions.

She had none to give them.

"It's so dratted frustrating. There's basically nothing we can do until Tahal gets here with his army. And then we have no idea what he'll do with them."

"He seems to have done well enough in the South."

Divo turned his head to look at his brother. "Where there wasn't a battle."

Ovid nodded. "True. We might not have a battle here, either."

"If I read Prince Tahal correctly, that will be bothering him."

"We can agree on that."

"And we know what that means."

They both turned to face Marisola, mild surprise on their faces. "Is something...wrong?"

She smiled. "Oh, no, but if the two of you have an argument, it must be something worth listening to."

"Not an argument... a discussion."

There is a stir in the castle. Riders approaching.

"And that will be his outriders." She stood. "Well, my friends, the war enters a new stage, and we have no idea where it will take us now."

24.   Skirmish

There was no flash or polish in the troop of horsemen that filed up the road to the castle. They kept a good pace though, and the horses, tired as they may have been, still had their heads up and their ears scanning the noisy atmosphere of the forecourt. The baggage wagons were right behind, and soon tents appeared on the lea west of the drawbridge.

While his men dismounted, Prince Tahal stayed on his horse, flicking a finger or speaking a word to direct some underling. It was a good demonstration of a fighting force at the height of its efficiency.

Finally the prince swung down and, after a slight stagger to get his legs working again, strode over to where Lord Waldheim and Marisola waited. "And here we are again."

Marisola shared his grin. "Older and wiser, my Lord?"

"I would have to agree. Your idea was a good one."

"My idea?"

"Yes. An army that size, even of nomads, cannot move swiftly. We caught them the third day and hounded them down the border, refusing their scouts access to the hinterland. We used our time well while they bashed themselves against the Maridon heavy cavalry, and when they made a try for our border, we had picked our battleground and we were ready for them."

With hands on their shoulders, he turned them into the hall. "I could use a drink before I tell the rest."

But he had not gone five steps before he took up his tale again. "They didn't even try. From what the scouts say, they lost about a third of their men against the Maridons, and their hearts weren't in it anymore. So back up the trail we came, shadowing their every move. We only pulled ahead yesterday. They're spread out along the valley, with the leader pushing to get north, and the wounded trailing a day or so behind."

"When do you think they will arrive in the camp?"

"The leaders might come in late tonight. The rest will trickle in over the next two days." He sat at the table in the workroom, took a huge gulp of ale, and regarded them. "What's the situation here?"

Waldheim deferred to Marisola, and she outlined the developments of the last three days.

"Hmm. So this Husam is in perfect position. Both his brothers have made a hash of their battles, so he can take charge. He didn't wait for the brother to get back from the South, but started moving. But not too far or too fast, so the brother can't complain that he took action without consulting. Very clever, our Husam."

"That's about how we looked at it, my Lord."

He regarded Marisola. "Oh, I'm sure you have it calculated. What do you see happening next?"

She tried to hide her surprise. "Well...he moves the line about a mile every day. Probably something to do with the grazing of the flocks. He's certainly in no rush."

"When will they get within striking distance of Waldheim?"

"They're a league or so away right now, so that means three days."

"That doesn't give us much time to make any decisions." He turned to Waldheim. "Are the peasants taken care of?"

"Yes, my Lord. Most of the farmers have gone. The crops are harvested and stored in the castle or taken south with them. There is little for the enemy to live on."

Marisola shrugged. "Except their flocks, which will find gleaning a harvested field better than their usual dry land forage. At the pace the horde is moving, they can graze along cheerfully and keep up."

"My men and horses need tomorrow to rest. That gives us time to make plans." He leaned forward and stared earnestly at each of them. "We have to find a way to slow this horde. A place to attack them that makes them think twice about moving."

He leaned back and cracked his knuckles. "I sent a messenger across to Falkengard when we passed by. Our army is slow in forming, as we expected. If the horde decides to pick up and move faster, we won't be able to field all of our forces in time.

"I sat in with Guevejar and my father in the initial planning. We must stop the Ulaan at a line connecting Visgard, Falkengard, Quentar and Oliveres. South of there, the mountains open up and the horde can spread over the whole central valley."

A short silence allowed them all to think of the consequences of that.

Then, with a quick shake of his head, he brought his attention back to Marisola. "Have you any recent news?"

"We speak to Falkengard every evening, now. As of yesterday there was no change. Perhaps tonight…"

He nodded and sipped his drink. "We'll sleep on it." Then he flashed them a grin. "With all these intelligent minds attacking it, the problem doesn't stand a chance."

* * *

There was no good news from Falkengard, so Marisola and her team spent several fruitless hours that evening discussing various attacks.

The following morning they made their report to the prince. "My Lord, we have only come up with one possible plan. It will not be definitive, but it may help in the long run."

"I don't hear a whole lot of enthusiasm, my Lady."

She shrugged. "It is a simple plan, based on the usual activities of Lord Waldheim and the other border lords. They close up safe in their castles, wait for the enemy to pass, and then harass them from behind. Quick raids, cutting supply lines, stealing supplies and the like."

"But the nomads have no supply lines."

"But they do have herds we can stampede. We are counting on Husam al Din to be an intelligent man. We should start that kind of activity early to show him the troubles that confront him. We have no illusions that he will stop, but he will have to move slower to consolidate the territory he has taken and pull men off the front lines to protect his herds. Our objective is to slow him down, and that should do it."

The prince pondered a moment, his head slowly nodding. "Yes, I see the value of that sort of harrying. It would be a good idea to start immediately."

He smiled. "But I can hardly expect my knights to be harassing sheep with their lances. I need a more definitive result."

By which he means a result that brings him more fame.

Quiet. Let's hear him out.

"I have learned from the Maridan campaign. The knights had a great advantage over their smaller, lightly armed foes in any situation where the geography confined the battle. If the Ulaan can spread out and attack from many directions, they do much better against us." He walked over to the map on the wall, gesturing. "For example, if we were to assail the nomad line from the front, we could only overwhelm a small number of them, because they are spaced so far apart. They would then circle around us with their superior numbers and pull us apart.

"However, I have a better idea. As the enemy penetrates deeper, the valley narrows. Their line becomes shorter and more crowded. Just the sort of situation that will work for us. Instead of attacking the line at a right angle, we should come in from one end and sweep along it. We set our knights in a crescent moon configuration, with the tips sweeping ahead to fold the enemy in towards the centre where the main mass of our charge will roll over them." He flattened his hands with his thumbs overlapping, creating a "C" shape, which he swept from east to west across the map.

He is completely out of his mind.

Yes, but we can't tell him that.

She pretended to consider the map. "I see the fighting advantage on flat ground, but here the geography will be against us."

"How so?" He peered at the map. "Ah. The creeks. I don't recall that any of them were deep enough to stop a horse."

"No, it's the hills and valleys, which all run north-south. With an east-west sweep we'll be constantly crossing them, uphill and down."

"Hmm. Show me where the line is tonight."

Kitten brought up a picture in her mind, and Marisola traced it across the map.

"And one mile from there?"

With Kitten's help, Marisola was able to make a prediction of the best place for the line for the following night.

I suppose the advantage is that Husam wants his perimeter to be as solid as possible, so he will use any east-west flat spots.

Well, we're not going to tell Tahal anything of the sort.

"I watched you draw that line. If Husam works the same way, he'll pick places with level ground running east-west. That's to our advantage."

Drat. He really is rather intelligent.

Kitten sent an image of spitting out a hairball. *When his ambition isn't making him completely stupid.*

Marisola stood looking at the map, waiting. *Whatever I say, he's likely to take it as encouragement.*

He gave her a disappointed glance, then forged on. "We scout the line at nightfall and put it on the map. Your Sword can carry the picture with her like she did on the last raid, and we'll use the same technique to keep the Sensitives in position. The rest can follow them."

The next pause lengthened until Marisola had to say something. "Well, we have all day to think about it." She shrugged. "At least it doesn't take us long to get to the Ulaan line any more."

He regarded her. "I don't hear enthusiasm for this plan either, my Lady."

"It's not for me to say, my Lord. This is your kind of warfare. These are your men, whom you have been leading successfully. You have been through the terrain where you will fight. My Sword and I will do our duty."

"For the good of Inderjorne."

"Exactly."

He frowned. "I have been regaled with the praises of your Sword's knowledge and experience in battle. What does she say about my plan?"

What shall I tell him?

That you don't hear a lot of enthusiasm from me, either.

"She is concerned about the terrain, as I am."

"Thank you. Subordinates who are afraid to question their leader's plans are little use to me. We will scout the area this afternoon. If the undergrowth is too thick or the hills too high, then we will go out and worry sheep instead. Good enough?"

She found a smile. "A fine plan, my Lord."

* * *

By that evening the Ulaan line had crawled to precisely where Marisola predicted.

Tahal was jubilant. "We have them where we want them, and we're one step ahead on our planning. They'll be demoralized and disorganized with the return of the defeated army and the wounded to deal with. Has anyone come up with refinements to our plan?"

"Put lancers on the tips of the horns." Marisola made the same pattern with overlapping hands and wiggled her fingertips. "They can maneuver better in the bush and up the hillsides."

"I completely agree. Anything else?"

"What shall we tell Lord Ecmund when we make contact?"

"Let's not tell them anything. It will be a pleasant surprise when we announce our victory."

"Whatever you say, my Lord."

"Still no enthusiasm?"

She shrugged. "To concern myself with decisions that are not mine to make is to waste time and energy. I am concentrating on doing my best to hold up my end."

"What do you see as your role in the battle?"

"My Sword's main function is to act as a beacon for the troops to focus on. Our best position is at the rear of centre. The role of my men is to protect me. We will leave the killing of the enemy to you."

"Fair enough. I ride at the front of centre so we will be nearby in case we need to communicate. My guard can protect you as well."

She smiled. "The Ulaan tend not to bother me, and my own guards have proved sufficient, but I will not turn down more protection on the field of battle. My Sword will do a

203

better job if she is not distracted by having to help me defend myself."

He grinned. "Well, there we have it. You get a pleasant outing in the countryside, and my men will do the heavy lifting."

Her smile disappeared. "I doubt if it will be pleasant for anyone, my Lord."

He nodded slowly. "No, I don't suppose it will." Then he brightened. "But we have sixty knights and thirty lancers, along with assorted scouts from Lord Waldheim. That's a hundred trained fighting men and a good battle plan. We will prevail."

* * *

The communication with Falkengard that evening went smoothly, although Kitten could feel Ecmund's reservation about the prince's story that they were, "thinking of ways to slow the progress of the horde."

Due to her close relationship with her former Hand, she was able to overlay a tone of cynicism at that point in the sending, which she was sure he picked up.

"That's fine, my Lord. I'm sure you will do as you see fit. Just don't waste your men. We will need all the experienced fighters we can rally for the big battle to come."

"Don't worry about me wasting men, my Lord. If any die, it will be for the glory of Inderjorne."

No one wanted to tell the prince the obvious response to that.

After they had closed the merge and Tahal had bounded out, full of enthusiasm, to give his men their final orders, Kitten brought Marisola and her troop together.

Are we all clear on our duties tomorrow?

"We heard our Lady...we are to protect her...nothing more...nothing less."

Jesco barked his old laugh. "And if protecting her means we keep young Tahal alive, well, that's his good luck."

Marisola frowned. "I hope none of you have the idea that he is expendable."

"Of course not...but if he runs up against...his own foolishness...we know what our choice will be."

"That is fair. If we can help him to succeed, it would be to the advantage of the realm, no matter how we feel about him and his personal glory."

His glory would be a small price to pay for victory.

Ovid reached out and laid a fingertip on Kitten's hilt, and their unified minds spoke directly. *Kitten, we do not hear any prediction of glory on the part of the Cloud Cat.*

I am refining my ideas on the usefulness of glory. Tomorrow is not the day for great deeds. Survival will be enough.

Jesco added his touch, and they shared a moment of determination.

Survival will be enough.

* * *

In the dim light of the early morning torches flickered in the bailey as the knights mounted in semi-darkness and filed out to line up in front of the castle, the lancers behind. Marisola sat Tariq off to the side, her troop at her back.

As Tahal jogged his destrier out to face them, Kitten's fur stood on end, and she hissed an oath. *No! No, no, no!*

What is it, Kitten?

Lances! Now I know he is out of his mind.

I suppose...

There is no suppose about it. Ride out there. I will speak to him.

Marisola did as she was bid and brought her horse alongside the prince's.

"Good morning, my Lady. Our men look ready for a fine day of fighting."

She wasted no time on salutation. "My Sword would speak with you directly."

The prince looked taken aback but nodded.

My Lord, no lances.

"What do you mean, no lances? The Maridon knights decimated the Ulaan with lances."

In a straight charge across level ground. You are hampered by tradition and habit, my Lord. You have seen the terrain we will fight in. I have two words for you. "Heavy brush."

"Oh...oh, yes, of course. I had not pictured that."

He raised his voice. "Sorry, men, no lance charges today. This will be tough sword work in heavy brush." He handed his long spear off to his squire, and the knights did the same, though not without grumbling.

"Anything else, my Lady?"

"Not until our scouts report in, which won't be until daylight."

"By which time we'll be in position to attack." He nodded to his trumpeter. "March out."

The clarion blared, and Tahal led his men up the road to the north, Marisola and her group swinging in behind him, the ten men of his personal guard immediately following.

Marisola squirmed to settle in the saddle, and Tariq hopped a couple of times in protest. "It's all right, my friend. Just trying to get this extra armour comfortable."

She was wearing a solid cuirass today instead of her usual chain mail shirt, and it restricted her arm and waist movement more than she would like. Her kneecaps and

206

greaves rubbed against Tariq's sides, enough cause for him to complain.

The breastplate is necessary in case of arrows.

Of course it is, and the leg protection will be useful in the brush, but I don't have to like it. This isn't my type of war at all.

Then let's go out and win in a hurry and get it over with.

A fine sentiment.

She glanced over at Jesco, who wore his usual chainmail shirt. "Not worried about arrows?"

His lip lifted on one side in what might have been a smile. "When you reach my age, there's more pain at the end of the day from your own armour than from the enemy. I shouldn't be going to war. But who has a choice?"

"Exactly. Don't worry, I doubt if we'll see much action today."

"Said the inexperienced general before his plan hit the battle."

"Remind you of anyone else?"

The old swordsman spat on the ground and jogged on.

The prince had arrayed a thick screen of outriders, interspersed with local guides, so their little army was able to reach their chosen point at the east end of the Ulaan line without any alarm raised. There, they formed up their crescent, and all heads turned towards the centre where Tahal sat his charger, his sword raised.

He spoke just loud enough to be heard. "No sense in advance warning, men. Let's keep it quiet as long as we can. Remember to focus on your Sensitives. They will be in position."

The start was around the curve of a hillside, and the lancers of the right horn clambered up as the centre passed through the easier going at the bottom. Kitten and Marisola strained their senses – Kitten's in her mind, Marisola with her eyes – to keep everyone within sight. The knights of

Maridon heritage were easier to see, with their bright reds and blues. The Inderjornese in their muted browns and greens blended in more with the foliage. They moved forward at a trot, and as the lancers came down around the hillside, they approached the first enemy outpost.

It was a complete surprise. Many of the Ulaan were dismounted, standing around a fire with a morning drink. The knights crashed through the camp, destroying everything and cutting down all opposition. A line of lancers followed to clean up any fighters lucky enough to escape the first charge.

Kitten and her troop trotted along behind, keeping their eyes and other senses wide open.

Now the brush closed in again, and it was more difficult to keep the crescent in its shape, but the knights ploughed on through the woods, overcoming three separate camps in the first rush.

The fourth camp was larger, and the enemy more prepared, but when a wall of huge, metal-clad horses roared down on them they broke and tried to flee. Ulaan war horns sounded their wailing cry, but the knights prevailed once more, and the advance picked up speed.

Marisola listened to the faint responses from other horns. *This won't last.*

I'm afraid not. If he'd turn and go home, now...

Do you see that in his mind?

What mind? They're running on emotion now. Nothing but death will stop them.

"We'd better catch up." She turned to catch Divo's eye, and he nodded.

They caught up all too quickly. The left horn of their crescent had splashed across a large creek, only to find a swamp on the other side. Their horses were ploughing through, belly-deep in mud, scrambling over fallen trees and stumbling into ponds of open water. Kitten signalled the other horn, and the whole army slowed to a crawl.

Marisola could picture the enemy horsemen gathering ahead and behind them.

You're right, Dear Heart. I can feel their mass.

"Where?"

All around. They won't group together.

Finally they escaped the swamp, and the panting left horn pushed raggedly ahead. The riders in the next camp stampeded away in panic, but...

No. That was too organized. Kitten grabbed the Twins and Jesco for their power and screamed out a warning. *Trap! Look right!*

Tahal reined in, his head up, as a scattered foray of a hundred or more nomads swept down on them. The knights of the right horn barely had time to turn as the lancers at their tip were swept away. Then the Ulaan were through and gone, sweeping around the left-hand tip and disappearing in the scrub forest.

The prince's herald sounded a "Reform," and the army paused. Tahal sent new lancers out to replace the right tip, and the knights started their ponderous way forward.

But now there was no surprise. Groups of nomads stormed in from every direction, refusing more than fleeting contact, did minor damage and scurried away. The next camp was empty, and a large squad of Ulaan hit them from either flank at the same time. The knights had to turn to fight, and the crescent dissolved into a melee of individual battles.

Now the Inderjornese began to take casualties. An individual knight, tangled in brush, was no match for three Ulaan horsemen, who picked and tore at him from several directions at once. Marisola saw three go down, and Kitten picked up many more than that.

Push up beside the prince.

Her troop all heard the command and turned as one. Tahal sat his destrier, pacing in circles, his sword thrashing uselessly. They confronted him, and he stopped, his attention swinging to them.

"A good time to take our small victory and go home, my Lord?"

He flipped up his visor, frowning at her. "No! We'll reform here, wait for a larger group to attack, then crush them. Now is the time for that Sword of yours to prove her worth."

I will do so, my Lord.

Kitten sent out an urgent call, and the knights began working their way towards the prince. In little time they formed a perimeter, the lighter-armed lancers interspersed between the heavier knights.

Tahal gave Marisola a satisfied nod and turned to his knights. "Listen up, men. They'll gather a larger group, now that they have time. Most of them haven't come up against knights before, so they'll think they can attack us. When they get close enough, we'll charge and decimate them."

My Lord, do not charge towards the enemy camp. That will be a trap.

"Wait for my signal, men, in case of a trap."

During the lull the squires and lancers were gathering up the wounded, the dead and their stray horses. It was a depressing number, and Tahal looked shaken. He designated ten lancers to form a guard, and the squires lopped down trees to make stretchers.

This is no longer a lightning raid. It is now a war of attrition, and it is our side with broken supply lines and poor transport. Now would be a good time to leave.

"He won't."

No.

Marisola and her troop sat their horses to one side of the wounded, with nothing to do but wait.

And wait.

The Ulaan mass charge did not come. Instead, a series of small attacks began, with groups of twenty or thirty horsemen probing the Inderjorne line, doing minor damage, then pulling away. But the minor damage mounted up. Soon there were twenty still forms on the ground or seated on logs nearby, some dead, some wounded. More than one brightly clad warhorse was pulled away by triumphant nomads.

Kitten observed it all, sharing her thoughts with her friends. *This will continue until Tahal realizes his position. Then will start the running battle to get away. If he makes his move soon, we will have no trouble. If he waits until he has not enough men to move and protect the wounded and fight off the main attacks...then he will have tough choices to make.*

She used her senses to observe the battle again, but nothing was changing. Then she became aware of something else. A powerful emotion was building nearby. A familiar emotion. She centred on it.

Jesco was getting angry.

Both Kitten and Marisola focused on him, but he sat his horse, unmoving, his face a mask. Only the searing power of his mind betrayed his feelings. In Kitten's experience this could only mean one thing: an explosion.

Jesco...

The swordsman turned towards them, barely controlling his urge to strike out.

You know what needs to be done.

"Right!" Jesco jumped from his mount and strode to the midst of the wounded men. "You! Get two men and start loading bodies. Three to a horse."

They gaped at him, and he stepped forward, one hand on his sword. "Move it! We're getting ready to leave." He turned. "You two! Figure out which of the wounded can ride. You four on the stretchers; start loading them. The sooner you finish, the better chance you have of living, and they might even make it as well."

In short order the wounded and dead were all accounted for, and the lancers who could be spared were ahorse, patrolling the perimeter again. Jesco stared around and nodded, then strode through the milling knights to where Tahal still paced his charger in circles, his frustration boiling.

"My Lord, the dead and wounded are ready to travel."

The prince started, then looked down at the man on the ground. "I gave no such order."

"No, I did. At the moment we have enough men and horses to transport the wounded, and five lancers left for protection. If we wait until there are more injured, you will have to take more fighting men away from the perimeter to carry them. I'm sure you can do the arithmetic." He paused. "My Lord."

A cloud formed on Tahal's brow, but then he began to look around. His horse no longer paced fretfully.

He's doing it.

What?

The arithmetic.

Well done, Jesco. Now get out of there.

Jesco did a smart about-face, marched back to his troop and mounted.

It did not take long. The prince finished his calculations and nodded. His head came around, seeking Marisola. "Get your Sword to call our people in. I will lead, and you follow right behind, giving me the route. The wounded can stay with us under the protection of my guard. That will free the lancers for battle."

He turned back to confer with his Guard Captain, and soon the Inderjornese party was on the move, trotting as smartly as they could in the bushy terrain, but following the clearest path Kitten could find.

The nomads seemed hesitant, perhaps still afraid of a full charge by the knights. They continued their forays, but did little damage.

Soon the remains of Tahal's force reached the road south and stepped up their pace. The nomad attacks faded out, and more lancers were available to clear their path.

It was a dejected force that limped its way back to Waldheim Castle. Three wounded died along the road, and two slipped from their horses and had to be carried on stretchers as well.

Dinner was late that night, and no celebration. When it was over, the leaders retreated to Waldheim's workroom to discuss the day. For a moment they all sat there, staring into their drinks.

It is up to Tahal to speak. It was his debacle.

Finally the prince raised his glass. "To those who gave their lives today for the glory of Inderjorne."

They all drank.

For the glory of Tahal, which he didn't get. Not a good reason to die.

Hush, Kitten. It's too late for that.

Tahal took another sip. "Except for the first rush, that was an incredibly frustrating day." He looked around. "None of them came anywhere near me. It is an exasperating feeling to be losing a battle with no opportunity to do anything about it."

Like retreat? Like use your brains?

Keep it down. At least he admitted he lost the battle.

"It was a bitter pill to swallow, but we can learn from the experience." The prince laid his hands on the table.

"However, that's all water under the bridge, now. A messenger came in from Falkengard while we were gone. We have new orders."

He glanced around the room in satisfaction as they all gave him their full attention. "General Guevejar will reach Falkengard tomorrow with the bulk of the army. In the coming days, they will survey the area and choose our ground for the final battle. With the advance of the enemy, our best move is to join him. There are few in Inderjorne with more experience fighting the Ulaan than those assembled here."

He turned to Lord Waldheim. "We leave this castle in the best state of preparation that is possible. More men would just use up more supplies."

The older lord nodded.

"So. Tomorrow we will be on the road early, because carrying our wounded will slow us. We are to survey the other three castles as we travel, to inform my brother of their condition. There will still be time to send them aid, should they require it. In four days we join the rest of the army and then," he spread his hands, "the decisions will no longer be up to us."

And about time, too.

Marisola ignored this last sally and regarded the prince. "Do you have any suggestion about us? We could stay behind and monitor the Ulaan advance because we have instant communication with Falkengard."

He shrugged. "Why don't you discuss that with them when you speak tonight? As your very polite term 'suggestion' implies, you are not under my command, so you must do as you see fit."

"Thank you, my Lord. I'm glad you see it that way."

He gave a wry smile. "After my brother hears of my latest accomplishment, I doubt if he'll be giving me command of anything soon."

"Since you bring up the topic, my Lord, may I comment on today's foray?"

He shrugged. "I suppose I deserve it."

"Not entirely, my Lord. There was a point, fairly early in the battle, where my Sword said to me, "If we pull out now, we will have done what we came for."

"But I did not pull out, and it all went downhill from there."

She shrugged and raised open hands.

"We are all new at this." He glanced down at Kitten. "I will remember your Sword's wisdom in the future."

A valuable lesson in itself.

"I heard that."

You were meant to.

Tahal smiled and rose. "I must see to my men and check the wounded. I hope you will carry the conversation with Falkengard tonight. I have no desire to place today's actions before that combination of brainpower and experience."

She nodded. "They are a more forgiving group than you might expect."

He tilted his head in response, then left.

Well, you certainly let him off easy.

"He has learned from today. At least he's willing to take responsibility and listen to others."

Now, he listens, after a battle with eighteen dead and twenty-three injured. Not to mention the six horses, complete with their armour, stolen out from under us. Oh, the Ulaan will be happy with those.

"You heard him. Next time he'll listen harder."

He says, now.

25.   Retreat

It is a good thing the nomads advance so slowly.

Marisola regarded the winding line of refugees ahead and behind her small troop. "We certainly aren't moving very fast."

There was a chuckle behind them. "Yes, a small cat...just passed us."

She dropped her gaze to the Ambassador, who leapt up on a cart loaded with sacks of grain. He was sitting on the top, looking like a king on his throne, except when a wooden wheel lurching into a pothole stirred his regal balance.

"Glad someone is having a good time."

"He takes...his duties...seriously."

Sure enough, the little animal swooped down onto the seat beside the driver, rubbing against his arm in friendly fashion. The man petted him, then sat straighter on his bench and cracked his whip. The oxen moved fractionally faster.

The Ambassador hopped down and tumbled ahead to the next wagon, attracting a snort from the lead ox as she passed.

They had caught up with the first refugees south of Lesser Walden, and now the road was plugged. Marisola looked back to where Tahal's standard strolled along with everyone else.

He wants to speak with you.

"Thank you, Kitten. How does he feel to you?"

Kitten considered while Marisola turned and trotted back along the side of the road. *Frustrated, but rather resigned. Perhaps he has realized that much of a soldier's life is slow escort duty, as opposed to charging to glory at the head of sixty knights.*

"A good response. He could have pushed his way through and headed south at a trot."

He could have. But he is more concerned with his reception at Falkengard. This is a chance to re-establish his loyalty and commitment to the people of Inderjorne.

"Do you have to put it in such negative terms?"

History, dear one. Plus my extensive knowledge of human nature.

She sighed. "Well, since you can see into everyone's heads, I suppose you have a cynical attitude towards our selfishness."

Do you have to put it in such negative terms?

Point taken. She pulled Tariq around beside Safiy. "How goes the journey, my Lord?"

He looked down at her with a twisted grin. "About the same speed as a slow ox cart, my Lady."

"It's good of you to stay with them."

He gave a large enough shrug that his armour creaked. "I can't do much else, with these bands of foraging nomads ranging around. No, we'll plod along behind, at least until we pass Woldbarg. Then we'll see."

"Did you have something for me to do?"

"Yes. What I can't. Please cut along and get to Woldbarg in good time. It's the smallest castle on the route, and I don't want to give them any surprises. Tell Lord Chlodomir we'll bivouac, and we have our own supplies. Also poke around and get your Sword to give us her opinion on how well Woldbarg is defended. It didn't look good when we came north a month ago. Ask Jesco, too. I appreciate the old man's experience."

"We'll throw all our weight against the problem, my Lord." She grinned over her shoulder. "Anything for a chance to move!"

Kitten sent a warning to her troop, and when Marisola trotted back up the line they were already sliding aside. They moved off in single file, dodging carts and slowing down for families with small children scattered over the road.

It's a good thing there's no traffic in the other direction.

"Nobody's that crazy."

Now they moved at a better rate, and it was mid-afternoon when they approached Woldbarg, a tidy little castle built on the banks of the river that provided a water-filled moat. Mindful of their assignment, they sat their horses and looked it over.

"What do you think? It looks sturdy to me?"

Jesco frowned. "I wouldn't like to attack it with only horsemen."

It could be done.

"The walls are...not high."

Jesco surveyed the castle again. "Ladders?"

If you have overwhelming numbers of attackers, the defenders can't push the ladders down fast enough. It's not that easy to push a ladder weighted with several men away from a wall.

Kitten waited while everyone took in the situation

We have seen enough.

"Right. Let us proceed."

They pushed their way along the road, winding between camps, individual tents, parked wagons and mobs of people. A mass of bodies surrounded the castle gate, and soldiers with pikes stood shoulder to shoulder, monitoring entries.

Marisola pushed Tariq through the throng and tipped a salute to the officer in charge.

His name is Thrúd.

"Good afternoon, Thrúd. Message for Lord Chlodomir from Prince Tahal."

"Important company coming, my Lady?" He motioned them to ride through, and the pikemen stepped aside.

She nodded and led her party in.

Lord Chlodomir appeared as they were dismounting. He was a tall, thin man with shoulder-length hair and moustaches to match, which gave his face a droopy look. There was nothing wilting about his attitude, though.

"Good afternoon, my Lady. Pleasant to see you again. I gather the prince is on his way?"

"Merely impeded by several hundred refugees, my Lord."

Chlodomir smiled and swept a hand at the scene outside the castle. "We have some experience with them, ourselves."

Marisola passed on Tahal's message and explained her own assignment.

The lord nodded. "We are a small holding, that is true. But Woldbarg has withstood her share of sieges in the past."

"But never by several thousand men."

"I have to admit that bothers me." He gestured her to follow.

Leaving their horses in the charge of the stable hands, they did.

Up on the battlements, they could see the castle layout: a simple, square tower on the river side of a semicircular curtain wall that enclosed the bailey. The gatehouse contained a portcullis and an inner door, protected by the drawbridge when it was raised. The top of the wall was wide and level, allowing good movement by defenders. Various pieces of equipment stood handy, most involving fire.

The lord gestured. "Our main defences against men with ladders are the simple ones. Pike poles to push them away,

219

hot liquids to pour on them," he patted a pile of stones beside him, "and the simplest of all. Rocks on their heads."

"Assuming they can get their ladders to the wall, with all that water down there."

"The moat is fifteen feet deep. Given time, an enemy could bridge it or fill it."

"We don't expect to give them that much time. Once our army is gathered, the battle will begin."

"Any word on that?"

Marisola gave him the latest reports of the wrangling.

He snorted. "We have no problems like that up north, here. Maridons don't like our cold winters." Then he glanced at Jesco's dark hair. "No offense."

Jesco merely gave a tilt of the head and his crooked grin.

It's all a matter of men. How many ladders can be put against this length of wall, so how many men do you need to push them off? Say, three men against each ladder, a ladder every six feet.

"How long is the curtain wall?"

"Eighty feet this side of the gate, seventy the other side."

"So, one hundred and fifty feet, they could put, what, twenty-five ladders up?"

"No one has ever managed to get ladders up."

"So, really, the only way they could take the castle is to catch you with the drawbridge down."

Chlodomir shook his head. "And we have to lower the drawbridge to send out sorties. It could happen. We'll have to make sure it doesn't."

"Ah. That's why castles have a barbican on the other side of the moat. To keep the enemy out long enough to get the drawbridge up."

The Twins weren't saying anything, and Kitten knew there was no point in asking.

They slipped down off the wall and retrieved their horses.

"What are your plans now, my Lady? We're quite crowded, but I'm sure we can find room for four."

"No, we would be more useful back up the road. Our leaders will want to monitor the tail end of the refugees. I'll report to Prince Tahal when I meet him, then go on. We'll camp overnight and come down in the morning, tailing the last of the rush."

"Very thoughtful, my Lady."

She shrugged. "They are our people. What else can we do?"

* * *

So Kitten and her troop went back and made their report to Tahal, who continued south at a faster rate. Kitten's party slowed their own progress, shepherding refugees and discouraging the Ulaan raiding parties that threatened them. Her ability to appear out of nowhere, strike and disappear without a trace seemed effective, although rumours spread of groups attacked and robbed, often with loss of life.

"Have you noticed? We haven't seen a raiding party all day." Marisola looked at her three companions as they sat around their campfire near a small refugee camp to the north of Woldbarg. No one answered.

Before you ask, we haven't missed them. They now stay off this road.

"A change of tactics, perhaps?"

Fear is our greatest weapon.

"Plus the fact...we are now about...three days travel ahead...of the horde."

They had consulted with locals and scouts they saw, and the picture was not optimistic. Marisola shook her head. "If the gossip up and down the road is true, the Ulaan have picked up their pace. We're only two days ahead of them."

"That means the horde's well past Waldheim." Jesco frowned in concentration. "Ought to be near Lesser Walden about now. Hope they were able to hold out."

"The huge plume of smoke that scout reported bothers me."

"The Ulaan have...not been burning...farms or villages."

She shrugged. "They're not raiding. They're taking over the land. They want to keep it."

"Except for a castle." Jesco tossed up a hand. "I can't see the nomads having much use for walls of stone."

"But there's not much to burn in a castle."

"There is if you ...look for it. They are...barbarians."

"Should we go up there and find out?"

There is no point. I am reading intense emotions from the north. Triumph and despair mixed. A battle or the like, with many Sensitives involved. But since both our people and theirs are Sensitive, it's impossible to tell who won.

"Then we need to go!"

No use, Marisola. We could do nothing, and one small castle more or less will make no difference to the outcome of the war.

"That's heartless, Kitten!"

That's war, Dear One. We do not waste valuable resources we will need at a later date.

"I feel so useless!" Her shoulders slumped.

Like the rest of us. Nothing is sometimes the hardest thing to do.

They all sat in silence for a long time.

* * *

Early the next morning the bad news came through, in the person of Lord Walde and a ragged troop of men, escorting a mob of footmen and servants and three wagons of wounded.

Kitten heard them coming from far off, but waited until they were near before rousing her party.

The survivors of Lesser Walden are approaching.

Marisola jumped out of her sleeping roll, dragging on her boots. "How many? How near?"

Not many, and you have time to put a pot of water on for tea. They will need rest.

The refugees staggered out of the woods, their horses stumbling. Those walking looked half asleep. The wounded in the wagons were silent, lost in their misery.

Marisola stepped out to the road. "Come in and rest, Lord Walde. Have you been on the road all night?"

The lord sat straighter in the saddle and looked back. "We have to keep moving. I must save those I can."

Marisola held a quick back-and-forth with Kitten.

"There are no Ulaan on the road behind you. Let your people rest, and we will guard."

"Just how...oh." His glance dropped to Kitten's hilt. "Yes...if you would, my Lady."

She smiled. "Take over this campsite. We're almost ready to go. I'll be back for the kettle in a couple of candles."

He raised a hand. "But we must get the news out...?"

"Already done. You rest your people, and when I come back we'll decide what's best."

The lord slouched to a log by the fire and sat while one of his men took over the kettle.

During this conversation Kitten's men had packed their camp in their efficient way, and soon her party was trotting northeast, taking a wide swing to search for raiding Ulaan. At regular intervals they stopped and all made contact with

Kitten's hilt so she could scan as far as possible. Ulaan presence was everywhere, but nowhere did they feel a concentration near enough to threaten the road.

Except perhaps that group moving northwest. Rapidly. I wonder what they are doing?

No one had an opinion, and the riders moved out of range, so they rode on.

They returned to their overnight campsite before noon. Walde's men were spread around, wrapped in saddle blankets and cloaks, unmoving blobs on the ground.

Let them rest. We'll slide in quietly.

Marisola allowed the lone sentry to see her and waved a friendly hello. They loosened their girths and quietly made their noon meal, their eyes scanning the somber scene.

Let's check the wounded.

Marisola lifted the cover at the back of a wagon. Four men lay there, and Kitten scanned them. One was dead; the others looked close. She clambered in, and the three survivors roused. Two had sword cuts, one an arrow through the thigh. The arrow had been removed by the simple process of pushing the barbed head through and drawing the shaft out behind it.

Both entry and exit wounds are clotted. He is in no danger. Time will tell. Infection will mean amputation.

"Eirlin is at Falkengard. She and Fang will deal with it."

They settled the men with encouraging words and moved to the next wagon, rousing a couple of soldiers to remove the dead man. They visited the other wagons and Kitten did what she could for each victim.

When they had finished, Lord Walde was awake, staring into the fire over his forgotten mug. He looked up as she approached, shoulders hunched as if expecting a blow.

"No danger near. The Ulaan are avoiding this road, and their main army is still two days to the north. If your people are able, we should move on. You will either make it to Woldbarg or get close enough that we can bring you supplies. Don't push yourselves. There is no danger nearby. I will go hot-foot to Woldbarg and send mounted men and scouts."

His shoulders relaxed.

"Could anyone follow your trail?"

He shrugged. "We came roundabout in three groups through the farm lanes and hit the main road in the middle of the night. It's hard to brush out tracks in the dark."

"So far, nobody seems to be coming this way. We'll start out now. You come whenever you can get your party together. We'll meet you on the road."

They did not push their horses because they had a long day yet to go. At Woldbarg they gathered up an aid party and set out north again in mid-afternoon. The fresh soldiers were anxious to push ahead, so Marisola let them go.

They need to feel they're doing something. The waiting is very hard.

"The sooner they find Walde's men, the safer they'll be."

They jogged along the road in the afternoon sunlight, the peaceful scenery belying the horrors that prowled.

Jesco pulled his horse alongside Tariq. "When do you think we'll meet them?"

"Your guess will probably be better than mine. Kitten?"

A large group a long way ahead. One, not two.

"The Woldbarg men must have caught up. Good."

They jogged on.

No, now I'm feeling another group. That's strange. Why would I be sensing another group now?

Jesco's face dropped into grim lines. "If they were coming down from the north."

With a soldier's curse, Marisola jammed her heels into Tariq's sides, and he spurted up the road.

Don't outpace your escort. They can't keep up to Tariq.

She allowed the steed to slow, and soon they were a compact group again. She glanced behind her. The Twins had loosened their swords, riding with one hand on the hilt.

Marisola did the same, but for a different reason. This allowed Kitten to combine their power to scan further.

The Inderjornese group has picked up speed. They have discovered the enemy behind them.

"They can't go much faster. We'll have to do something."

The enemy is not catching up. Perhaps their horses are tired.

"That group we sensed. They must have been tracking and lost the trail for a while. They circled back, found it, and now they're pressing on."

We will meet our friends around the next bend. Let them go by. We'll have to find a way to slow the Ulaan down.

"Any ideas?"

Strike from behind. Harry and run. Pull them apart and cut them down.

"I like it."

Marisola pulled aside, waving the weary troop through. They were striding out at a reasonable pace, although Kitten wondered how the wounded were doing, bumping along in the unsprung farm wagons.

The officer of the Woldbarg troops pulled up alongside. "One of our scouts got up on a hill for a view. There's a party coming down the road behind. Not fast, but strong."

"So it's not another group of Walde's people."

"He says not a chance."

"Then keep going. You know the area. Run or hole up as you see fit. We'll go back there and harass them, slow them down."

"Be careful, my Lady."

"I intend to be."

He trotted away, and she turned Tariq north again.

Time to leave the road.

They pulled aside and Kitten misted their presence. Soon she could feel the enemy approach. *Ulaan. Thirty or so. A strong group. Determined minds, confident. Nobody familiar. We'll have to see about that.* She sent the order, and the Twins strung their bows.

The Ulaan troop came into sight. The leader was a short, heavy-set young man with a scowl. He sat his mount like a caged animal, his energy trying to escape from this impediment that held him back.

The horse trotted gamely, but sweat darkened its chest and shoulders. The nomads filed past, their eyes fixed on the road ahead.

Once they had passed, Kitten made her move. The Twins loosed two arrows each, then they all broke into a gallop, swords swinging. Each of them took down one of the trailing riders, then they spun and galloped away up the road, leaving the enemy troop in confusion.

Off to the left, now.

They circled around and got ahead of the enemy. Soon two scouts stomped through the trees towards them. They hid and watched them pass.

No more outriders on this side. Let's take them on the flank.

Once again they hid until most of the Ulaan had passed. Then they made the same charge, taking down another five or six.

This time they cut back into the woods and thundered away, pulling a troop of riders after them.

Now we ambush them. There are only ten. We are the leaves on the bushes. We are the wind in the trees.

The nomads paused, puzzled at the disappearance of their prey. One of them called out for silence, and the whole group froze, listening. Their attention was rewarded by the buzz of arrows, and another three riders fell.

Now we take them!

Kitten reached out to the minds of her followers, merging them into a single force. They slashed through the scattered nomad troop, Tariq using his superior strength to plough the ponies under, Kitten singing her battle song as she hewed with all her might.

Three nomads made it back to their troop, and only because Kitten had taken her party off to the east of the trail, riding ahead to lie in ambush again.

This time a screen of outriders preceded the main mass, and again Kitten let them go by.

Let us observe. This man interests me.

The nomad troop was walking their horses, now. Half of them had bows out, arrows strung. The leader's face was even sterner, and his eyes pierced the undergrowth as if he could physically push it aside.

Divo, take the man on his left. Ovid, on the right. I will help your aim.

Two arrows whirred; two nomads fell. The leader, suddenly unprotected, did not flinch. His flat stare zeroed in on their group.

He knows where we are. Get ready to ride. We are small forest animals, playing in the grass.

The nomad leader reined his horse over, and it paced towards them.

The single thought came from the Twins. *Take him?*

He has better armour than the others. Divo, try for his leg. Ovid, kill the horse. NOW!

Again two arrows buzzed, but somehow the Ulaan knew. He jerked the reins, and his mount spun as two arrows drilled into its flank. It stumbled three steps and fell, the uninjured Ulaan leader jumping free.

His men flung their horses to circle him, staring outward, bows fully drawn.

Very gently, now. Fade.

Their horses, used to this drill, backed away and turned quietly.

When they had retreated far enough, they broke into a trot, cutting south towards the road.

"Do you think that will discourage them?"

Jesco pulled up to her shoulder. "They don't matter. We have to discourage him."

"Have we just met Third Brother?"

"Not much doubt in my mind. I thought he would set the brush on fire with the power of his stare."

 The Twins pulled up close behind. "Now, why did someone...with that strength of...mind allow his less...imposing brother...to rule?"

Their traditions are firmly entrenched. Plus having that kind of personal strength doesn't make you a leader.

Jesco grunted. "Have to agree. I wouldn't want to be under his command."

They trotted south along the road for a while.

They are not following.

"Are they moving?"

Give me a moment...yes, they're getting fainter. They must be heading north again.

"Don't count on it. I don't trust this man."

Jesco, ever the optimist. But I do agree. I'll remember him. He is quite Sensitive, and his aura spreads a long way.

As they travelled, Kitten kept in touch with both groups. Finally she found the right place. *Pull up here. We'll rest the horses, and I can feel both our men and the enemy. Both are moving away at a slow pace.*

Wait...what's that?

A rush of fear, anger and pain shot through them. Then nothing.

We know what that was. The Twins' aura was grim.

Kitten slipped into Marisola's mind. *Do you?*

He killed someone, didn't he?

I'm afraid so.

Her thoughts swirled. *It didn't feel the same. We killed ten men, but it's completely different!*

The Twins rode up on either side, and each put a hand to her shoulder. *That was war. This was murder. Now we know what kind of man we are dealing with.*

Marisola took a deep, shuddering breath and let it gust out. "We do. Kitten, if it's safe, let's go and tell everyone else."

It is safe.

"Then we should move quickly and tell Lord Walde he can slow down. No sense jouncing those wounded men any more than we have to."

26.   The Last Tally

Two days later they topped the final rise and looked out over the valley to Falkengard. The scene was so different from their last view that they just sat their horses and stared.

Falkengard Castle still poised its brooding presence over the valley, but its walls were now topped by roofed hoardings that protected soldiers from arrows and allowed them to shoot and drop things straight down on anyone at the base of the wall. In contrast, the dry moat and the area immediately around the castle were now barren, giving no cover whatsoever to attackers.

The village of Falkenby had also reinforced the exterior walls, and a hoarding sat above each gatepost. Thatched roofs facing the wall had been covered with boards or raw hides to protect them from flaming arrows.

And all the flat spaces nearby were filled with soldiers. Tents, horse lines, latrines, kitchens and training grounds scattered haphazardly around, and a seething mass of men went about their business through it all.

Jesco spat on the ground. "Home, sweet home it isn't."

"At least they're here." Marisola stood in the stirrups and peered. "I've never seen so many people in one place."

Not enough.

"But there's thousands."

And there are thousands more Ulaan. If we do not have many more on the way, we are in deeper trouble than I thought.

Marisola shrugged. "Then let's get up there and find out." She kicked a heel into Tariq's side, and he pushed up to a trot.

Inside the castle it was even more crowded. New structures, all with heavy roofs, had sprung up around the bailey, most holding stock and bins of grain. The rest were smithies and weapons storage.

A loving welcome awaited them, in spite of the grim reality that faced the realm.

This is the first time the whole family has been united in many years.

Ecmund dropped a warm, rough hand on Kitten's hilt. *You have done well, Ailur.*

We have done well, my former Hand. This whole gathering is the result of our work for the past forty years, and the continued survival of Inderjorne stands within arm's reach of us at this moment.

Ecmund gazed at his family. Jandro and Xavier had pushed in to embrace Marisola heartily, her mother standing aloof with a proud smile. Tyrbrand and Eirlin made a more decorous greeting to the Twins, but the power of their magic and the warmth of their love shone around them.

Ecmund tucked an arm around his wife's shoulders. "Not a bad bunch, if I do say so myself."

She batted his chest with her free hand as her other arm sought his waist. "Don't take all the credit."

He nodded. "And thus I avoid more than my share of the blame." *Kitten?*

Yes, my Lord Ecmund. The time for human sappiness is over. She spread her voice to all of them. *Come, my friends. Now the real battle starts.*

Faces fell and emotions settled. The iron in the souls of the Inderjornese seeped into their spines. Shoulders straight, the family of the Falcon filed up the stairs and into the meeting room.

Ecmund waited until all were seated.

"Kitten has brought me up to date on the situation to the north, which is about what we expected, although the loss of Lesser Walden was a blow. Lord Waldheim has commenced his harassing tactics with some success. The enemy riders have slowed their advance.

"General Guevejar has taken counsel with everyone and is in the process of choosing the battleground. It will probably be the pass between here and Ulvalla. There is open ground for our knights to maneuver, but the valley is narrow enough to confine the nomad riders and make them an easier target."

"How are our levies coming, Grandfather?"

"More are arriving daily, and more are on the way. Guevejar left a reasonable force on the southwest boundary. A good move, I think, because those who are more concerned with their own protection from their neighbours wouldn't have come this far in any case.

"And after all, we can't be positive that King Albanches of Marida wouldn't take advantage of the situation to push his objectives our way. There are enough of Inderjornese extraction in that area to keep our Maridons from plotting treachery. Our backs are well enough covered."

It is our front I am concerned about. How many men can we count on?

"Our best estimate is six hundred knights, plus lancers, scouts, archers, mercenary heavy infantry, peasant infantry and all the quartermasters, cooks, servants, pages, squires, equerries, and everybody else. At least we can count on everyone in this part of the realm to fight. If they arrive in time, we can probably field two thousand men, most of them well equipped and trained."

Accuracy is impossible, but our best estimate of the Ulaan is four to five thousand riders. It could even be more, although those are not all well equipped, and most are not trained as we use the term. If Waldheim and the other border castles are having effect, it might cut the numbers down some. But the Ulaan backs are against the wall the same as ours are, and they can count on all of their people just as we do.

"We have not counted the Leute. There may be as many as a thousand. I hear all their people fight, women included."

Do not count on the Leute. They have little reason for loyalty to Inderjorne. Their language is more akin to that of the Ulaan. Their defence is to disappear and wait for better days. Which they are doing. Leave them out of your story.

"But Kitten..."

No, Marisola. Leave them out of it.

The Hand grabbed her hilt firmly and drew her from her scabbard, slamming her down on the table. "No. You must tell them."

It cannot be! Even if there is a chance that it will save the realm. There is a far greater chance it will tear us apart.

Lord Ecmund raised a hand. "No, Marisola. Those of us who understand have agreed with Kitten. A merge in battle is too dangerous."

His glance sought the eye of the Magician, who nodded. "Far too dangerous."

Marisola shrugged and returned Kitten to her scabbard. "Then we fight as we always have. Outnumbered, but with the heart of Inderjorne within us."

There were heavy nods around the chamber. After a brief silence, people began to rise.

"When General Guevejar arrives, we will meet again." Ecmund offered his arm to Perica, and the lord and lady of Falkengard led the way out into the castle.

* * *

The following three days were a blur of movement, as an outnumbered people organized themselves with grim determination for the fight of their lives. Guevejar brought two hundred knights, four troops of mercenary infantry, a mob of peasant footmen and archers, and no hope of more.

"That's all we can gather. My father and mother have done their best. We have wheedled, threatened, and made all sorts of deals. We could not leave the Marida boundary undefended, so that is that."

Jandro was toting up numbers on a slate. "That pretty well confirms what we predicted. We have about two thousand fighting men of all types. To face five thousand Ulaan."

Ecmund shrugged. "If we had a good place to defend, that would be more than sufficient."

The general nodded. "But we do not. The line from Visgard to Oliveres is twelve leagues long, and crosses three easy routes into central Inderjorne. Our scouts are keeping us informed, and it doesn't look like the Horde is using the other valleys, but is massing in the one that leads here. I don't understand why, but it seems to our advantage."

Marisola grinned. "We know the reason for that. The Great Leader Husam has two fractious younger brothers. They have already squandered more than half a thousand men on unwise attacks. He is keeping his army under close control."

"I wish him all the family rivalry the gods can bring him. But even this valley is too wide. The Maridons succeeded in a much narrower field, and they only faced two thousand enemy."

Jesco made eye contact for permission to speak. "The only place we can meet them is north of the village of Langstrich, half way between here and Ulvalla. The valley narrows to less than a mile, all open farmland to give our knights a chance to keep in formation."

Guevejar glanced around the table, receiving nods from everyone. "That is where we meet them. Is there any reason not to move there tomorrow?"

This time the responses were all negative.

"Good. Then we move out. We'll start early tomorrow and survey the area. By the time the supply trains reach us, we'll have decided where to set up the camps. The knights will move on their own schedule, and the footsoldiers can come over the next two days as more camps are set up. Lord Jandro, I'm counting on your experience in this area. Let us make a more detailed schedule while everyone else arranges their own plans. Lady Marisola, the timing of the enemy's approach is critical..."

"I will take my troop north to scout the enemy."

The general turned to Lady Perica and Lady Caterina. "And the hardest job is for you."

"The refugees. Any idea how many more?"

Eyes turned towards Marisola. She considered. "There is less and less room for them to be anywhere but here. The last ones should be straggling in tonight." She regarded her grandmother. "The logistics must be horrendous."

Perica gave a wan smile. "Food, sanitation, medical. Some even need beds. We do what we can."

Guevejar slammed his fists on the table. "Whatever they get here would be better than the alternative. Let's make sure that Horde never reaches them. We all have our duties. Now is the time for Inderjorne to prove it is worthy of a space in the world."

The meeting dissolved into purposeful action.

27.   Meeting the Leute

"There is a small roughness a hand's breadth closer to my hilt. That's right. Ahh. That feels better. Thank you."

Marisola ran the oiled rag the length of Kitten's blade. "There you are. Good as new."

Far better than new. I was so young and naïve, then.

"I was young and naïve a month ago. We're growing up fast."

We must. The war is not going well. I find it frustrating that I cannot use my skills on a larger scale. It is as War Leader Husam predicted. I cannot protect more than my own family.

"That's the problem. No matter what we do, the Ulaan edge forward like oozing mud. Why don't they attack and get it over with?"

They are in no hurry, consolidating territory as they come. Moving with their supplies — flocks, tents, and families — takes longer, but it is a convenient way to run a war. However, I have good news.

"Why do you have news that I don't?"

Because you don't listen closely enough. I have just received an invitation to visit an old friend.

"Who has a thousand men-at-arms he's willing to lend us?"

His name is Polvijarvi, and he has a bit less than a thousand Leute, whom he has led for the last forty years. It seems they are willing to come and help me if I promise to destroy the Ulaan Horde.

"I know that story. What does he say? Besides the destroying the Horde part."

If we want more than that we must go to him. His people dare not come out of the mountains at this time.

"Then we go. Tomorrow sunup?"

We cannot run off and make alliances wherever we choose. It requires a more formal approach.

"It does?"

The official sanction of Prince Guevejar and Lady Perica, representatives of the monarchy and the Conclave of Peers, would be appropriate. Plus the other matter. We must not omit the possibility that the Leute will ask me to take charge of their merged tribes as I did once before. At the moment, if the Leute join the battle on their own, this may not be needed. Still, everyone must be aware of the situation.

"In that case, O mighty Sword, thy Hand will do thy bidding. We shall gather at the fourth hour past noon in the formal assembly hall as thou hast requested. Is that formal enough for you?"

If that's the best you can do, I suppose it must suffice.

* * *

The Sword surveyed the downcast group assembled in the usual meeting room at Falkengard Castle. Lord Ecmund, sturdy still, yet wrinkled and worn like an old stump, his arm around the shoulders of Lady Perica, hereditary ruler of the Demesne of the Falcon, supported by their son, Jandro, his wife Caterina, and their son, Xavier. Ostersund the Magician, lean and grey, the marks of his ordeal of Magic never faded from his gaunt visage. Eirlin the Healer seated at his side, paler streaks in her blond locks, but her face unlined and calm. General Guevejar, fast becoming an expert at the politics and managing of armies, but untried in battle. Jesco Half-Hand, a dark figure in the background and a dark presence looming in Kitten's mind. And her lions, their combined aura a constant purr in the back of her head.

238

Marisola faced them. "Ailur the Cloud Cat has asked to meet with us."

"Ailur?" Eirlin glanced down at the Sword. "Why so formal?"

It is a time for decisions.

"There are decisions left to us?"

I have received a summons from the Leute. From Polvijarvi.

Guevejar glanced around the room. "Who is Polvij...arvi?"

The Chieftain of Clans of the Leute. Ecmund met him, once.

"I would have thought he was dead by now. He must be ninety years old."

He was not perhaps as old as you thought when you first met him, Ecmund. And now he has sent for me. For us.

"But there have been no messengers."

Nonetheless.

"What can he want from us?" Guevejar's glance again compassed the room as he tried to keep up with this quick exchange of information. "The Leute bore the brunt of the first attack, but they have disappeared into the mountains. They harass the enemy from time to time, but have little effect. I can't see they will be much use to us, or we to them."

Eirlin's head tilted to one side. "I think Kitten has some explaining to do."

About what?

"Don't give me that innocent guff." The General frowned. "What is so important about the Leute? We're in the middle of a war that we don't have much chance of winning, and you think a few hundred wild tribesmen are going to turn the balance. You know something I don't."

Marisola put a hand to Kitten's hilt. "You know why the Leute want to see you. We know it frightens you, but we have no idea why. Make us see what it is, and why you are so afraid of it."

Think of the bond we hold. Feel it. Test its strength. Consider what it allows us both to accomplish.

"I am quite aware of the bond between us."

Now place that bond between you and me, and between Ecmund and me, and between Ecmund and Eirlin, and Eirlin and you. All of us, held together.

"The merge you use when we communicate. We all know about that. But holding even this small group together tires you out. And for some reason you don't like it."

Lord Ostersund and I have discussed this problem over the years. Tell them, Magician.

"We..." Ostersund cleared his throat, tried again. "We looked into why it is so hard for the Sword to focus the Power of a group. It seems that humans have very messy minds, as Kitten sees them. Full of conflicting ideas and desires. In order to focus a group on a single purpose, Kitten must control and direct each one of those conflicts. Our contacts from Falkengard to the Capital come through a merge of familiar people, all Sensitives trained in concentration, with a single, strong purpose. Even so, she finds it difficult. To control a troop of soldiers, for example, would be impossible."

Marisola frowned thoughtfully. "But somehow the Leute are different."

Their lives are bound closer together. It is part of their Clan responsibility and training. The whole Clan, man, woman and child together; it is how they survive in their rough domain. You felt it in our contact before the Ulaan attacked them.

"That huge, powerful presence. I'm beginning to see."

That isn't all. Think about being in control of that power.

"One person? In control of all of them?"

That's right.

"No one should have that much power! That's what you taught me. What everyone has been teaching me all my life."

240

You are correct. No one should.

"But you sound as if this already happened. You mean someone did?"

Yes, dear one. Someone did.

"And the results were...unhappy?"

"Unhappy," would be a feeble word to describe the results. I was very young and stupid in those days. I should never have allowed it.

"And you're so much older now?"

Don't be sassy.

Guevejar chopped his hand to the tabletop. "Will you do this or will you not?"

As the situation stands, I will not. But I must talk to the Leute.

The general nodded. "Then go and talk to them. Who will you take?"

Ecmund, too, surveyed the group. "Marisola, of course." He tossed a grin at Jesco and the Twins. "A good swordsman came in handy last time, I recall."

"Anyone else?" Eyes turned to the general.

Guevejar waved a negative. "I cannot be away from this mess of porridge I'm trying to grasp."

Less is better.

Marisola nodded. "We will be moving through enemy-held territory most of the way. Kitten can focus the powers of her friends easier than others, so extra people will slow us down and make her shadowing more difficult. Grandfather knows them the best of all of us. The six of us, I think."

"Five."

She turned to face Ecmund, words forming.

He grinned. "I'd just get in your way."

"But Grandfather..."

"You are the Hand, Marisola, and Polvijarvi wishes to speak to your Sword. My presence would be unnecessary and possibly disruptive."

"Fine. We leave at dawn tomorrow.

General Guevejar placed his hands on the table. "This meeting has been productive. Lady Marisola and her troop will meet with the Leute to explore their cooperation. Lady Perica and Lady Caterina will continue to coordinate the feeding and housing of the common folk at the refugee camp. Lord Jandro and Lord Xavier will aid me with similar problems for the military. The rest will keep themselves ready to receive communication from Marisola."

* * *

But their morning started before dawn. Kitten was roused by a feeling of dread that grated along her edge like granite.

Marisola. Something is wrong.

Her Hand came awake in an instant, hand reaching for her hilt.

Listen. Concentrate. Can you feel it?

"Something is going on. I feel surprise and anger."

And pain and fear. The agony of death. There is a battle going on.

"We must wake the others! Sound the general alarum?"

No, this battle is far away. I can't tell how far. Just wake the general and the family. Especially Wynna. This needs our best Listening.

Soon the Sword was surrounded by all the Sensitives: Tyrbrand, Eirlin, Fang and the Twins, Jesco and Wynna, Ecmund and Perica. General Guevejar would add something to the merge, and he must be included. Hands stretched to touch her hilt, and she sent her spirit out into Inderjorne.

242

The powerful emotions continued, rising and falling like waves.

It feels like it is close. Within a few leagues.

There was general agreement in the merge, but no one's concentration wavered.

I am getting something else. Something familiar. Follow my lead. She concentrated on the fine wisp of aura that permeated the surges. *There! Marisola, do you feel him? Divo and Ovid? Yes. It is him. We will leave the merge, now.*

They gradually pulled away and sat, looking at each other.

That person we felt. The malicious aura. That is Third Brother. He leads the raid, wherever it is.

Guevejar frowned. "Where could the attack be?"

"I would send scouts out towards Visgard and Quentar. If Quentar is safe, they can continue to Oliveres." Ecmund shrugged. "There are no other towns nearby large enough to cause that kind of anguish. I assume if the refugee camp had been attacked, we would know by now. It's only half a league south of here."

"How about a smaller town, closer in?"

I considered it, my Lord. It felt like more minds. More than a hundred. And farther away. I have little experience with a surge of emotion like that, so I cannot say.

The general nodded. "I will see to the scouts."

He strode from the room, leaving the rest staring at each other, horror in every heart.

Finally Ecmund rose. "Well, no matter what tragedy has occurred, we all have work to do. So we're getting an early start at it. I'm sure the cooks have something available to break our fasts. Marisola, I assume you will wait for news before you leave."

She nodded mutely.

"Then let us eat."

With little enthusiasm, they moved towards the main hall.

They had barely finished eating when word came. "Riders approaching."

Jesco grabbed the page by the shoulder. "From which direction, lad?"

"From the west, my Lord."

He turned to the rest. "Visgard, then."

They hurried to the conference room where Guevejar was just entering. "It was Visgard. Our scouts met a messenger. The Ulaan had a force of about two hundred. Tossed grapples up and climbed over the wall, thirty or more of them. It was risky because the guards cut most of the ropes. But five of them made it over, and three of those put up a suicide stand to let their companions lower the drawbridge. After that, there was nothing to do but fight and run. Many deaths."

What did the Ulaan do then? Kitten suspected what had happened, but she did not mention it. Yet. *Are they holding the castle?*

"We have no new information. The first messengers were outside and ran when the castle was attacked. I have sent Tahal with his knights and two hundred lancers, with orders to attack if possible."

Over the next few hours word filtered in from a stream of survivors. The Ulaan had taken the castle and given no quarter. They piled everything in the courtyard and set fire to it. Then they mounted and searched the area, methodically killing every person and every animal they found, burning every building.

Third Brother. Kitten flattened her ears, her claws flexing. *He brings his evil wherever he goes.*

According to the next report, the murderers overstayed. Tahal and his lancers found them spread out and killed at least seventy before the survivors realized there was another force in the area. The rest of the raiders then disappeared, presumably up the road to rejoin the Horde.

At that point, Kitten had endured enough. She forced herself to speak calmly to her Hand. *It is time to settle this. Find the General.*

Marisola quailed at the fury in her Sword's mind. She rushed to where Guevejar was organizing his troops.

"My Sword wishes to leave. Have there been any changes to the plan?"

"No. We must confront them as soon as we can."

True. Again, Kitten controlled her emotions to send clearly. *But this latest attack changes everything for me. Up until now we were dealing with a normal war, but now that has changed. If Third Brother were ever to take charge of the Ulaan, it would be a bloodbath as we have seen today. If the Leute are willing, I will lead them. My people are about to be wiped from the face of Inderjorne, and I WILL NOT ALLOW IT!*

Marisol shook her head, trying to stop the ringing in her ears that seemed to go all the way through her brain. "All right, Kitten. No one is arguing."

Then I will bring the Leute, my Lord General. We will meet you at Langstrich.

* * *

The only joy in their meeting with the Leute was the surprise of meeting the War Leader. As they approached, Jesco's grin widened. "It's him!"

Marisola glanced over in surprise. "It's who?"

"Kitten. It's him. Karvilanti. The one we fought that day."

"It is. I wonder how he survived this long. Probably something to do with Polvijarvi."

"Yes, that would explain it."

I imagine he'll feel the same about you.

245

"Probably something to do with a certain Cloud Cat."

They rode up and dismounted. Polvijarvi was bent and wizened, holding himself erect with the aid of a staff. His War Leader had aged, but still showed the physique of a warrior.

"Ah, the Cloud Cat has lions in attendance. How appropriate."

The Twins grinned at each other, and Ovid spoke. "We have always been awed at the story of Polvijarvi and the duel. It is an honour to meet those involved."

The old man nodded, then coughed. "I have little energy for the adulation of the young, no matter how well deserved. The Cloud Cat has come. Do you know why you are invited?"

Do you have time to acknowledge my new Hand?

"She is Hand to the Cloud Cat. All is explained."

Marisola, you have been accepted.

She inclined her head. "I welcome the chance to meet the legends of my family."

"Hah! A smoother tongue than the last one, as I recall. Come. Let us sit and talk about that which needs no discussion."

She is his granddaughter, the best that his line and my training can produce.

The old man led them into one of the canvas-covered belowground shelters the Leute used. When he was seated, he stared at each of them, his dark eyes glittering. "So. The Final Days are upon us. I had no thought to live to such a dark end."

Marisola frowned. "I have heard nothing of final days. It will be the final days of the Ulaan Horde if they come against the might of Inderjorne, aided by the Leute and their Cloud Cat."

The old man chuckled. "Such optimism as I felt at that age. But then the legends were young and hope was among us.

246

The Cloud Cat came, and her new demeanour lifted the last shadows of a terrible memory from our folk. Now the clouds of fate hang low over us, and we bow to the necessity of a return to the ills of the past. But the Leute do not fear. We have lived a long and a proud saga, and it is with great honour that we approach our most important part in it."

And your people are ready and willing to play this part?

Polvijarvi sighed. "Long before my time the Leute decided that our fate would be tied to the fate of Inderjorne. Oh, we did not tell you. That would have made you harder to control. But we knew. Now the time of Inderjorne draws to a close, and we are willing to follow to the end."

Marisola's back straightened. "And if Inderjorne has no intention of drawing to a close and rolling over meekly to present our throats to the predator?"

The old face wrinkled even more. "Then the Leute will be happy to do our small part to aid in your endeavour."

She nodded. "Good. Then let us drink the traditional drinks and sing the old songs, because tomorrow we march."

"Well, young Hand, my voice is weak for singing, my stomach for strong drink likewise and I cannot take the trail with you tomorrow, but my spirit is as strong as it always was, and I will follow you on the wings of the red-tailed hawk, my emblem."

Well spoken, my friend.

* * *

The Leute came down out of the mountains on the rising gusts of a northeaster that thundered and roiled around the peaks, stabbing at the stone with bolts of lightning. They travelled light, their supplies on their backs. Even the youngest children bore their small shares.

247

General Guevejar and his brother were there to greet them, along with his Senior Commander and knights from the leading families of Inderjorne. Marisola rode forward and dismounted, passing Tariq's reins to Jesco.

"Sir, we have delivered the Leute as ordered."

"I only count about six hundred fighters."

She smiled. "You only count the men."

"Of course."

"Be happy it is not your enemies you number with such credulity."

He looked closer at the file that strode past, heads high in spite of their recent trek. "Some of the younger lads look fit."

She smiled. "And...?"

He pretended to frown. "I know what you want me to say."

"Then it is unnecessary. The Leute are willing, my Sword is willing and this combination will save Inderjorne. With some help from your sturdy knights, of course."

"I'm glad you thought to include them." He smiled down at her. "They would be upset if they were left out of the glory at the end."

"There will be enough glory for any who survive."

His grin faded. "I will be happy if we survive. Glory is overrated."

"My Sword is pleased that you feel that way. It speaks well for your leadership."

He spun on his heel. "Thank you for reminding me of my duty. It is time to organize this mess into a battle. Come. The others are waiting."

Marisola signalled the Leute War Leader, and they headed for the command tent.

28.   Final Battle

General Guevejar surveyed his allies from the head of the table. "The order of battle." He nodded to his Senior Commander. "My Knights will form the first front, with archers to either side. We will sweep in a straight line down the valley behind a volley of arrows and crush the enemy's front. Once the first wave is over, the battle will break into skirmishes, where the lancers and footsoldiers will be more useful."

He turned to Ecmund. "This is where the Powers of Inderjorne will be crucial. If I have a strong Sensitive presence at my command post, I can direct my forces as I see fit." He glanced at Tyrbrand. "What say you, Magician? Will you join this battle?"

"I must. If there is a solution involving the Powers of Inderjorne, I will be here."

"Eirlin?" Ecmund shrugged. "There is little use for a Healer..."

"I have another role to play, Brother. I will come."

"But there will be killing. I remember you once said..."

"It was a long time ago that I said anything that silly."

Ecmund chuckled. "I don't think you were ever silly, Eirlin."

"Then let's say I was naïve and idealistic." Her hands came out flat on the table. "My people are in danger from a virile disease. I must excise that illness from the body of my realm. Fang and I will help as we can. We can move to the Healer's tents after the battle."

The only response from her Scalpel was a low, rumbling growl.

"How pleasant...a family outing...all together at the same sport."

Marisola glanced back at the Twins. They were not smiling.

"My Lord General, my Sword suggests a modification to your plan."

"And what is that?"

The Leute will centre the front line in the first attack...no, do not look so incredulous. I have heard you complain that this valley is too wide."

"The knights of Marida chose a defile that was half this size."

Though lightly armed, the people of the Leute are doughty fighters and they will stay together no matter what happens. You must also see them as the enemy will. Many of the nomads are Sensitive as well, and only a head of stone will be unaware of the combined strength of my merge. The Ulaan will view the Leute as an unbreakable wall down the centre of the valley. Your knights can crush their foes against this wall from either side.

The Senior Commander glanced to his leader. "It might solve our main problem."

It will solve your main problem. Plus it will destroy the morale of the enemy. The Third Brother seeks to unman us with fear and horror. He has no concept of the fear the Ulaan will experience on this battleground today.

Guevejar nodded. "I have been instructed to take the advice of the Cloud Cat seriously. What you say makes good sense, and recent experience tells me that you can do as you promise. The Leute will centre the attack."

Kitten sent a private thought to her family members. *He accepts direction graciously. He might make a king some day.*

The Magician's wry aura intruded. *He hasn't much choice, has he?*

Just be sure he survives. He is our hope for the future.

Guevejar, unaware of this exchange, swept a hand to the map on the tent wall. "We must place the reserve lancers and infantry."

Kitten sent Marisola a prompt.

"Sir, there is one other consideration. The Third Brother. He will not be in the front lines. He will have something else planned. It will be devious and cruel."

Jesco's grin was more of a snarl. "If he thinks to attack the families of the Leute, he'll be disappointed."

"It would be more like him to attack our command tent or our hospital. Maximum disruption, minimum risk."

"I had planned to place the reserve lancers and peasant infantry half way between the two." Guevejar pointed. "Behind the hillock where I will set the standard of Inderjorne, where they can appear from either direction.

What a clever general we have. Now Tahal.

"And my Sword has one last suggestion."

Guevejar raised his eyebrows. "I can't wait, my Lady."

"Give Tahal charge of the right wing."

The general's glance shot to his brother and then away. "Tahal? Would you say he has earned the position?"

"Failure is the greatest of teachers, according to the Cloud Cat. And Tahal has faced the Ulaan more times than the rest of you put together."

An explosive snort came from the younger prince. "And I have fifty knights under my command who respond to the Cloud Cat's orders on the instant."

The only fifty knights in this army that know what they really face today, and will fight accordingly. Put Tahal on the right where he will be most effective and let the knights on the left play their chivalric games. Perhaps they will come to their senses before it is too late.

The general shrugged. "Once again, I find it difficult to argue. Tahal, you will command the right."

Pride swelled in the younger man's breast, but he shot Marisola a worried glance.

Kitten sent the prince a private message. *In a few years he will be King Guevejar, and he will need an experienced and loyal general for his armies.*

Tahal's eyes widened, a fierce determination clamping over his mind.

Marisola squeezed Kitten's hilt, and they shared an inner grin.

"Then our forces are ready to deploy." The general put his hands on his chair arms, ready to rise.

Marisola spoke before anyone rose. "Uncle Tyrbrand, I need your opinion on something." She looked around. "Everyone's, I suppose."

They relaxed back in their chairs, observing her.

"Kitten and I have been watching events unfold, and we see a pattern."

Tyrbrand nodded. "That is often useful."

"But it is not a useful pattern. What I see is that all the problems we are having are showing up in the Ulaan horde as well."

Ecmund scratched his cheek slowly. "Difficulty in getting everyone behind us, made more difficult by younger brothers striving for independence."

"Everyone is acting exactly as expected. Even Kitten and her abilities. Forty years ago she showed up exactly when she was needed. Soon after, she discovered she had the talent she needed to stop the other Sword from taking over. Now that ability is exactly what we need to win this war."

I am beginning to wonder if these events weren't all planned somehow.

The Magician laughed. "Don't exaggerate your own importance in the grand scheme of Inderjorne, Kitten. The survival of our small realm in these violent times has often been due to our unique powers and our outlook on life. The creation of the magic Swords was merely one facet of this situation."

"But what about this war with the Ulaan?" She tossed her hands up. "It's like looking in a mirror."

"Very few leaders have the luxury of commanding an undivided people, and disgruntled family members are historically the first ones to cause trouble when the realm is in turmoil."

Perica grinned. "And if you think deeper, you will find that some of the situations reflect Kitten's talents precisely because Kitten caused them in the first place."

A very perceptive and unpleasant idea. Thank you, Lady Perica. I suppose.

"You're welcome, Kitten. Always happy to help you stay on topic."

"And while we're getting cause and effect mixed up," Ecmund held his hands as if balancing, "you might consider that these common weaknesses have made this war necessary. If one side or the other didn't have equal problems, then that side would already have won the war, and the loser would be dealing with the aftermath."

Marisola grinned. "And the last thing we want to do is relax, assuming that somehow fate will haul our irons from the fire at the right time."

"Exactly. An appropriate response."

"I've been hearing that from everybody since I was four years old. It must be carved inside every skull in Inderjorne."

So, in the opinion of our most esteemed Magician, we are on our own?

Tyrbrand nodded.

"We can handle it." Marisola caressed Kitten's hilt. "We must."

General Guevejar stood. "I will see to the deployment of the army. Lady Marisola, I assume you will deal with the Leute? They are beyond my comprehension and my command."

We will control the Leute, my Lord General, inasmuch as it is possible.

With a shiver of apprehension, Kitten turned her attention to her army.

* * *

Marisola handed Tariq's reins to Jesco. "This is not a day for horses." She stroked the velvety nose. "Take him with you to the command site."

"I still think I should be with you."

She reached out and ran her knuckles down the side of his face. "No, Uncle. A battle is not the place for you. We need a physical presence to look over the general's shoulder and warn him of mistakes. Keep the mounts nearby and bring them if we need them."

His frown softened. "Aye, Hand. I hear and obey." He mounted and led the three horses away.

Marisola and the Twins turned to view the forming battle. "Amazing how well ordered it all looks."

It will not last.

"No. What do you think of the enemy?"

"Perhaps fewer...than our worst estimate... Over four thousand for certain."

254

"Hmm." They stared up the valley at the mass of men and horses, details clouded by a mile's distance, moving at an inexorable pace towards them.

Our army forms. We must greet them with appropriate ceremony.

It had rained during the night, and the grass of the field was damp.

Another advantage. The unshod horses of the Leute are not used to wet grass.

The storm hovered over the mountains, dark clouds shrouding the eastern horizon, fingers of cloud reaching out towards the battlefield. In the early morning light, the Leute marched out to the centre of the valley, their women in the van, babies strapped firmly to their breasts. The leaders lined up in front of Marisola. She drew Kitten and held her in a ceremonial pose. They knelt. She motioned them to rise.

"Your presence is a great boon to Inderjorne. The king himself has asked me to thank you. It is his will, and the will of the Cloud Cat, that you place yourselves under the leadership of his generals. Let your War Leader stand forth, and I will give him his orders."

The grizzled warrior stepped forward. "I am Karvilanti, at your command, Hand that wields the Sword."

"It is good to meet again, Karvilanti. The generals have acceded to your request that the Leute people will hold the centre. However, there will be one change. Your best warriors will form the first wave. Your women will form the second wave. They will carry their children on their backs, not their breasts."

The War Leader's back straightened. "That is not possible, Hand of the Cloud Cat. This is the Final Battle of the People of the Leute. Our finest hour, our great moment in history. We will form our army in our traditional order that we may die in the manner of our ancestors before us."

Marisola regarded him for a cool moment, then raised her Sword. "I believe the Cloud Cat would have something to say about that."

Kitten felt for the glow of emotion in each breast in front of her. She gathered their fear, their pride and their longing into one, single, agonizing ache that oozed throughout their beings and soared into the sky above them, where thunder echoed in response.

A wailing yowl spread over the army, resonating into the corners of every mind. The Leute stirred as if the storm in the mountains eddied through them, and even the Knights of Inderjorne squirmed in their armour, tugging their prancing war steeds back into line. The War Leader quailed, struggling to keep his knees from bending.

I am the Cloud Cat and I HAVE MADE MY WISHES KNOWN!

The War Leader's head bowed. "It shall be as the Cloud Cat says. The women will form the second wave."

Marisola nestled Kitten back into her scabbard. "And if there is no need for the second wave?"

A wry smile touched the Warrior's lips. "Then we shall thank our gods, the Cloud Cat and the Hand That Bears the Sword, and return to our homes, rejoicing."

"I'm glad we have the story straight. We will destroy the Ulaan as the avalanche rolls over the new trees on the mountainside, as that storm over the mountains crushes all before it. Your women may follow, singing the song of triumph and dealing mercy to those in need. Your children will come, only that they may tell the story to future generations, and say with pride 'I was there.' So says the Cloud Cat. Do you understand?"

Karvilanti bowed low and returned to the head of his tribe.

Striding to the General, sitting on his huge destrier, his flags and his knights around him, she spoke in a voice that carried.

"Your Majesty, only one element of your whole army is truly prepared for this battle, and that is the Leute. Your knights and nobles still think this is just a border skirmish or another of their interminable chivalric squabbles. Do you not realize that none of them know fear?"

"Of course my knights know no fear!"

"Not fear for their personal safety. I'm talking about a greater fear. The fear for their homes, their families, their whole way of life. Your people are not yet aware that the future of Inderjorne and of every soul who lives there is at stake in this battle. If we lose here, we cannot regroup, reform, retrench, or any of those fine terms you generals toss around that make losing not seem important. If we lose, we lose, and that is the end of us.

"Look at the Leute. Understand why the women wanted to go into battle armed with their teeth and fingernails with their babies as shields. They are past fear. In their hearts they are dead, and their only choice is whether to die well or not. Your men need a little of that, your Majesty, and that is why they will not be in the van this morning. I will hold the front, with my Leute behind me."

"You! But you're only..."

"We are your only hope of salvation, General."

Can you speak to him, Kitten?

The time for teaching is past.

He'll have to learn with his eyes, then.

The knights on the left had been edging forward during this conversation, each eager to be the first, pushing the Leute back farther and farther.

"A slight demonstration would be in order, General. Who ordered your knights forward?"

Prince Guevejar grinned. "You know what they're like. A little over-eager, that's all."

"I call it undisciplined. Watch this."

All right, Kitten. Gather them.

Kitten reached out with greater strength, feeling the raw emotion surging through the souls of the Leute. She quailed at the memory of the last time she had done this. *This situation is very different. I must hold to that.* Once again the familiar glow coursed through her as the feelings of her people fed on each other. With a gesture as easy as pawing a feather, she gathered them. The whole mass of Leute straightened and slid closer together. Then, at one moment, every member of the tribe took one step forward. The knights reined in their anxious steeds, holding their ground.

The Leute people stepped forward again.

There was a shuffling of the ranks as the destriers began to edge away.

The Leute people made two more steps, then began their march. Soon they formed the van again, the restless steeds of the knights milling at either flank.

Thank you, Kitten. You may let them go, now.

That would not be wise, Marisola. The Leute merge is not a Power to be picked up and laid down again at a whim. My control is already beginning to slip.

Then I suppose the battle begins. Should I inform our General?

It might be polite. He's going to figure it out soon, anyway.

"There, Prince Guevejar. Now you understand. The first wave of Leute will now attack. Your knights are to hold their flanks. Bring your foot levies in behind the knights as you choose, but leave the centre clear for the second wave of Leute.

"But..."

"I'm sorry, sir, but the Leute are a force of their own. The Cloud Cat can barely control them, and their desire to fight is fierce. The more the emotion builds, the harder they are to handle. Signal your armies, sir. You have thirty heartbeats to prepare."

Marisola left the General hastily summoning his heralds and strode to the front of the Leute. She glanced right, to see Tahal holding his knights in formation, his face turned in her direction.

At least someone learned something.

She nodded to him. He grinned and dropped his visor, settling the butt of his lance on his stirrup.

Only then did she draw Kitten again: slowly, with ceremonial dignity. As the blade cleared the scabbard, a hoarse growl tore from the throats of the massed Leute.

Hold them, Kitten. Mold them. Force them into one unit, the hammer that will drive fear into the heart of the enemy.

Kitten could not respond. It took all her strength to contain the Power that flowed around her. She could barely see. Memories came back to her from long ago: the heat of the fire, the blows of the hammer. She could feel once again that glow emanating from her. She was now ablaze from hilt to tip, her Name glowing in fiery letters, lighting the sodden morning.

Marisola raised her Sword high and strode forward, her lions at her shoulders, and the Leute strode with her. Across the field, the mass of barbarian warriors continued their menacing approach.

As Marisola joined the attack, Kitten spread her consciousness over the battleground. The presence of the Leute surrounded her, their small, round shields held low, their leather helmets down over their brows. Each man held his own preferred weapon: sword, mace, hammer or lance.

Back at the command post the bright glow of the Power of Inderjorne lit up the ether as all the Sensitives molded their auras to Kitten's merge.

The knights settled into a trot now, holding back with admirable restraint to stay even with their allies. The mercenary foot soldiers pressed in behind at their grinding pace, stern and professional. As the Ulaan front neared, Kitten waited for the exact moment.

And then it came. Husam raised his sword and swung it forward, and in two paces his Elite Guard had heeled their ponies to full gallop. Kitten's order slammed into the minds of the Inderjornese heralds, and their trumpets blasted in unison. Flights of arrows filled the air in both directions. The Leute broke into a sprint, their shields held high, and the knights, slower to react, abandonned their pace and charged behind.

Now that the Leute were in battle array, their awareness merged even tighter. They were easier to control, and Kitten could reserve a slice of her own consciousness for the job of keeping her Hand alive. As the Ulaan neared, she sharpened Marisola's senses, strengthened her muscles, sent a wave of confidence coursing through her.

"What's going on?"

A battle is going on. What do you think? Concentrate, girl!

"No. Look at the Ulaan. What are they doing?"

Instantly alert, Kitten focused her senses on the enemy. Straight in front of them, the Ulaan War Leader galloped forward, his Elite Guard around him. But the rest of his army was acting strangely. They slowed, they wavered, they began to lower their weapons. At the exact time that the Ulaan Leader should have been gathering his people for the shock of the first clash, he realized that they weren't following him. He lifted his hand on the reins, and his pony hesitated in its pace. Members his Guard swerved, trying not to run him over. At the moment of contact the Ulaan centre was in turmoil, and the rest of the barbarian army was hesitating, ready for flight.

The Leute army swarmed through them, pulling men off their horses, cutting, hacking and trampling. Marisola and her guardians held their position in the centre, a rock rolling within the torrent of the Leute attack.

The knights recovered their surprise at the speed of the Leute charge and caught up, their massive weight overwhelming the lighter horses of the nomads, rolling them under like wheat. Soon the field was a mass of fleeing Ulaan and pursuing Leute.

A strange warbling sound caught Marisola's ear, and she glanced back. The second wave of Leute was dancing into the battle as promised, the women singing and swinging their freed and laughing babies high, then leaning down with their cooking knives to kill any wounded Ulaan who survived.

Kitten revelled in the victory. *Now my people take their revenge. The prey flees, but we are fleet of foot. They run, but we run faster. We strike with speed and power, and their blood enriches our soil. Now they pay for their attack...*

Kitten forged ahead, but voices kept distracting her.

"Marisola...what are you doing...you must slow down...too dangerous..."

"...can't. Something wrong. Kitten! Stop...!"

Kitten? What's going on? This is wrong...!

We must hunt down the prey. We must kill...!

Help! She won't stop...

"FATHER, MOTHER! WE NEED HELP NOW!"

A wash of light blasted through Kitten's senses. Strong hands gripped Marisola's arms, and her own mind was grasped by a powerful force. *No! Let go! I must fight...*

The voice of the Magician came through, strengthened by the powerful minds of his sons and the soft strength of the Healer. *Kitten, you must control yourself.*

I am no kitten. I am the Cloud Cat of the Leute, with all the power of my people behind me. Who are you to bid me stop?

You are Kitten, and you are family. Can you not feel the love that surrounds you? You must control yourself, or what you feared most will happen again.

She returned her mind to the battlefield. Sure enough, the more Sensitive of the Ulaan were returning to the fight, their faces twisted with emotion. Wild screams tore through the din as the songs of the Leute women keened higher and higher and their knives dropped. Now they slashed with sharp fingernails at the faces and eyes of their victims. The babies' screams of terror ran an aching counterpart high above.

I...I cannot stop. It is exactly like before, like my dreams. Let me go! I am Cloud Cat, and I must...

Again the Magician's voice fell like a blanket over her emotions. *No, Kitten. You are better than that. You can control yourself and control your army. Last time you were alone. We are family, and now we are here to help.*

I cannot...

And if you cannot, Tyrbrand's voice took on a tremor, then firmed, *I will oppose you with my dying breath. Ailur, Cloud Cat of the Leute and final masterpiece of Hanflaed the Smith, I call upon you to fulfill your destiny. You must not fail your people or your family. You must overcome yourself!*

From somewhere closer by a smaller voice wrapped itself around her. *Come on, Kitten. Be what you taught me all these years.*

Kitten seized on the feeling of her Hand, the love and care between them. She felt the solid strength of the people of Inderjorne, stretching back through the years to an old Swordsmith with a quiet voice and a shaking hand. Slowly she pulled herself back, forcing the anger and terror away, yearning for the warmth of her family.

Kitten came to her senses in a wide circle of bodies, hewn and slashed beyond recognition. Before she could understand, a new wave of attackers galloped at them, and

262

she was immediately busy keeping her Hand alive and trying to maintain control of her army and her own emotions. The lull had allowed the Ulaan a chance to regroup, and more were turning to attack...

Wait. Something different...

What? The Hand dodged a lance and chopped at the arm that held it.

There is a new feeling in the Leute...over...there!

Marisola downed a swordsman and slid back between the Twins so she could scan the battle. From the enemy flank on their far right a spearhead of horses raced forward, bonded together in the kind of charge a fearless leader can inspire. Screaming their war cries, the attackers swept around to take the Inderjorne army from the side. Disorganized riders from the main body of the army began to fill in behind them, and the rout threatened to reform into a flank attack.

Dividing her attention, Kitten tried to help Marisola fight a horseman charging her, at the same time sending a desperate plea to all Sensitives in the Inderjorne heavy cavalry. *Tahal! Turn right. Danger right! TURNTURNTURN!*

Her cry was taken up by the Sensitives at the command post, and the right wing of her army slowed, heads turning. It took a moment until the non-Sensitive knights became aware of the new danger. Then the notes of the Tahal's herald cut through the battle, screaming the order to wheel right. Marisola's herald belatedly sounded the same call.

At least someone was listening.

"Sorry. Forgot about the heralds."

We did pretty well with our usual methods.

The knights began their charge, trimming up their line as they hit their stride, Prince Tahal's bright banner in the lead. Another trumpet call, and the reserve lancers rushed from hiding, their lighter horses sweeping swiftly against the far side of the Ulaan attack, their long spears darting out. Then the mass of solid metal struck the enemy line, upending the plains ponies, sending their riders flying. The leaders of the nomad charge were cut off from their troops and hewn down.

We know who was leading that charge.

I hope for the sake of both our peoples that he faced the consequences.

Marisola turned her attention to the Ulaan War Leader who stood facing her, his sword drawn back, his free hand open to her in invitation. His Elite Guard lay decimated around him, and now he stood alone, his horse downed, his lips drawn back in a frozen snarl.

"Time to surrender, Great Leader."

"I will never surrender!"

"That's fine. Don't. We'll stop attacking you."

She half-turned to the herald who followed her. "Sound the 'disengage,' if you please."

The man frowned. "Only the General can order that call, my Lady."

Her Sword swung to point at his midsection. "I believe I gave you an order, soldier. Sound it or I'll disengage your liver."

The man sounded the call, immediately taken up by the other heralds. The din of battle began to fade, to be replaced by the moans of the wounded and the screams of injured horses. And over it all, the lilt of the Leute women, singing again and playing with their babies as they searched for enemies to slay.

Marisola turned to the Ulaan War Leader. "Have I made my point? The battle is over."

"You must kill me now." He lowered his sword and shield.

"Why would I kill you? You're kind of cute. I might take you as my first concubine."

His lip curled, his head rising. "This is not a matter for jokes. If you do not kill me, I will return. And next time..."

"Next time don't bring your playmates with you. They spoil the party. Come alone and you might get a more friendly reception."

She couldn't help but smile at the shock that crossed his face.

She means it, Great Leader.

Marisola reached out and ran one fingernail down his cheek hard enough that the blood flowed. "I have put my mark on you, Husam al Din. Now you must return."

His hand went to the wound and he regarded the blood, rubbing it between finger and thumb. His eyes rose to her face.

"And then perhaps I will make good on my promise to help you regain your rightful lands. The Ulaan need powerful friends, these days."

A thoughtful frown creased his forehead.

She smiled. "Now, I believe you have a retreat to organize, and your power to re-establish. If all our gods are with us, your youngest brother did not survive that melee. If he did, you have a harder path ahead of you. You may go." She flicked her fingers towards his routed army.

His eyes snapped open and his muscles tightened but her gesture froze him. "Don't even think about it. Take what is left of your Horde and remove them from my realm. We ask no hostages; we demand no treaties. Such civilized deals mean nothing to barbarians. All you understand is defeat, and I have made yours very clear.

"This is your one chance to leave with dignity. If I unleash the Power of the Cat against you, your men will run screaming in terror." She rubbed Kitten's pommel reflectively. "Perhaps I should do that. Perhaps you need a little reminder of what awaits you here."

Kitten eased out a yowling whisper, echoing back and forth in their minds, rising and falling, only to rise again with exquisite delicacy.

I begin to appreciate the skill of the violinist.

Just keep it up, Love. I really don't want to fight him. He might polish up quite presentably.

Your wish is my command, Dear One.

The barbarian nodded. "I will see you again."

"I look forward to it." She replaced her sweet smile with a frown of command. "Now go."

Once again shock flickered over his face, but he mastered it, nodded more sharply and turned on his heel. The tatters of his Elite Guard struggled to keep up with him as he strode to a nearby horse, flung himself on and wrenched its head around.

A thundering of hoofbeats, and all that remained of the attacking Horde was a cloud of settling mist. The merge of the Leute faded as each fighter became aware of his own surroundings. The crash of thunder from the mountains eased to a rumble, and the sun broke through scattering clouds.

Kitten ruffled Marisola's satisfaction. *I have a message for the Leute. From Eirlin the Healer.*

What is it?

She says, "Please tell your women to leave a few wounded for us to practise on. Many of those they are giving mercy to would survive with a little Healing."

Marisola chuckled. *Well, go ahead and tell them. The Leute warriors don't listen to me. I sincerely doubt their women will.*

29.   What's in a Name?

There was scant celebration in the Great Hall at Falkengard that evening. By the time the exhausted warriors made the long trek from the battleground, all they had energy for was food, and in large quantities.

When they had finished eating, the leaders retired to Perica's workroom. Extra chairs crowded the space. Guevejar sat at the head of the table with the lady of the manor on his right, his brother on his left, his Senior Commander next. The rest of the family lined the sides, with Marisola and Kitten at the foot, the Twins and Jesco at her back.

The prince gazed around the room, then raised his goblet. "A better result than I dreamed possible. All honour to those who died in the defence of Inderjorne this historic day."

They all drank, and there was silence.

"And thanks to the Cloud Cat, her Hand and her Leute allies, without whom the day's results would have been much different."

Again the goblets were raised. Marisola, her face red, glanced around, unsure where to look.

Back straight and proud, Dear One. You deserve this.

"And thanks to the demesne of the Falcon." The prince stood. "Once again you come to the aid of the realm and her rightful rulers, all the people of Inderjorne. I raise my cup in acknowledgement of my duty to protect that trust." He swept his goblet in a gesture that encompassed the room, then emptied his drink and set it down.

"And now I go to my bed in safety." He shook his head. "A novel concept." He strode out, followed by his retinue.

Only the family remained.

Ecmund exchanged glances with Tyrbrand. "All the people as rightful rulers. An interesting turn of phrase."

The Magician nodded. "It gives one hope for the future."

Perica chuckled. "Now that we have one to look forward to."

It is time to speak of the future.

Marisola drew Kitten and laid her on the table before them. All eyes turned to the Sword.

This war, unfortunate as it may be, will change Inderjorne forever. How that change happens and what direction it takes is under our control,

Ecmund nodded. "You are correct, Kitten. Our kingdom has been brought closer together than at any time in the past two centuries. Those who rallied to the defence of the realm have gained immeasurably. Those who held back are discredited."

But not for long. We must plan carefully and act quickly or the old habits will return. Jandro and I have spoken of this.

All eyes turned to Marisola's father, many in surprise. He reddened, then straightened his shoulders. "Yes. Very soon we must present a positive and optimistic strategy for the future. We can use the euphoria of the victory to fuel the rebuilding of the realm in a new form. Construction and cooperation will become our watchwords. Those who support us will prosper, and those who hold back will notice and fall in line."

Perica looked across the table at her son. "Another surprise to end a day of surprises. And you and the Cat with Many Claws have this already planned?"

He straightened his shoulders. "No, we were too busy preparing for war. But just as you worked hard to get the realm in the right mood for battle, we must also arrange the realm for the peace that follows. We must not allow the old, destructive sniping and competing to rise again. Peace does not just happen. It is built, stone by stone, and requires a solid design and master craftsmen and women to execute the plan."

Caterina laid a hand on her husband's shoulder. "So, while we were all preparing for battle, you were planning what would happen afterwards?"

He gave a twisted smile. "I even had a plan for what would happen if we lost. But now we can forget all that." He ran a hand through his hair. "I don't wish to take away from those who created this victory. This is your day, and you deserve all the honour and applause. But the time for the builders is upon us, and speed is of the essence."

Marisola grinned. "The Falcon was fully involved in this war five days before the rest of the realm knew it was coming. There is no reason why we can't be just as far ahead on what happens afterwards." She glanced at her brother. "I know how frustrating it was for you Xavier, having to stay behind and not take part in the battle."

There was a pause, and she shrugged. "Well, now it's my turn to fade to the background. I have no idea what use Kitten and I will be, but we'll back you in any enterprise."

She raised her goblet. "I'm a little tired at the moment. Could we have one last drink together and save the planning for tomorrow?"

Everyone drank, grinning. As Marisola put down her cup, sharp claws pierced her sleeve, and a small cat appeared on her shoulder, rubbing his jaw along her ear.

"Aha. My Ambassador and Chief of Protocol tells me that the meeting is over."

A nudge in her mind and a slight hand gesture from the Magician, and Marisola stayed where she was while the others filed out. The Twins looked back, but she motioned them to go ahead. When the room had cleared, Tyrbrand gazed down the table at them.

"There is one more discussion required."

"There is?"

"Yes. Only Kitten and I know how momentous this day has been, but the cause must remain unacknowledged in the greater world."

"In what way?"

Warmth swept the length of Kitten's blade. *The Cloud Cat of the Leute has performed a miracle that no Magician or Sword has ever achieved. Never in all the history of magic has such a merging of the minds of so many people occurred. And safely.*

The Magician gave a wry smile. "That is probably true."

It is true, my Lord Magician...with substantial help at a key point, I am pleased to admit.

"It is truly a moment to go down in the annals of magic." Tyrbrand paused. "What does that mean to you, Kitten? Do you think another Name is necessary?"

My Name is Cloud Cat. Now that I think about it, it always was; I just didn't realize it. The torn and bedraggled body that Hunflaed found in the alley was a cat of the forest and the mountains. What happened the last time I visited the Leute, tragic though it was, served to prepare me for this test. Now the challenge is met, and it was the Cloud Cat who succeeded.

Tyrbrand had a strange smile on his face, the one that said he knew more than he was telling. "And your other Names?"

All the other names are useful frippery. It is more important to be what I am, not to try to be many things to many people in a vain search to please them all.

"I see. Then how will you deal with your Names?"

People will call me what they like. That is the nature of humans. Thus over the years I will have many names. Each name will have significance to me because it aids me in dealing with the group of humans who gave it to me.

My real Name, the one that tells the world what I am, will always be Cloud Cat of the Leute, because that is what I was when I accomplished my greatest achievement.

But that is only what I am to the outside world. She sent the Magician a pat on the cheek with a soft paw. *Who I am, deep inside? The name I think of myself as? My real name will always be Kitten. That is who I am to the people who count the most in my life.*

The End

More from Gordon A. Long
Available at most online retailers

"Ocean of Grass" Petrellan Saga 1
"Waves of Stone" Petrellan Saga 2
"Zoysana's Choice" Petrellan Saga 4
"The Innkeeper's Husband" Petrellan Saga 5

"Out of Mischief" World of Change Book 1
"Into Trouble" World of Change Book 2
"Mountains of Mischief" World of Change Book 3
"The Trouble with Tents" World of Change Book 4
"Queen of Mischief" World of Change Book 5

"A Sword Called...Kitten?"
Romantic Comedy with an Edge
"The Cat with Many Claws" Sword Called Kitten #2
"Sword Called Kitten: The Early Days" Short Stories
"Factory 4-80" Science Fiction

"Why Are People So Stupid?" Social Humour with a Point

Look for Gordon's books, selected reviews, poetry and
short stories at <airbornpress.ca>
Gordon's opinions on humanity are at the
"Are People Stupid?" blog
Find his weekly reviews and his ideas on writing at
"Renaissance Writer"

About the Author

Brought up in a logging camp with no electricity, Gordon Long learned his storytelling in the traditional way: at his father's knee. He now spends his time editing, publishing, travelling, blogging and writing Fantasy, Sci-Fi and Social Commentary, although sometimes the boundaries blur.

Gordon lives in Tsawwassen, British Columbia, with his wife, Linda, and their Nova Scotia Duck Tolling Retriever, Josh. When he is not writing and publishing, he works on projects with the Surrey Seniors' Planning Table and is a staff writer for <indiesunlimited.com>

www.ingramcontent.com/pod-product-compliance
Lightning Source LLC
Chambersburg PA
CBHW052034240626
47153CB00006B/2080